A Murderous Crow

Iron Wraiths MC
Book 4

A.J. Downey

Published 2025 by Second Circle Press

ISBN: 978-1-95022-59-9

~

Editing & book design by Maggie Kern @ Ms.K Edits
Cover art Dar Albert at Wicked Smart Designs

Dedication

To Tee, I never would have made it through these last few books without your Alpha reading as I go along, demands for more, and snarky wit when there's been no more for me to give. You're invaluable to the process, babes – and everyone should be grateful.

Prologue

Corvus...

I dropped the paperwork onto my desk and sank into my seat behind it, feeling mixed emotions.

Savvy Savannah Davenport was *hot* – sure, but just about everything about the bitch annoyed me. Not least of which was that she was doing *better than I was* when it came to the real estate game here in Savannah, Georgia.

She was tall, and elegant, and a royal pain in my ass.

Just about every time our agencies clashed, I was the one to deal with her – partially because she was easy on the eyes, and partially because I *loved* riling her up.

She was a rich bitch, just like every other disposable darling that'd come in and out of my life. There was no substance there. No passion. Just a competition and a certain amount of ruthlessness.

I could appreciate the last, especially in a pretty package.

I stared at her smiling face in the full-page ad lying on the corner of my desk, about to fall off it and into the trash, and tsked to myself.

She was old man Beauregard Calhoun's cash cow, and she had come out of nowhere from some elite place with a fake-as-hell steel magnolia personality and exaggerated southern drawl with her kitschy-as-fuck tagline – *Savvy* Savannah.

From the moment she'd introduced herself, all saccharine sweet, holding out her hand with its gold watch and its tiny, barely readable face. Her nails were manicured to perfection and painted with a classic French tip, but with a thin gold line between the white and the natural color of her nail bed. I had instantly disliked her.

My dislike had turned me cold, and her competitive when it came to the real-estate race. She seemed determined to show me up every chance she got, and that had just made me dislike her even more – but at least she was good for two things – looking good, and being a good sport. She tended to turn the usual game of checkers that was real estate in this town into a game of chess, and I could appreciate the challenge.

So, she did have her uses. I'd give her that.

Chapter One

Savannah…

"Aggravating prick," I muttered under my breath, and set my phone aside on the linen by the sparkling cutlery.

I hated dealing with Corbett Prescott. The douchebag was old money – born with a silver spoon in his mouth, with a line going all the way back to some of the first settlers and maybe some Vanderbilt blood built in. Whatever it was about his lineage, it was all the *worst* parts of the American aristocracy flowing through his veins.

Arrogant, insufferable, brash, and cocky.

I *hated* working across from him on deals, but alas… it's where we were on the Duffy listing. My clients were the homeowners. His were looking to buy, and they were picking on things to the nth degree, stalling literally *everything* at *every* turn, to the point it was just turning into one big quagmire. *Ugh…* it was only around a 900k listing, and he was making me *work for it.*

I sighed and checked my watch. It was gold and had diamond chips at the 12, 3, 6, and 9.

A gift from my grandfather to my grandmother on their wedding day. I flipped over the face, and on the back was inscribed, *never enough*... as in there would never be enough time spent with her.

I hoped that someday someone would think of me that way, but I wasn't counting on it.

I heaved a sigh and was just about to consider this meeting *dead on arrival* when a harried man, led by the maître d', arrived at the table.

"I am so sorry I'm late," he rushed out with a clipped, foreign accent, as the maître d' held out his chair for him and he slid into it. I gave the maître d' a nod, and he snapped a curt bow and strode back to the front of the house.

Yes, this place was *that* kind of place.

"No trouble at all, sugar." I put on my award-winning smile, as much as it pained me to do so.

"Please," he said. "I mean it. I do apologize. I was held at a rather volatile board meeting. Anyway, I'm Hal Lindstrom. It's a pleasure to finally meet you." He held out his hand.

I gave it a light, girly shake and said, "Savannah Davenport, and the pleasure is all mine." I laid my southern accent on thick. Hal here was from Sweden or Norway or some such country. He was looking for that slice of Americana that was in the movies.

He'd likely watched *Midnight in the Garden of Good and Evil* one too many times, and had been enamored by the whole southern hospitality and weird sort of vibe that was Savannah in the 1980s and early 1990s... but I was twenty-nine. Born in nineteen ninety-five, so all that sort of culture was lost on me.

Savannah had settled some. All the women who'd made it a wild place back then were in their fifties and their sixties now. Some were pushing into their seventies. There was a reason that *Slow-vanna* was what she was called today. The city had mellowed considerably in the intervening years, but there was no big Hollywood blockbuster film out there to reflect that nowadays. It was all the ballad of ornery old Jim Williams and the lore of the Mercer-Williams house.

It was still murder, and the mayhem of characters like the Lady Chablis – God rest *her* soul... who'd passed in two thousand sixteen.

It felt like the wild vibe of Savannah's rebellious era had gone to rest with her, and now it was a slower, calmer, more sedate place to be – a lovely walk down historic streets, past old and historic homes, with a sense of nostalgia steeping in the sultry air; permeating everything.

But Hal wasn't here for that. He was here for the Savannah of at least thirty years ago, and that was fine by me.

He was looking for the perfect property to steep himself in that Williams kind of vibe, filling it with antiques and a maximalist style, which was, at least, the vibe I had gotten from his emails.

At first, I had wondered why anyone would wish to immigrate to the United States under the current political landscape. But then he took his seat across from me, and I realized he was exactly the perfect archetype that the people in charge wanted around these parts now.

Blonde-haired and blue-eyed, and as the Lady Chablis would say... *'stinkin' motherfuckin' rich.'*

It was quickly obvious as he described what he wanted to me that I could likely add *insufferable* to that category as well.

I thought about it as he droned on and on about the kinds of property he was seeking, that he would have been much better off with Corbett Prescott as his buyer's agent. But Corbett could and would pry the commission I was looking at from the sale of the type of property Hal was looking for out of my cold, dead hands.

Still, this was the game.

Only one person out here knew what I was doing, and that was my assistant, who was older than me! Fabian was pushing forty, but with his skincare routine and generally bubbly personality, he might as well be twenty to my *almost* thirty.

I could picture him at home in his light, sheer silk robe with its copious mounds of ostrich feathers surrounding the collar and cuffs, a facemask on his face, and fingers dripping with jeweled rings as he texted me back; his manicure clicking against the screen of his phone as he took notes on a legal pad nearby.

I relayed the information, and he would have a series of properties to review by morning that were up for grabs and fitting Hal's whims and desires.

I would find Hal what he wanted at a better price than he had ever dreamed of.

It was the Savvy Savannah way.

I just hoped it would be enough.

Chapter Two

Corvus…

I lived separately from the Manse, which most of the club called home for a reason. As much as I would have loved shacking up with my old dorm-mates from our boarding school days, it wouldn't do with how many… less-than-legal fronts we had dealings with. If the Manse ever got raided and Syn taken in, I needed plausible deniability to remain firmly on the outside so I could continue conducting business. Besides that, I was their best point of contact to secure the entire team of lawyers they would need.

Speaking of which, it was time to sign off on those monthly retainers.

As far as the outside world knew, the retainers we paid on the regular were for business dealings, legitimate to the above-board business we each ran on a daily. Good enough cover. Decent enough to keep a whole contingent of lawyers a phone call away for any criminal court services we may need them for.

I sat at my desk in my townhome off Charlton Street. I could see Troup Square from one of my upper-floor spare rooms' windows if I angled right and looked hard enough.

The townhome had cost me just a little over a million, and I was its first new owner in sixty years. To be honest, the three-bedroom, two-bathroom place was a little big for me, but it served me fairly well. One bedroom was reserved for the odd occasion that one of the guys had a clash of personality over at the Manse and needed a place for a night or a few days in order to get whatever beef had arisen properly quashed. The third bedroom wasn't used as a bedroom at all, but rather as my home office.

There was a smaller office space downstairs that I kept as a library with all manner of law books attributed to real estate law, and some personal reading material as well. It held nothing but shelves and a ladder to reach the top along a brass rail, and an overstuffed and comfortable chair with a reading lamp over it.

A cozy, if rarely utilized space.

One of the charms of the place was the exposed brick and open-beamed ceilings, which were great for anyone who loved historic charm. I did not. I preferred sleek, black, and white – preferring modern and minimalist myself – but it was a sacrifice I was willing to make to have the carriage house at the back of the property with enough garage beneath it to house both my car and my bike.

Above was a simple mother-in-law apartment, fully furnished, but empty. The guys referred to it as my "fuck studio," which they weren't wrong to do. It was where I brought the insipid, but at least pleasant-to-look-at, women to fulfill my needs, but kept them separate from my permanent dwelling.

I liked keeping my space my own.

I let them believe the carriage house apartment was where I lived to keep them from knocking on my actual door. Still, there was the odd occasion when it happened. Hence, my multitude of security cameras. And thanks to Requiem, I always knew who was where and what was happening on my property with a few taps on my phone's screen.

An invaluable tool.

All was quiet as I worked through my morning ritual, pomading my hair back from my face and taming my beard with its own balm and a hot comb. I was what you would consider a "dirty blond," my hair more bronze than golden, too dark to be a true blond but too light to be considered a brunette, either.

I thought it suited me well enough. My eyes stared back at me, a whiskey brown with more gold and amber to them than brown, depending on what I was wearing. Today, I wore a dark suit, but in just the white shirt, they were molten caramel, the gold notes plucked out harder when I laid the neutral gold tie around the back of my collar, working it into a pristine Windsor knot at my throat.

I cinched it up, laid my collar down over it, and cracked my neck from side to side, cracking it, rolling my shoulders to settle the fit of my shirt.

I pulled on my vest – I tended toward three-piece suits. I liked the classic fit and the old-time vibe. Today, it was a navy suit with a gold tie, brown shoes, and a gold sock that was in tune with the tie.

It was a bit matchy-matchy, but I didn't care. A white pocket square and a few tugs to get the jacket to lay right, and I was as ready as I would ever be.

I felt a bit of a twist of regret as I passed up my bike to get into my Porsche, but it was what it was. There would be time for a ride later tonight. First, I needed to get through the day.

I drove to my family's set of offices on the riverfront, parked in my designated, bought-and-paid-for spot at the side of the building, and got out, briefcase in tow.

I gave Specter a nod as I walked past the corner where the club's gambling op was held in the old warehouse building's basement.

"Long one?" I asked.

"Too fuckin' long," he said, flicking his cigarette butt into the gutter, and hocking back whatever was in his sinuses and spitting right behind it.

"You could always get a real job," I suggested.

"And make my daddy remotely proud? Yeah, I'll fuckin' pass," he said, and we shared a laugh.

I stepped over his mess and shook my head. "Have the prospect clean this up. I don't need prospective buyers getting the wrong idea about our town."

"Whatever, you prima donna," he said, giving me the finger behind my back, which I caught in the window of one of the gift shop doors opening up before me. I also caught him opening the door behind himself and heard him holler, "Prospect! Get out here with a broom or some shit..."

I stopped at the non-descript door with the etched brass plate of my father's realty company and took my keys out of my pocket.

It was going to be a long day today, and I just wanted some more fucking coffee.

"Morning, Mr. Prescott," Ashleigh, my assistant and one of our junior real estate agents, greeted me as I came through the door upstairs into the too-small, what served as our waiting room in our suite of offices.

"Morning, Ashleigh," I said, and she traded me my briefcase for a rich black cup of coffee.

Good girl, I thought silently to myself, but I had no interest in Ashleigh. She practically threw herself at me at every turn, begging for my attention like an overly friendly, starved puppy hoping for some scraps.

Which was disgusting, considering we were cousins – granted, it was like third or fourth cousins and it was by marriage or something – but still cousins, and while I was a southern boy, I wasn't *Alabama* southern. I was Georgia born-and-bred aristocracy, or as close to American aristocracy as you could get.

I hadn't hated it as much as some of the others in the club, like Specter. I had instead leaned into it, however, I didn't give two fucks about whether I made my father proud or not. We weren't like that. We'd never been... *affectionate* like that in our household. We'd always been purely transactional.

I wasn't even sure my father and mother knew what love was. If anything, their marriage was just another contract drawn up by their parents, and likely their parents before them. I wouldn't put it past the family line to make an arranged marriage, but for certain, my parent's relationship felt purely transactional.

They were quintessential boomers in every regard. My father refused to retire even though he was in his seventies, pulling up the ladder behind him, lamenting about my generation's lack of work ethic, and attempting to leave no crumbs behind when they finally did do us all a favor and shuffled off this mortal coil.

I couldn't care less.

I'd used my position here at my father's real estate company to leverage every bit of wealth I could, and if he'd bother to look up from any of his deals to scrutinize mine, he'd realize that I far outdid him. When he finally did croak? I would do just fine, if not better, without him.

His empire was mostly my empire now. I just didn't think he realized or noticed.

I let him continue to believe that all was in order and mostly in his control, but he had, honestly and unwittingly, signed almost everything over to me, a little at a time. He really shouldn't have trusted me so blindly when I'd put papers before him.

For as cunning as he thought he was, I had done plenty to outfox the old fox.

"You're in early," Ashleigh said, preceding me into my office and setting my briefcase where I liked it. I took my seat behind my desk and rolled myself up under it, setting my coffee on the coaster set out for it.

"Early bird gets the worm," I said with a gusty sigh. "Old man in yet?"

She rolled her eyes. "He doesn't get in much before ten anymore, you know that."

"That, I do..." I muttered, moving the mouse on my PC to wake it up.

"Anything for me to do?" she asked.

"Not right now," I told her.

She pushed off the edge of my desk where she'd parked her shapely ass and said, "Holler if you need anything." She arched one dark brow over her shoulder at me suggestively.

"Will do," I said distractedly, scanning the emails up on my screen for anything that needed my immediate attention.

A new one popped up at the top from Savvy Savannah Davenport, and I scowled.

We had a meeting at three o'clock this afternoon, a phone call about the old Shriver's place. Old man Beauregard was selling, my clients were buying, but it was a mess of what my clients could and could not modernize due to its place on the National Register of Historic Places. Thus, the negotiations had gotten… sticky.

It annoyed me that she was emailing me to confirm this afternoon's appointment, like I'd forget. Avoiding confrontation was one of my father's favored plays, but I was not my father. I relished the back-and-forth, the bargaining, and the sparring.

I loved the thrill of the chase, the hunt, and lived for the capture and the triumph of having the opposition bow to my will.

It was my thing, and when it came to the old Shriver place? Savvy Savannah was in my fucking way.

At least she was pretty, as far as prey went.

Chapter Three

Savannah…

Corbett Prescott was nothing short of incorrigible, and it was getting on my last *fucking* nerve! I shot him a text back, noting that I was about to show a place and that there was nothing more to discuss. That *no*, the current owners weren't willing to go forward with the sale to his clients. They wanted to ensure their property went to someone *responsible* when it came to the property's *historical* husbandry.

His buyers had lost them, and the sale would not move forward. There honestly wasn't more to discuss. Now kindly let me get on with my day… *Jesus H. Christ, typical male, he wouldn't take "no" for an answer!*

I put my phone on silent, texted my assistant back, and told him where I was – the Habersham property. It was one of ours, so I wouldn't have to deal with Corbett Prescott or any of his bullshit. It was just a question of whether Hal Lindstrom would like it.

His budget was *very* forgiving, but by the same token, he was looking for just himself. He didn't want or need anything so grandiose as a five-bedroom, *but* he still wanted something historic, and that would allow him to live that Jim Williams, *Midnight in the Garden of Good and Evil* type fantasy.

I'd scoured listings and found something to start with that I thought might suit him. It was a one-bedroom, two-bath home for just under a million in the heart of the historic district, just off Columbia Square near Colonial Park Cemetery. There was plenty of fine dining and entertainment well within walking distance, however, it was on-street parking only. Still, while unassuming from the front, its two stories had beautiful porches overlooking a small patio garden in the back with huge potential for elegant entertaining within its twelve-hundred-square-foot footprint, and it had once belonged to the prominent Lane family. It checked more boxes than it didn't where Hal was concerned.

I had gotten lucky and found parking on the street, right out front. I looked fondly at the 1995 Silver Jaguar XJS. It was the car my grandparents had bought the year I was born to celebrate their semi-retirement.

My grandfather had *loved* that car, and my parents had taken ownership of it after his death. It'd barely been driven, and upon my college graduation, it had been gifted to me, just as my grandmother's watch had been gifted to me by her at my high school graduation.

I loved both so much and missed home with a fierce ache in my chest. But that ache was one that would have to be pushed down and ignored, as a sleek black Tesla pulled up and stopped in the middle of Habersham Street, essentially double parking beside my Jag and flipping on its emergency flashers.

Ah, Hal's Uber is here, I noted, as the man himself climbed out of the back and let his gaze critically eye the property's front. I stood on the small front porch, forcing a smile as he slowly closed the door and stepped behind my Jag and up onto the low curb.

His Uber pulled away just in time, as the person behind them looked like they were about to lay on their horn to get them moving.

"Savannah, good evening!" Hal called out from the sidewalk, and I could hear the trepidation in his voice.

"Good evening, Mr. Lindstrom! Come on inside. I know it doesn't look like much from the street, but once you're inside, I'm sure you'll be pleasantly surprised." I laid my accent on thick as golden honey, and Hal didn't bat an eye.

He came up the steps to the modest front stoop, and I pushed open the door to let him pass me into the cooler interior of the old Lane house.

"This is not..." he faltered, and cleared his throat as he passed into the living room, and I closed the door behind him.

"Oh, now, don't you worry about a thing, honey." I playfully patted his arm. "This is just the first of many properties I have to show you. This is just to get an idea. Now, I know it doesn't look like much from the front, but just look at this, right here!"

As you entered the home, there was a hall that led directly into it – a living area off to the left with an upright piano against one wall and a modern working gas fireplace. The home was full of big, beautiful, tall windows, allowing plenty of natural light, and the stark-white walls made it feel voluminous.

It had a quaint dining room and a modern kitchen, both open to the living room, but, more importantly, to the vast entertaining space of the lower back porch and the small back garden.

Hal didn't like it, I could tell, but I pressed on with my bubbly routine of hyping up all the positives about the place. He was warming to parts of it. Even if he wasn't sold on this particular property, I was taking notes and getting a sense of what he was after.

We stood in the kitchen, and I marked things on my legal pad, scribbling notes for myself as we discussed and he described more of what he had in mind.

One thing about real estate was that it wasn't for the faint of heart. Clients you thought would be a dream could turn into a nightmare, and the ones you fully expected to be trouble could turn on a dime and be your dream client in disguise.

I was having trouble getting a read on Hal Lindstrom. At times, he was pleasant, but at others, he was cold and very nearly unreadable. By the end of this showing, I couldn't tell you exactly what it was about him, but my woman's intuition was subtly and cautiously peeking through with alarm in her eyes.

I ignored her, made it through the upstairs, and onto the top porch where I leaned a hip against the railing in the deepening gloom and asked, "So, final verdict... what do you think?"

"It is not what I am seeking," he said and looked chagrined at having to make the rebuff.

I put my hand on his arm and said, "That's alright, that's alright! What did you like about it?" I asked, prepared to take as many notes as it took to get things right.

Too modern, is what it boiled down to. Too much paint. He wanted more wood trim and classic elegance. All things that I could and would work with.

For now, it was back to the drawing board, as they say.

We parted ways. I locked up, and once I was seated in my purring vintage Jag, I started to feel much better.

I headed home, which wasn't likely what anyone would expect from me. As I was pulling into the small, detached garage on the property, my phone lit up and started to sing *Cabaret* at me. That could only be one person.

"Fabian," I said warmly, dropping all pretense and fake accent.

"You alive, Savvy?" he asked me, and I chuckled.

"Oh, I'm alive, and as suspected, the Habersham property was an absolute no-go."

"Lemme guess, Mr. Lindy has a real hard-on for the classic, antique-filled elegance a la the movies?"

I sighed and said, "Either hold on, or let me call you back. I just got home."

"Girl, call me back when you're comfy. You know I've got all night," he declared, and I barked a laugh.

"Okay, gimme five," I told him.

"Take ten," he ordered.

I tsked and said, "You're getting soft, you old Queen."

He chuckled, and it was very contrived and mirthless. "I'll get you later for that one."

"Talk soon," I said.

"Byyyyeee!"

I hit the red button to end the call and retrieved my phone from the magnetic mount it was stuck to.

I got out of the car and went to the back of the garage, pulling down the overhead door and pressing it until it latched.

The house I was at was a grand old Victorian outside of the city, near the river, but I didn't live in the big house. No, I lived in the tired, old, worn-down carriage house next to the garage. It looked like a shed, really, and was a far cry from the expensive and lush properties that I hawked all day long. But I wasn't here for any other reason than it was *cheap* – allowing every last red cent of commission I earned to go right back into what I truly loved back home.

I went around and unlocked the door under the sagging roof of the old porch that had seen better days.

It was a world of difference on the inside versus the outside. While the teal-green paint on the clapboard siding, which sagged with rot on the outside, peeled and bubbled, the inside of this place was a pristine oasis.

I pulled my sensible kitten heels off and opened the closet door by the front door, putting them on the rack inside.

I set my keys in the bowl on the entry table across from the closet and took my phone and my folio with its notes and such with me into the first doorway on the right that led to my little kitchenette.

I set things on the one sparse bit of counter space next to the stove and opened the fridge to pull out my chilled wine and pour myself a glass.

Three sips later, I was unwinding and taking everything into the small but cozy living room.

The fireplace didn't work anymore, but that hadn't stopped me from making it the centerpiece of the room, anyway. I had put a small space heater with a fireplace effect into it and had sealed off the chimney by taking a board backed with insulation and stuffing it up into the fireplace, holding it in place with spray foam – you couldn't see any of that mess from in here – but it did the job, sealing out the damp and the draft. With just a flick of the switch on the side of the small heating unit, the glow effect of the false fire made this little house feel like a home.

I had done a majority of the restoration of the inside of this place myself. My dad had come to help me with some of the tougher stuff, such as tiling the bathroom and fixing some of the plumbing.

Did I ask permission to alter the interior of this dump? No, but I *had* made it livable on the cheap and had probably raised the property value considerably for the slumlord I rented it from.

Not that the curmudgeonly old fool would ever know. It's not like he ever came to inspect or to fix anything.

I dropped onto my Wayfair-purchased, cream, boneless couch and sighed with relief, setting my glass onto the glass-topped rescue French Provincial coffee table I'd stolen off the curb up the street. I had spent a weekend restoring, sanding, puttying, sanding *some more*, and painting until it looked like a piece out of *Home & Garden Magazine*, all for the cost of some masking tape, primer, and a crackle-effect spray paint.

I pulled my dusky rose faux chenille throw over my lap and set my laptop onto it next.

I dialed back Fabian, and he asked me, "You drinking your dinner?" by way of greeting.

"You know I am." I rolled my eyes, and he chuckled.

"I've trained you well – so, what did you learn?"

"I have a much longer list of what he hates than what he likes," I told him.

"Typical," he said, and I could hear his mouse clicking on the other end of the line. "Let's have it."

And that was how we spent another fun-filled Tuesday evening – looking through listings online and coming up with a short list of properties to email to Hal Lindstrom in the morning.

It was the Savvy Savannah way, after all.

Chapter Four

Corvus…

She was ignoring me.

I hated it when she did that. It was childish, and it also stirred that part of me that wanted to hunt, to stalk, and to pin her up against a wall and *make* her listen to what I had to say, even if I already knew it was a nonstarter. Our respective clients were two very different kinds of people. No matter how in love with it my clients were, they weren't going to get away with making the changes they had in mind after taking possession of the place without an uproar and lawsuits hitting them left, right, and center from the local historic societies.

Sometimes, it was about protecting your clients from themselves as much as it was about protecting the agency from becoming legally liable during a sale for making bad-faith investments and sales.

Still, I appreciated Savannah's spitfire attitude and general stupidity in not backing down from me. She could be feisty when she wanted to, and it gave her hot looks an edge with personality that just did things for me.

Not enough to want to keep her around for anything but a casual fuck – I didn't tend to do shallow and insipid for very long. Like I said, there was something about Savannah Davenport that screamed *fake*. Disingenuous. She certainly could mean girl and be as cutthroat as the best of them, but I didn't tend to dig it when it was a woman's whole personality.

I set my phone aside, put my feet up on my ottoman, and took up my glass of cognac, breathing deep its rich aromatics.

My phone started buzzing across the small side table, and I let out an explosive sigh. "Jesus Christ," I muttered, and picked it up, half expecting her name to flash across the screen – but no, it was worse than that. Much worse.

I grimaced and answered the line. "Renaldo, to what do I owe this pleasure?" I asked.

Renaldo Benitez was the foot soldier for Benito Castañeda, our primary contact and boss for one of Colombia's more notorious cartels. No, we didn't deal in drugs – but we did deal in guns, and it wasn't time for our monthly cache exchange for cash out in the middle of nowhere. So, a call was... out of place, and out of place was never a good thing when dealing with the cartel.

"We got a situation," he said. Holding the phone away from his face, he rattled off in rapid-fire Spanish to someone in the background.

"What kind of situation?" I inquired, trying to suss out whether it was one that involved the club, or was just a problem the cartel was having and was coming our way, looking for a solution.

"The kind that requires the right tools to fix – if you catch my drift."

I did indeed catch his drift. He needed weapons, and he needed some now, before the usual drop. I heard someone make a query in Spanish and Renaldo tell them, "*El parche*." I knew what that meant. It meant posse, or group of friends – roughly.

"So, you help us out?" he demanded.

"Let me take it to the table," I said. "Get back at you within the hour."

"I'm gonna need an answer sooner than that," he said.

I nodded, realized he couldn't see it, and said, "Noted. Holler back at you in a minute."

I ended the call and dialed up Syn forthwith.

"Yeah?" he rasped on the other end, and he sounded out of breath. This time? He was likely fucking Madisyn into next week.

"Renaldo called, wants to, ah, borrow some tools."

"Borrow?" he asked.

I cleared my throat, and he grunted.

"Timeframe?" he asked.

"Like fuckin' yesterday, apparently," I said.

Syn swore, and I heard Madisyn groan, then yip after a sharp report – likely his hand landing on her ass. I got hard just thinking about it.

"Call him back, tell him rendezvous at the third worksite in..." he checked the time. "Forty-five, and he better not make this a fuckin' habit."

"Copy that," I said, shaking my head and pinching the bridge of my nose. Syn hung up on me, and I dialed Renaldo back.

"Third worksite in forty-five minutes," I said as soon as he answered.

"We'll be there," he said, and the line went dead.

I sighed and swirled the amber liquid in my glass, holding it up to let the light shine through it.

That was a little too easy, I thought... and I was sure that Syn would impart the rest of his message himself.

I scrolled down to the text exchange with Savannah and huffed a sigh.

She was showing a place on Hamblin. I wondered if it was the old Lane place – if so, good luck selling *that* one. It'd lost most of its historic charm, and there weren't many willing to shell out just under a mil for a one-bedroom, two-bath, especially not now.

The wave of new money, typically from online influencer money, required *space,* studio setups, and a myriad of other bells and whistles that the old Lane place just didn't have.

It was charming, sure, but it wasn't really what you thought of when it came to Savannah – at least not without an eye for and a budget for restoration.

I closed my eyes and settled back in my seat.

I'd have another chance to spar with Savvy Savannah another day.

I didn't have any doubts about that.

Chapter Five

Savannah…

This was the sixth property this week that I was to show Hal Lindstrom, and I swear to God, the man was a vampire and would *not* set a show time before sunset. It was making for a *very* long week – and my dogs were barking, *but…*

I stood in front of the Dickinson-Exley House on Duffy, just steps away from Forsyth Park, and had a feeling that if this place didn't move him, no place would.

Was it brick? No. Was it a mansion? Oh, *hell yes!*

Going for a cool one-point-four-two-five million, the Dickinson-Exley House was an 1890 crown jewel of a Victorian, complete with witches' peak and a unique one at that. It wasn't a room under the witches' hat. It was a round sitting porch, and it was *grand.*

She was a *gorgeous,* historical, three-bedroom, three-bath, with parking on the property. Three thousand eight hundred and seventy-one square feet of historical elegance with *beautiful* pressed copper ceilings throughout, working gas and wood-burning fireplaces and stoves, and golden glowing wood trim and banisters throughout. She had shelving everywhere inside, from bedrooms to sitting rooms to a lovely and cozy in-home library or office space. While the people living here now were rather minimalist by comparison to what I felt like Hal was looking for, this place had spaces, nooks, and crannies aplenty just *begging* to be filled with antiques.

She even had classic cast-iron tubs and fittings in more than one bathroom, as well as beautiful stained-glass windows.

She had been impeccably restored and maintained throughout her lifetime, and she was just *perfect* if I did say so myself.

Her current owners were overseas on a trip, which was just fine by me. I sat in the beautiful kitchen, my Jag parked out back, and worked diligently, looking through listings for my next client, just sure I'd be putting in an offer on this one for Hal within moments of his arrival.

He arrived with a light rap on the kitchen door to the back of the property, which, I confessed, scared the life out of me! I jumped, pressing a hand over my heart between the panels of my halter-style jumpsuit.

He'd startled the hell out of me, but it took me no time at all to shake it off and to clack across the kitchen's stone tiles to unlock the back door with a laugh and a toss of my long hair over my shoulder.

"You got me more nervous than a long-tailed cat in a room full of rockin' chairs, honey!" I greeted him gaily, and immediately I noticed that he was a man aglow with maybe slightly too much drink.

He greeted me familiarly, a hand at my lower back as he leaned in to kiss each cheek, which I didn't think much of. He seemed relaxed, and it was a typical European greeting.

"Now this!" he exclaimed, sweeping out his arm, and I smiled warmly.

"Yeah?" I asked. He followed me in, and I shut the door behind us. My phone, laptop, and keys were on the kitchen counter, and I took up my phone and slid it into my pocket.

"This is beautiful!" he exclaimed, taking in the pressed copper ceiling and the gleaming stone countertops. He slid a hand along the counter, and I swallowed hard as he looped his index finger through the ring of my keys and swung them, catching them in his palm. He fidgeted with my keys, and though I wasn't alarmed *yet,* my intuition was stirring again.

I shoved her away and said, "Come see the rest of the first level. If the kitchen impresses you, I can't wait for you to see the drawing room."

I toured the home with him, and with each room, he seemed more and more enamored. My hope and excitement grew that this might be it – and that I could put in an offer. As far as most clients were concerned, this hadn't been too bad, but then, it all went pear-shaped all too fast.

He wrapped an arm around my waist and pulled me in, trying to kiss me – for real this time – in one of the upstairs bedrooms. I turned my head, pushed back, and said, "Hey, no." But he persisted, and I ended up, in a desperate bid to get him to stop, coming down on his foot in one of my spiked heels. I was grateful that even though my feet hurt like hell from being in them all day, that I'd chosen the unconventional shoes because I hadn't bothered to have this jumper hemmed, and these were the only shoes that would allow the outfit to work for now.

Ridiculous fashion over function saved the day, because he shouted and let me go. He balled his fist around my keys and, hand wrapped around my upper arm with bruising force, sank his fist into my gut, crying out, "You little bitch!"

I doubled over, winded, and he dropped me. I went to all fours, trying not to gag and vomit from the blow, while trying desperately to draw air. He thought I was down, and yeah, I may have been – tears pouring from my eyes and unable to breathe – but I was already *moving* for the hall, scrambling on all fours.

He swore behind me and launched himself at me, tackling me around my waist, but sliding over the tan linen pantsuit to my knees. I kicked and kicked again. My heel caught him in the cheek, and he let go. My keys fell to the carpet, but I didn't go for them, because that meant going *closer* to him, and *no fucking way!*

I scrambled to my feet, still retching, trying to breathe, chest feeling like it would explode, and I made it to the stairs. Unfortunately, they were the ones going *up* because he burst out of the room, face bleeding under one eye and making another crazed and savage grab for me, but I was up the stairs.

He caught me around the ankle, and I went down, screaming, kicking, my lungs finally working as I lost a shoe and he lost a grip. I made it to the top of the flight and in a door, slamming it closed between us, throwing the lock, and backing away.

I took my phone out of my pocket and scrambled to text Fabian and managed to get out – *He's going to kill me – 911 – 911! 14 W. Duffy*

Crash!

I screamed and dropped the phone. The door held, but I didn't know how long it would.

"You get out here, you *fucking little bitch!*" he screamed. His accent was so thick with his anger and drunkenness that it was barely comprehensible.

"Mr. Lindstrom, stop!" I cried and tried to reason with him as my butt hit the tile and I scooted back toward the tub and scooped my phone back up. The screen was cracked in half, and the lower half, where I would dial, was flickering green and then black, while the top half remained normal.

"I'm calling the police!" I lied, but I couldn't. My phone was damaged, so I couldn't dial. I prayed my text to Fabian made it through and that the police were already on their way.

Chapter Six

Corvus...

I was in the Porsche, just about to leave the Manse after a late dinner with the boys, when my phone buzzed twice and the screen lit with an incoming text.

I had texted Savannah just a little earlier – to annoy her about a matter that really could have waited until tomorrow – but I was feeling petty, as she'd disturbed me days ago with an equally petty text after hours.

The message I got was *not* what I had expected.

He's going to kill me – 911 – 911! 14 W. Duffy

I started the car, and the engine roared, the shifter moving smoothly, as I worked the pedals, tires screaming against the drive as I pulled around, fishtailing and damn near running my ass end into the gate on the way out.

Synister would be pissed about the rubber I laid on the drive, but I would have it fixed later.

I tore ass around the back of the Manse and screamed around the block and down Whitaker. She was lucky. She was barely two blocks away, and I knew the 14 W. Duffy property. I turned down West

Park Lane and went up the back of the houses, turning into the back lot.

As soon as I hit the pavement after flinging open my door, I could hear the faint shouting and screaming coming from up and away inside the old Victorian. I didn't hesitate. The back door leading into the kitchen was locked, so I busted out the pane of glass by the doorknob with my elbow.

I reached through carefully and threw back the lock, letting myself in.

I could hear loud crashing, as though someone was trying to take down a door, a man screaming in something that wasn't English, but wasn't a language I recognized. I went for the stairs, lunging up them, two and three at a time.

My gun was in the back of my waistband, but I didn't bother with it yet. I didn't know what I was dealing with.

I found a blond man beating his shoulder into a closed and locked door on the third floor, and could hear muffled and hysterical crying from the other side.

"Hey!" I barked. He turned, sweat-soaked, disheveled, and with blood dripping down one cheek.

There was a woman's shoe lying forlorn on the floor between us.

"Back away from that door slowly."

He rushed me, and I clocked him in a smooth, controlled motion – all muscle memory, and one hundred percent reflex and training.

He went down, skidded to the top of the stairs along the runner, and came to a halt, half lying down them, his legs on the landing, his waist over the top step.

He didn't move.

I did. I glided up to the door, listened to the heaving breaths of the frightened prey behind it, and took a deep breath.

I knocked.

"Savannah?"

"Who – who's there?" she demanded. "Is it the police?"

I bit back a laugh.

"Open the door, Savannah," I ordered.

There was a dragging sound, some scuffling, a little shuffle, and then *click!*

The door opened inward just a crack, and a wild blue eye looked up at me, her mascara smeared in a muddy track down to her chin, her hair a wild and tangled mane, half-hiding the other side of her face.

"Corbett?" she squeaked, and she sounded horrified.

I cocked my head. "You texted that you were in trouble. I was less than two blocks away. You want I should leave and let you call the police?" I held a thumb over my shoulder, and she thrust open the door and nearly took me out, hiding her face in my chest, her arms wrapping around me like steel bands as she clung to me like I was her last known hope in the world.

The scent of peaches and adrenaline tickled my nose, and before I could catch myself, my arms went around her.

"Easy," I ordered, but she was sobbing brokenly and blubbering what, I couldn't understand.

"He tried to get me, he tried to hurt me, thank you! You came out of nowhere, but thank—" She shrieked, and reflexively, with one arm around her, the other went to the small of my back, as I turned us to the side and emptied three shots into the lunatic charging us.

She held onto me, screaming. I swore and turned to her and shook her a little more violently than I intended, but her mouth snapped shut, and my snarled "Stop it, right now!" seemed to get through to her.

She stared up at me, horrified, and I swallowed hard, knowing just how to turn this situation to my advantage.

Emotionless, I told her, "Stop your screaming." As soon as it was safe to do so, I traded my gun for my phone and pulled her in so she could hyperventilate in peace against me, and I could get the job done.

I dialed Requiem.

"Yeah," he answered on the first ring.

"Cleanup on aisle thirteen," I said, deadpanned.

"Aw, fuck. How bad and where?"

I rattled off the street address and told him, "Get Reaper over here with you."

"Shit, man, was that *you?*" he asked.

"Aisle *thirteen,*" I reminded him. It was the unluckiest number, so he knew it meant there was a witness, if not witnesses.

"How many?" he asked.

"One, and one," I told him.

"Shit, right. YO, REAP!" he hollered, and I pulled the phone away from my ear and grimaced. He came back in his normal tone, "On it, be right there."

"Thank you," I said, and the line went dead.

"No, it's okay. This is okay," Savannah reasoned with herself, staring in horror at the man I'd just killed. "It was self-defense, or defense of others. The cops will come... it'll be okay," she said. She looked up at me, beseechingly, with that sexy-ass gleam of true fear in her eyes and silently begged me to make it all better.

The trap was sprung, and Savvy Savannah Davenport was firmly in my grasp.

I cupped her cheek, rubbed a thumb through the muddy tracks along it, and said, "No cops. It's too late for that now."

"What?" She sounded as though I'd stolen her breath.

"Corvus!" Requiem boomed from down below.

"When are the homeowners due back?" I demanded before calling down, "Yeah, we're up here!"

"What?" she echoed. She was starting to stir, starting to realize I wasn't the savior she thought me to be.

I seized her up tighter against me and snapped at her, "*Focus!*"

She gasped and went still, nearly boneless in my grasp.

"The-they're abroad, um, uh, it's in my calendar on my laptop downstairs."

"Good."

"Shit*fire*, mother*fucker*." Requiem stepped up and around the dead body.

We could hear sirens in the distance.

"Don't worry about it," Grim said, coming up behind Requiem. "Syn already called in and made a false claim that it came from Forsythe, more toward the other end. Go on and get out of here."

"Let's go." I cajoled Savannah in the direction of the stairs, and she gasped.

"Come on, sweetheart, let us help you," Grim said carefully, putting on his funeral director's cautious airs. He knew how to handle fragile women.

"Give us the deets as soon as you can," Requiem said. I nodded and passed Savannah off to Grim, who handed her down past him to who could only be Reaper around the bend in the stairs.

I met up with him, took her from him, and led her carefully down to the main floor.

"What's happening?" she asked, and she was ghostly pale.

"They're handling it, and you're coming with me," I told her, while scooping up her laptop on the way out the door.

"Wait," she protested, and I stopped and looked at her.

"It's either me, or the cops. And I promise you, that you don't want any of that mess."

She swallowed hard and went with me. I felt like a spider, winding its prize into ropes of silk to stash away for later.

I can't tell you how much that got me off.

Chapter Seven

Savannah…

A strange sort of hollowness, I didn't know how to describe it, overtook me. No, that wasn't right. I didn't know how it came to be. All I knew was that one minute we were out the kitchen door, Corbett Prescott carefully lifting me over broken glass and not putting me down until we were on the driveway, and then we were at his rather ostentatious yellow Porsche. He shoved me into the passenger seat.

It was dark now, well past sunset, and I stared in horror at the shadows moving around up in the windows along the stairwell on the third floor.

"What's happening?" I asked, and he set my laptop and its cord in my lap.

"Don't worry about it," he said, and I jumped as the engine fired up and he swept us backward out of the lot and onto the lane, heading for… *shit.* I didn't know where we were going.

"Where are we going?" I demanded.

He said again, "Don't worry about it. Tell me what happened."

I coughed and stammered things out, waffling back and forth

between events, and meandering through the things that'd happened that were all a shaken mess in my mind.

"Okay, so shoes, keys, the Jag is yours – anything else?"

I pulled my phone out of my pocket and said, "I broke my phone – after I texted, before I could call 9-1-1."

"Shit happens, buy you a new one," he said, and I shook my head.

"Who were those people?"

"*My* people, and that's all you need to know about it," he said.

I asked quietly, "Are you going to kill me, too?"

"No," he said and pulled into a carriage house on a street I knew I should know, but *fuck*, everything was a blur.

"Come on." He got out of the car and came around, opening my door for me. Taking me by the elbow, he led me across the courtyard, out from under the carriage house to the main house.

A common structural thing here in Savannah.

He brought me into a small but cozy kitchen, then through into a sitting room that was part library, and sat me down in the wing-backed chair in the corner, switching on the lamp overhead.

"Let me look at you." He gripped my chin and tipped up my face, turning it this way and that, in the light. "Good girl," he murmured, and asked, "He hit you?"

I reflexively wrapped my arms around my middle, clutching my laptop over it like a shield, and said, "He gut-punched me."

"You got him good with your heel, yeah?" he asked.

"Yeah... um... where *are* my shoes?"

"Dates," he reminded me firmly. "When do the homeowners get back?"

Oh...

I opened my laptop and looked for him while he poured a drink out of one of the nearby decanters.

"Two weeks," I said. "In exactly two weeks."

He took my computer, set it aside, and replaced it with the drink.

I didn't care what it was. I downed it.

"Easy there, tiger," he said and looked bemused.

"I want to go home," I said and stood.

"Easy," he said and took the glass from me, setting it aside.

"I mean it," I said. "I want to go *home*."

"And I'll take you there," he said. When I went to walk past him, the room sort of swum, and I blinked and shook my head. My heart was still thundering in my chest, my blood still raced, and I felt my respirations pick up again as the swimmy feeling intensified, and my hands and feet suddenly felt like lead.

"What did you do?" It took entirely too much to get the words out, and they felt slurred around the edges.

"Just a little GHB, to take the edge off. You'll be out before you know it, and trust me – you're good."

My legs crumpled, and I slid down him to the floor. He came with me, kneeling beside me and whispered, "Don't fight it, just breathe and let it happen."

"*What the fuck did you do to me?*" I demanded and tried to bat his hands away, but I honestly didn't think any of the words came out right.

"*Shhhh,*" he soothed, and I fought – oh boy did I fight it, but it was no use.

Chapter Eight

C**orvus...**

She was out, and I sighed with relief. This would be much easier with her *compliant.* I called Requiem first.

"Yeah?" he answered, and he was out of breath.

I gave him the rundown.

"Jag is hers, she's missing her shoes, and her keys. He had hold of them, playing with 'em in one of the second-floor bedrooms when he ambushed her with a sucker punch to the gut."

He muttered, "Son of a bitch." I heard something hard hit something soft and could only assume he'd kicked the corpse.

"Said his name was Hal Lindstrom. He's a foreign national. Eventually, they're gonna come looking," I said.

"Security system is a basic one," Requiem replied. "Won't take much to erase what's here and make it look like a glitch in the system."

"Nothing taken," I told him. "This wasn't a robbery. They come looking, I'm going to tell them they parted ways. He wanted to put in an offer on the house, and the next morning, she couldn't get a hold of him. Just make the motherfucker disappear."

"She trustworthy?" he demanded.

"I have her right where I want her," I said, looking down at her, prone on my living room floor.

"Shit," he muttered. "You fucking better. Syn'll have your balls if you go rogue on this and it fouls up the club."

"Requiem..." his name held a thread of warning.

"Yeah, yeah," he said unhappily. "Make sure the canary doesn't sing. Where you at? The Manse?"

"My place," I said.

"Bring her Jag to the carriage house?"

"Yeah. Burn the shoes. I'll take care of what she's wearing. Find her place, and bring some clothes."

"You don't ask much," he said.

"Divide and conquer. You have the dream team there."

"Yeah, that I do," he said. "See you by morning."

"She'll be out until at least then," I said.

"TGIF," he said, and I rolled my eyes.

"Friday doesn't always mean a fucking thing in the world of real estate," I reminded him.

"Guess you better check her calendar."

"Guess I'd better."

I hung up and checked her laptop, which was still open and conveniently logged into. While her phone's screen was indeed fucked, I texted her assistant, Fabian, from her phone link on the laptop and pretended to be her, saying the showing went well, and he bit. I also told him I dropped my phone and would be offline until midday the next day, when I could get a new one.

It'd only taken scanning through their texts that afternoon to find her "voice" and Fabian, likely already into his cocktails on a Friday night, just told her goodnight and to not let the bedbugs bite.

Ridiculous.

"Looks like it's just you and me," I murmured, looking down at her, thinking *just the hunter and his prey.*

I made sure she was in the recovery position, so that when I went back and forth to tend to things – namely, building a fire to dispose of our clothing- she would be safe in her unconscious state.

I fired up the fireplace and stripped her down, scowling at the dark shadowing under her skin, starting to ripen into a putrid hematoma where he'd sucker punched her.

I burned what she was wearing and spent an extraordinary amount of time untangling the decorative combs from her hair to set them aside.

I took off all her jewelry, including that gold vintage watch I never saw her without, noting the inscription under its face. *Never Enough.*

Curious.

She was beautiful, her form perfect. I appreciated that she was a woman down there, and didn't shave herself to resemble a little girl's pussy, or give herself a landing strip like some sort of porn star. I hated that shit.

It was awkward, picking her up, but there was a bath waiting upstairs. I wanted to make sure she was scrubbed free of makeup and get a look at her fresh-faced, as much as I wanted to destroy any potential evidence she bore from our newly minted crime scene.

She'd been right. It'd been self-defense, or defense of others, and no court in the country would convict. But I wasn't about to waste time on all of that, nor was I itching to be under any kind of scrutiny by the pigs.

She stirred as I lowered her into the warm water, and I shushed her as she whimpered and fussed, trying to climb me like a kitten to avoid the bath. She settled with some careful and quiet cajoling, and she was out of it to the point that I didn't suspect she would remember. But I was curious, so I tried to engage her in conversation to see if she could and would make sense.

"How do you feel?" I asked.

She muttered, "Warm, and tired."

"Warm is good, tired isn't bad either."

"Have you killed many people before? Because I sure haven't," she mumbled.

"Yes," I told her simply. "Having never been a party to murder before, I can understand how it might make you tired."

I dipped a washcloth into the gently steaming water, soaked it, wrung it out, and covered my hand before working it into her face as though she were a toddler after a birthday party.

She sputtered and batted at my hands ineffectually. It was adorable, really.

"What are you doing?" she demanded sharply, and I chuckled.

"Getting you ready to sleep," I told her.

She squeezed her eyes shut and tried to sit up before it seemed to dawn on her... "Did you get me *naked?*"

I laughed, and nodding, said, "I did."

"I don't want to be naked," she said aghast, and I laughed again.

"You won't be for long," I promised her.

"What are you doing to me?" she demanded, struggling through her drug-addled confusion.

"Giving you a bath," I said gently. I didn't want her to get too riled up.

"I don't know you," she whispered, and twisted away, her face flaming. I thought to myself, *GHB is supposed to lower inhibitions...* and found that her reluctance, even under the influence, was both adorable and intriguing.

"You will," I promised her. "This is only the beginning."

She turned to me then, and asked, "What if I don't want to know you, Corbett Prescott?"

"That's a good question, Savannah Davenport," I murmured.

"Kittridge," she said, and sounded confused. "My name is Savannah Marie Kittridge."

"Kittridge," I repeated, rolling the sound of her name across my tongue. "I like that better than Davenport."

She covered her face with her hands, and her voice, muffled from behind them, said, "Ohhh nooo, why did I tell you that? I wasn't supposed to tell you that!"

"Your secret is safe with me, Savannah Kittridge. Now tip your head back for me." It took my hand at the back of her head to get her to trust enough to lie back into it. I held her up and dipped the pitcher I kept under the sink up here to rinse the deep cast-iron tub, into her bathwater, then gently poured it over her head, carefully slicking her hair back from her makeup-free face.

"There you go." I worked some of my shampoo through her long locks, shifting so I could kneel between the end of the tub and the wall to work the lather through her hair.

She whimpered faintly, and I asked, "Too hard?"

"No, that's nice," she whispered, and I wondered if a man had ever washed her hair for her.

I asked, "Anyone ever take care of you like this?"

"Not since my mom, when I was little," she confessed.

I thought to myself, that was a shame... and then thought, it was a shame she likely wouldn't remember this at all. I mean, she could, but GHB could be unpredictable in that arena. I'd tried to tell her to take it slow. The bourbon I had laced was some expensive shit that was meant to be sipped, not downed like a shot.

You'll just have to do it again, I thought. *When she's properly conquered.*

I liked the idea of her loose and easy, pliable in my hands and bending to my will while I fucked her.

At this point, I had her trapped, for sure, but it would be awhile before I could break her. She didn't seem to be the kind of woman to easily break. I wondered what it would take.

After witnessing how hard she'd fought her assailant, I was beginning to think there was more to her. Her confession that Davenport may be some sort of alias led me to believe there was a lot more there that I'd perhaps misjudged about her.

I wasn't in a hurry to find all her secrets. I was curious now. Could I dig online and do some searches? Sure... but I'd rather she tell me. Running her to ground and capturing her, bending her will to mine sounded like so much more fun, didn't it?

It did to me.

I had always been into a sort of primal sport with women in the past. I liked the thrill of the hunt. The chase. I'd yet to be satisfied into complacency by any of them. I doubted she would wind up being any different, but I could enjoy things while they lasted until I grew bored.

I helped her rinse, made sure that she was warm, and kept her compliant. It was a trick getting her up out of the bath, but she did manage to stand on her own enough so I could dry her off and pull one of my shirts around her. She slid her arms through, and I buttoned around three buttons in the middle to keep her remotely modest, before I led her to my bed.

I folded back the blankets while she leaned on me as though drunk, and she crawled into bed willingly for me, scooting to the edge and promptly passing right the fuck out.

I let her sleep, and showered myself, pulling on a pair of lounge pants in time to my phone vibrating off the edge of the black marble counter and into my sink. I picked it up and answered Requiem's call.

"Jag drives nice, but open up, fucker."

"Be right down," I said, looking in on my guest and deciding she was out and secure for now. I padded down the stairs and went out through the kitchen, across the courtyard, and hit the switch through the arch of the carriage house.

While the garage door worked its way up, I pushed my bike through and out into the courtyard so he could squeeze her Jaguar in beside my Porsche.

He barely made it out and around to me as I leaned the bike onto its kickstand as the door wound shut, sealing us into my little compound.

"We got a problem," he said, and held out the rectangle of her license to me.

I looked at it. It was a South Carolina license, and sure enough, it read *Savannah Kittridge* on it, but the address was clearly old.

"Where is this at?" I asked, tipping it toward Requiem.

"College dorm," he said with a shrug.

"Shit's that old?" I asked.

"Yeah," he said with a sniff.

"So, no clothes?" I asked.

He rolled his eyes and went back to the open door of the Jag and pulled out her purse, and a black paper bag from one of the designer boutiques around here.

"She's taller than Mini-Syn, but she's skinny as hell and damn near flat as a board where Mini-Syn is not, so they might be the same size... ish?"

"Madisyn for the win." I sighed.

"Now for the big question on everybody's mind..." he trailed off and gave me a flat look.

"She'll keep her mouth shut," I said.

"She'd better," he said.

"She's not stupid. She will," I told him.

"She got a golden pussy?" he demanded.

"Don't know yet." I shrugged and crossed my arms over my chest, the bag dangling from my fingertips.

"Fuckin' A, Corvus. You're not one to take risks," he said and shoved her purse into my chest. I grabbed it to keep it from falling, and he dropped her keys in the top.

"New phone with all the tracking software is in the bag. You can activate it for her tomorrow," he said.

"I've got this," I told him, and tried to sound reassuring.

"Aliases, and old addresses... how we know she ain't running?" he asked.

"I don't," I said. "But I *do* know her, sort of. I've been working across from her for over a year." I shrugged. "I'll find out."

"Yeah, well, you better. This is way off the fucking reservation as far as you're considered, and I, for one, don't like it. Syn's not worried – yet – but the big dawg is distracted these days."

"Questioning Syn's ability to lead?" I asked.

He scowled at me. "Fuck no! But after this? I'm starting to question *yours*. Don't make me doubt you, bro."

"When have I ever before?" I demanded.

"First time for everything," he said.

"The foreigner?" I asked.

"Handled," he shot back. He slid through my side gate and out onto the night-darkened street, whistling as he made his way down the block, turning to go back behind my carriage house on a brisk walk back toward the Manse.

I wasn't one hundred percent that I was the one who shit in his Wheaties. Requiem always had several things to be irritated about at once – my little dust-up and slightly left-of-center behavior may just be a straw too many for his camel's back.

Still, I would be sure to handle little miss thing in my bed, and then get back with him to touch base.

I was usually the dependable one to keep myself out of any drama, so yeah, tonight had been impulsive and out of character. As I reentered my house and returned to my room, I couldn't help but think that Little Miss Savannah Kittridge had gotten under my skin, and I hadn't even noticed when it'd happened.

Chapter Nine

Savannah...

I was warm, and slept on a cloud, but it definitely wasn't my bed at home, and it definitely wasn't a familiar arm around my middle pulling me back into an equally unfamiliar hard chest.

It *was*, however, a familiar voice in my ear as a man nuzzled my hair just behind it.

"Welcome to your indentured servitude, Ms. *Kittridge*."

I closed my eyes and went very still in Corbett Prescott's arms.

"So, you learned my legal name, so what?"

"Why did you hide it?" he asked, and I rolled my eyes and twisted in his grasp to meet his whiskey-colored gaze.

There was a coldness to them, an empty guardedness, that set my teeth on edge.

"I'm a woman who lives alone in Savannah, Georgia, with my face and name splattered in the paper, and on bus stop benches. What woman in their right mind in this day and age *wouldn't* operate under an assumed name under those set of circumstances?"

He chuckled lightly and said, "Touché."

"Why can't I remember how I got here?" I demanded, and a thread of panic threatened to choke me.

"You had a rough night," he said, and I swallowed hard.

"So did you," I observed, and he lifted one shoulder in a shrug and let me turn in his grasp. I lay on my back in his bed, and had no idea how I'd gotten there, no matter how hard I tried to think. It was like a gray-black haze, worse than the time I'd gotten blackout drunk on a pilfered jar of my pa-paw's peach shine.

"It wasn't rough for you at all, was it?" I accused.

"I've been through rougher," he confessed, and I blinked.

"I don't know what to say," I finally said after a protracted silence in which we simply *stared* at one another.

"'Thank you,' is a good start," he said dryly.

"Thank you for saving my life." I could concede that one. "But what the hell did you just say? Indentured servitude?" I raised an eyebrow.

"For a while," he said.

"So, I owe you for saving my life?" I demanded and tried to remain focused on his impassive face and those cold and contemplative eyes that should have been so warm for their color.

He smoothed a hand down beneath the comforter over me, and up under the shirt I wore underneath. The feel of his hand on my skin sent a conflicting wave of sensation through me. I shuddered, and I swear every hair I had stood on end. He pressed over my solar plexus, and I cried out with the pain of it, "Ow!"

"Let me see," he ordered as I pushed his hand away and he pushed back the blankets. I immediately covered my chest, and he chuckled.

"Suppose you don't remember these hands all over you in the bath last night," he said. "You didn't complain then."

I felt myself blush violently, as the memory, faint as a whiff of perfume from another room, passed through my head behind my eyes of those hands buried in my hair, thick with suds as he'd washed it.

I swallowed hard and said, "I told you my name... You drugged me!"

"A little GHB to calm you down and make you compliant. Rest assured, it's out of your system by now."

"Who *are* you?" I demanded, aghast, and those eyes of his turned molten with his... anger? I didn't know what to call it, but the look he gave me made me fear and feel all of three inches tall.

"Right back at you. Now *let me see,*" he ordered, and I moved my hands. He popped the three buttons holding the shirt I wore closed and parted the expensive fabric just enough to see, but kept two sides closed enough to cover my breasts. There was a terrible purple-red bruise down low, in the notch below my sternum, where things went soft and my ribcage met in the middle.

I tried to strangle my gasp, but it came out as this sickening little noise that made it seem like I was about to throw up.

"He got you good," he murmured, and he didn't sound happy about it.

"I don't understand," I said.

"Let me spell it out for you then." He quickly buttoned the shirt I had on, and I blinked, wondering how he'd done it one-handed and so swiftly, as he still lay beside me, his other hand propping up his head.

"You saw a side of me that no one should see, last night. You're privileged enough to live to tell the tale – but you won't," he said. "If you talk, and I'll disappear you, just as quickly as I disappeared your assailant."

"Okay," I said carefully. "So, you've bought my silence."

"I want more than just your silence," he said.

"What do you want?" I asked.

"You," he said. "At least until I grow bored enough to let you go. *If* I grow bored enough to let you go. You know how indentured servitude works, don't you?"

"It's a form of slavery," I answered. "Lasting for a period of time, traditionally seven years, until your debt is paid off, and then you receive your papers, and you are free to go..."

"Yes, well, that *was* how it worked," he said.

"This isn't that," I said. "There's no such thing as slavery anymore."

"Oh, that's not true," he said, and he sniffed. He'd been holding his free hand, just above me, trailing it over my body as though he were feeling the nervous energy coming off me.

"What are you talking about?" I demanded.

"You're mine to play with, to lick, to suck, to *fuck* as I want to until I get bored," he said. The *way* he said it had part of my libido sitting up and saying, *uh, YES please!* While the rest of me positively recoiled in horror. It was an interesting dichotomy.

"You don't know anything about me!" I argued.

He grinned, an almost feral thing, and said, "You're right, I don't, and I don't care. I like what I see, and I take what I like."

He rested his hand on my hip, and I batted it away, off me, like it was a spider crawling on me, which made him burst out laughing – loud and raucous like a murder of crows, the timbre of his voice richer and deeper somehow.

"This is sick," I whispered aghast, and he gave me a lopsided grin.

"Then I'm a sick man," he said. "But don't pretend you aren't aroused, or that you aren't squeezing those thighs together at the thought of me getting between them. Because I may be a sick man, but I'm an honorable one, mostly, and honor abhors deceit, and I really don't like liars."

"If I say no?" I asked.

"You're in no position to say no," he said. "Or did you forget you're an accessory to murder?"

"I didn't kill anyone!" I chirped in objection.

"No, I did, but you didn't exactly call the cops, did you?"

I remained silent because, well, he wasn't wrong.

"I'm not going to pin you down and fuck you right here, right now," he said. "So loosen up."

There was a sparkle of mirth in his eyes, and I felt myself relax, incrementally, until he seemed... pleased.

"I don't know what to do," I murmured.

"You don't need to *do* anything, except make yourself available when I call."

I swallowed hard and felt my eyes well, and the whispered words were out of my mouth before I could stop them. "I just want to go home."

He looked thoughtful for a minute and said, "First things first." He rolled onto his back and reached down beside his side of the bed and brought up a black bag from one of the boutiques downtown.

"Clothes," he said, and reached into the bag and pulled out a new phone. "And a new phone to replace the one that broke."

"I can't afford—"

"Hush," he countered. "You're mine for the time being, and I didn't get to the part where I tell you that comes with some perks."

"Like what?"

"Like a new phone to replace yours. Who's your carrier?" he asked.

I named the carrier I was with.

"Easy," he said. "Let's get that sorted, first..."

I blinked in amazement as he brought around his phone and my broken one from his nightstand, and we sat up in his bed. He bizarrely fixed my phone. Using his to call the carrier, while he did the work of switching SIM cards and used my computer and my old phone to download apps and transfer data like he was born to it, politely kibitzing like my granddad would with the representative on the line until everything was securely moved over and operational.

He hung up with my carrier, which I guess happened to be *our* carrier, and handed me my new phone. It was several models newer than my old one, and I didn't have a case for it, but that was a relatively easy fix.

"Thank you," I murmured.

"You're welcome," he said simply, and then he got out of bed and disappeared into the bathroom up here. I swallowed hard as I heard water hitting water, and I listened to him sigh.

I peeked into the bag and found an elegant black dress inside. Something sheer over a flowered material beneath.

I lifted it out and found a dress that *might* fit me.

Divesting of his shirt, I pulled the dress on quickly. It fit, hitting me below the knee, but it clung to my figure and gaped dangerously if I bent over, showing *everything* if I wasn't careful. As though it was meant for someone with a much bigger chest than mine.

The toilet flushed, and he stepped back out into the room with me.

"Where are *my* clothes?" I demanded, and he stopped, mid-stretch, and the play of his muscles beneath his skin was both a sight and an intimidating one at that.

"Burned them," he said with a shrug.

"*What*?" I blinked.

"They might've had evidence on them."

My knees weakened, and I was absolutely mollified by the gravity of my situation.

I sank to the edge of the bed and blinked slowly. "What if someone comes looking for him?" I asked. "I don't know what to say..."

"That part is easy. You tell them you showed him the house, you parted ways, and he told you to put in an offer. You do that today, and you do all the things you're supposed to do, and then you call him. And then you call him again, and then you call him *again,* and you do that for a few days, and then you drop it."

"Why would I call him when I know he's already dead?" I asked.

"Because you *don't* know that. You do it to establish your alibi. You're the last one to see him alive, but to *not* do those things now? It will point right at you later on down the line."

I nodded slowly in understanding.

He held out my new phone. "Call him and leave a voicemail. Tell him you're putting in the offer today, as promised. Put on that fake-ass accent of yours and lay it on thick, girl. I'm going to go make us some coffee."

I blinked, long, slow, and stupid, and he winked at me and went out the door. I heard him thunder down the steps a moment later.

I called Hal Lindstrom and waited, and waited, and waited, through what felt like endless ringing until his voicemail picked up.

I held my breath, waited for the beep, and, acting as though my life depended on it – which it *did* – I left a message.

"Hi, Mr. Lindstrom! It's Savvy Savannah, and I just wanted to let you know I'll be putting in that offer on 14 West Duffy later on today for you. You have a great day, now, Sugar! Bye-bye!"

I hit the red button with shaking fingers and felt like I was going to throw up. I was flying blind as a bat here, and I knew if I didn't do it right, I was likely going to die, too, and then where would the Kittridge line be?

I dragged myself to my feet and thought to myself, *I just want to go home.* Instead, I squared my shoulders and took myself downstairs to face a monster in his kitchen and drink coffee like a civilized person when there clearly wasn't a civilized bone in Corbett Prescott's body.

Chapter Ten

Corvus...

Her muted steps fell on the stairway's treads as I went through the motions in my kitchen, making us coffee. She looked thoughtful, troubled, and I liked the way the look wore on her beautiful face.

"How do you take your coffee?" I asked, and she stared at me, as though I'd spoken Alien translated into Greek in her direction.

"I just want to go home," she said, and I nodded.

"Your car's out back. Looks like you found your purse – sorry about no shoes, but I'm sure you have plenty others. I don't think I've ever seen you wear the same pair twice."

Her expression went from wide-eyed innocence and scared to absolutely mollified.

"What do you *want* from me?" she demanded, and she slipped into one of the seats at my small dining table.

I smirked and asked once more, "Coffee?"

"You seriously expect me to drink anything you'd try to give me from now on after *you drugged me* last night?" she asked archly.

I grinned wolfishly and said, "I'd tell you to keep your panties on, but I know you don't have any at the moment."

I watched her blush furiously, and she stood up.

"Oh, relax!" I chided. "Sit down, have a cup of coffee, get it together, and then you can go."

"I can go now," she argued.

Letting my gaze turn molten, I snapped at her, *"Sit down!"*

She sat, abruptly, and swallowed hard, and her obedience pleased me. She was afraid – but still stared at me, resistance and impertinence in her deeply troubled blue eyes, and I fully admit I enjoyed having the upper hand.

"How do you take your coffee?" I demanded curtly.

"Two creams, two sugars, but you're wasting your time. I'm not drinking that."

I gave her a look of consternation, then turned back to the pot, pouring two mugs, opening the fridge, adding half and half to one, tossing in two spoonsful of sugar, before sliding it across the table at her.

She sat and simply stared at me.

I raised my coffee to my lips and arched my eyebrows at her over the rim of my mug as I took a deliberate swallow and willed her silently to stop being so fucking obstinate.

She wrapped her hands around the mug in front of her, more for the warmth than out of any desire to actually drink it, and stirred it, which at least satisfied me that she was keeping with decorum.

"I like you better without all that fake shit," I muttered, and she arched one eyebrow at me, bristling.

"Pretty stupid blondes and sex appeal sell more houses," she said flatly, and I huffed a laugh.

"It also gets you whatever the hell that was last night," I countered.

"You're seriously going to blame me for Hal Lindstrom's bad behavior?" she countered. There was some of that fire she held banked inside – the embers and coals sparking to life.

I cocked my head and set my coffee on the counter beside me, leaning my hands between the counters, pressing my hands flat and lifting myself off my feet in a stretch, as I contemplated what she was implying. I had to admit, she was right.

"No, you're right. That was all him. You tell a dog to sit and stay in the presence of a prime piece of meat, and it tends to have more self-control than your average man these days."

"Did you just compare me to a piece of meat?" She gave me an ugly look, and I barked a laugh.

"Now you're reaching, princess," I told her. "I was agreeing with you and walking back my prior statement, but you won't even give me that, right now, will you?"

She shook her head.

"No, I won't. Not while you're standing there all blasé about drugging me and... and..." She was trying to find it when it was so blatantly obvious, so I helped her out.

"Sexually blackmailing you?" I supplied.

"Yes," she said, and she sat back in her seat as though I'd whisked the sheet off and displayed the stark horror that lay underneath.

"I guess I'm not such a complicated guy after all." I shrugged and took up my mug for another drink.

"Certainly, no better than the dog," she muttered.

"Although I do have more self-control," I said. "Right up until I don't..."

"I don't see the difference," she said.

I grinned. "The difference is that depending on *your* behavior, this gets to be as pleasant or unpleasant as you want it to be."

"What in the *Cruel Intentions* warped reality are you talking about?"

"Not as airheaded as you pretend to be on the regular, are you?" I shot back.

"What?" She looked confused.

"I like to play with my toys, and you're quickly catching on," I told her.

She closed her eyes and shook her head. "And if I don't want to play?" she demanded.

I laughed at that. "Then you wouldn't be playing like you are," I said. "You would have left by now if something in you wasn't at the very least... curious."

She swallowed hard, took up her coffee, and drank a big swallow.

She set it down and then seemed to realize what she'd done because she looked up at me with those eyes, so wide, and showing too much white, and I couldn't help myself. I howled with laughter.

"Give it a minute," I told her and took another swallow of the black liquid gold in my mug. "You'll see I didn't put anything in it."

She propped her elbows on the table, covered her mouth with her hands, closed her eyes, and trembled finely. I appreciated the beauty of her discomfiture.

"I'm going home," she said finally, and when she opened her eyes, the bottom lashes were thick with gathering tears.

"By all means," I said. "Keys are right there." I gestured to her keys in front of her. "Laptop is in the living room."

I watched her slowly get up and gather her things and said, "I'll walk you out."

"I can manage just fine," she tried. I smiled and chuffed a laugh, shaking my head as I held open the door off the kitchen into the courtyard.

"You need me to open the carriage house garage door for you."

"Oh." She cringed as she slid by me and carefully stepped out onto the patio brick in her bare feet, her toes perfectly manicured to match her fingernails.

She clutched everything to her chest, awkwardly, as though it would somehow shield her from my presence.

I opened her car door for her, and she looked at me, blinking in surprise, the door suspended between us as she still clutched her belongings as if they would somehow save her from me.

It was far too late for that, but if it made her feel better...

"Remember, I call and you answer."

High spots of color appeared on her cheeks, and she didn't say anything, just got into her car and tossed everything onto the passenger seat, most of it spilling onto the floor.

I made sure she was in before I shut the door and stepped back, hitting the switch to open the garage. She stared at me, starting her car and waiting so that she could pull out.

She was careful, and I was glad for that. It was a nice Jag. Looked like it didn't have many miles on it. She pulled out onto the street and, once clear, left in a hurry.

I hit the switch and walked back across the patio and into my kitchen, taking up my phone off the counter and checking the tracking software I had installed on her new phone.

I watched her dot move along the lines of the streets she took, satisfied it was working, and wondered just how all of this would play out.

Chapter Eleven

Savannah...

I went back to my little mother-in-law hovel and immediately went in to shower. I stood under a punishing hot spray and couldn't help but let my mind wander to the feel of Corbett's hands in my hair.

It'd been a long while, and even if my brain was like, *"ew, God no,"* it seemed that my heart and my body had other ideas about it.

I *longed* to be touched like that for *real,* which was honestly wishful thinking with how men were these days. I'd given up entirely on dating in college after some harrowing dates.

Men were just... *ugh,* anymore.

While I genuinely found Corbett Prescott *irritating* before all this, now I found myself... I didn't know – three-quarters terrified, and at least one-quarter intrigued.

Still, the terror was totally winning right this minute, and I honestly couldn't get into the shower fast enough, like it would do something to wash the horrors of the night before down the drain.

I stood under it, washing thoroughly with my comfort-scented potions and lotions that held the sun-drenched smell of peaches.

The fruity scent hung in the steam that filled my bathroom. When I got out, I felt marginally more relaxed than when I'd entered. I wound my hair into a towel, dried myself as thoroughly as possible with the other towel, hung it to dry, and shrugged into my soft, fluffy robe.

It was one of those cheap, microfiber bathrobes that was soft and almost furry against the skin. It was one of my most favorite things to cozy up in, especially in the winter months.

I didn't bother with slippers, I just went out into my bedroom with a sigh and tried to soak up my solitude – basking in it, like a lizard under a heat lamp.

I loved being alone. Especially after spending all day, every day putting on airs for these unbelievably snobby and wealthy people – fooling them into believing I was one of them when nothing could be further from the truth.

My family had always been firmly in the middle class – maybe *upper* middle class at some points, but just barely.

These people I worked with and for were a whole different league of *rich* – and even though they believed I was one of them, I didn't feel it. At all. Ever.

Yes, I was pulling in the kind of money to put me on their level – but I was living way below my means, as modestly as possible, for a reason.

The truth was, I was just a country-bumpkin farm girl who knew how to thrift where the rich people lived so I could cosplay as one of them.

Last night had definitely opened my eyes to just how out of my league I was.

There was no reason not to call the police. The more I thought about it, the more it freaked me out that Corbett had been so... cavalier about *not* calling them. Like, in what world is it more convenient to dispose of a dead body yourself versus just calling the police and telling them the truth about what had happened?

I made myself some sunshine in a cup. A warm and comforting

peach tea blend I'd found in one of the Savannah tea rooms that a client had insisted on meeting at.

My hands trembled and shook, and I didn't know what to do with all of this except go through the motions of making my tea, and go sit with things for a while. Tomorrow was Sunday, and while there was usually plenty of business to keep me going seven days a week, I was religious about taking Sunday off, even though I wasn't a subscriber to any one particular church or faith.

I had been raised Christian, but I didn't really belong. My family was religious, and my mother and father attended church on Sundays, but I didn't think they really cared about it so much as they cared about my grandmother and *her* love of the church.

I hadn't been raised the kind of stringent Christian – church three days a week, youth group, and all of that kind of mess – but more of attending on holidays and with my grandparents when they had me for the weekend.

I didn't think Corbett Prescott would survive setting foot inside a church. Given what I'd learned about him last night, he was the devil himself, and to do so would set the church ablaze – he would be fine.

Still, my main concern in all of this wasn't him or even me. My primary concern was how I was going to keep going at the clip that I was in order to pay Uncle Sam to keep my family's farm out of hock or whatever.

You see, my granddad was a good farmer. He grew and sold some of the *best* peaches South Carolina had to offer! What he was not was a businessman, or good with numbers – and we had discovered, after his passing, that the farm was in trouble when it came to the back taxes that were owed on it.

My mom and dad had taken on the management and day-to-day operations, but farming wasn't what it used to be. It'd been a long, long time since the farm had turned enough to support *all* the things, and for some reason, my grandpa had decided the taxes were the thing that could wait... and wait... and *wait, and wait, and wait.*

We needed money to make regular payments, and to keep those

payments up, or Uncle Sam would take the whole thing. Thus I put myself through college and took on the challenge of keeping our heads above water.

I was handling it – but barely – and I was getting to where there was a glimmer of light at the end of the tunnel. But it had required that I become the best at what I do, and to maintain being the best, you had to put in the work. I didn't know if I could afford the distraction that was Corbett Prescott and this *indentured servitude* he seemed to delight in having me under.

While I didn't know what I was going to do, I knew what I was *not* going to do – and that was panic. I was so not going to panic. Not yet, anyway.

I'd juggled so many things in the past that this was just one more thing, and I could do it. I was sure I could do it... But lord, I needed to stop, take a minute, and breathe. I couldn't fully assess what juggling this would entail until I knew what it looked like, and so far, it looked like I didn't have to really do anything until Corbett called. Lord knew when he would do that.

At least, hopefully, not any time soon.

I curled in the corner of my overstuffed, boneless couch and stared into the faux flames of the space heater in the fireplace, my hands wrapped around my mug of steaming tea as though a blizzard blew outside.

I was definitely in the freeze portion of fight, flight, freeze, or fawning, and freeze was okay for right now. I knew that I had plenty of fight left in me should it come to it. I wasn't about to fawn, and there was no running. My family's legacy depended on me staying right here and following through.

Chapter Twelve

Corvus...

I picked up my phone off my desk and texted Savannah *Davenport* while turning her real name in my mind... *Kittridge*. It sounded *vaguely* familiar, but for the life of me, I couldn't place it.

I tapped out my request, read it a time or two, considering it. I wanted to draw her in further, so I softened the wording and moved one of my pawns on the board.

What's your calendar look like for Friday night at 8pm?

I stared at the screen, waiting, waiting, and just as it tried to go black, it lit up with a return message.

Irritated, I unlocked the phone again and tossed my head back, exasperated that it was a spam message and not from her, just as the device buzzed in my hand, alerting me to another message.

I have a client showing at 7pm, depending on how long that takes, I may still be with them at 8.

"I am not an unreasonable man..." I muttered, but still, she intrigued me.

So soon after last week? I asked her.

Time is money. Her response made me bark a laugh.

Touché. Meet me at The Olde Pink House at 9. Dress for dinner, valet your car.

I wasn't asking, but I was being accommodating. I wanted her to meet me at eight, but I could do nine.

I prefer to park my own car. I'll be there at 9, regardless.

"*Ooo*, the kitten has teeth," I remarked to myself. "Put those claws away with me, sweetheart."

I love how you think I was asking. Valet the car under the reservation for Prescott. I'll see you at nine.

I tossed my phone back on my desk and breathed deep, letting it out slowly. I did love these little games. She could either do as I ask or suffer the consequences. It was on her – although it honestly didn't matter that much to me whether or not she parked her own damn car. It was a fun little test to see how she would be, and I was sure I could come up with a fun little punishment if she didn't want to obey. Something light enough to establish the boundary but heavy-handed enough to delight me.

My palm positively tingled at the thought of it making contact with her supple ass. Suddenly, Friday couldn't get here fast enough for me. Pity it was only Wednesday.

Friday dawned as it ever did, and the slog of paperwork and other real-estate-related business had been a real drag, but now the moment was upon me.

I sat in the private dining room in a not often used upstairs portion of The Olde Pink House and waited, surprisingly, not so patiently, for my prey to arrive.

I checked my watch. *Seven minutes to the appointed hour.* Frustratingly, irritation thrashed my heart as though she were already late, and I couldn't identify if it was my own impatience or something akin to nervousness.

While I sat and tried to pick apart my own Gordian Knot of feelings, working to solve a puzzle I hadn't even known existed, a runner entered the room and handed me a scrap of card.

I smiled to myself as he hastily exited, and I tucked it away in my inner pocket. She had done as I'd asked and had valeted her car. I took out my phone and texted the prospect to bring it to my place.

I was tearing a page directly from Synister's playbook on handling my first dalliance with Savannah, much the way he handled things with Mini-Syn – by at least buying her dinner first. What's more, I had a little gift for her... hopefully enough to buy me at least a little goodwill.

I glanced at the box beside my plate. It was navy and wrapped in a white ribbon with silver edging.

It wasn't much longer before I heard the smart clack of heels marching resolutely behind our host for the evening, the manager of The Olde Pink House. The door to this little private dining room opened up, and he ushered Savannah through, who did not disappoint in her attire.

She was dressed to the nines in some designer halter dress, the skirt flowy and fluttering on the breeze she generated as she walked.

Her heels were high and did great things for her legs. The outfit suited her. The dress was dove gray, printed with magnolia blossoms and foliage.

Her hair was half pinned up and curled to perfection, her makeup light and understated. She was beautiful in what appeared to be innocence, but given that she'd entered into this contract with me by way of her continued silence throughout the week and her presence here, I knew that I'd peeled at least a few layers of that innocence away.

I stood and held out a hand gallantly. She reached out and took it. I brushed my lips across her knuckles and told her the truth. "You look lovely."

"Thank you," she said stiffly, as the manager pulled out her chair for her at the ninety-degree angle from which my place was set. I wanted something a little more intimate than a table between us.

She took her seat, and he helped tuck her beneath her place setting.

I took my seat as well, as she unfolded her napkin and laid it upon her lap.

"Thank you for coming," I said as soon as the door whooshed shut behind the manager, closing us into the candlelit space.

"As if I had a choice?" She arched one eyebrow and looked at me plaintively with solemn blue eyes.

"I've brought you something," I told her. "A gesture of goodwill, if you will." I handed over the jeweler's box, and she took it.

"Really now?" she asked, and her curiosity was so obviously piqued.

She pulled the sash of the ribbon, and it unraveled elegantly. She lifted the two pieces of the cardboard box apart and set the top aside, turning the velveteen box out of the bottom. I took the liberty of taking the ruins of the ribbon from her and the bottom of the box as well, tucking the ribbon into my pocket for safekeeping, and setting the bottom part of the box aside without taking my eyes off her.

She cracked the lid of the box she held in her hands, and it folded open and back from the glittering gold within. She gasped and looked from the old watch to me, her eyes filling with tears.

"I thought I'd never see it again," she said.

"I took the liberty of having it cleaned and fine-tuned at the best place for it in town. I could tell by the engraving on the back that it held quite a bit of sentimentality. What does it mean and who was it from?"

It had been a burning question of mine. I reached out, took the watch from her trembling fingers, and she held out her delicate wrist so that I could clasp it for her.

"It was a wedding gift from my grandfather to my grandmother," she declared. "It meant that no matter how much time he had with her, it would never be enough."

"I take it one or both of them has since passed?"

She nodded, but remained mute, staring at the glittering watch on her wrist. Her lovely face was shuttered, her emotions hidden behind a mask of stoicism, but for the glitter of tearing in her eyes. She took a moment to look at the pressed tin ceiling in here to breathe through so they wouldn't spill and ruin her makeup.

"Thank you," she said finally. "I thought you had burned everything."

"I had to be sure, but no, I simply had things cleaned. Your necklace, earrings, and bracelet are here." I handed her the bag from the jewelry company I'd had them tended to, and she took it.

"I appreciate it, but these don't hold a candle to the meaning of this." She flashed her wrist at me, the candlelight glinting off the watch.

"Perhaps you might forgive me for my misstep with the drink last week."

She nodded carefully, but I could tell she was still guarded.

"Are you allergic to anything?" I asked. "Or is there anything you dislike immensely?"

"No." She shook her head. "I'm not allergic to anything. As for dislikes? I can't say I'm a particularly picky eater either, as long as it's not bugs or insects."

"Not a fan of escargot?" I asked with a fleeting smile.

"No." She shook her head, and a little laugh escaped her.

"Neither am I, so you're safe on that front." I unfolded my napkin and placed it into my lap. "There's no menu. I decided on a four-course meal."

"Sounds lovely," she said, and I smiled.

"I took a gamble on seafood," I said, and her smile grew slightly, and she nodded.

"I do believe it paid off. I love seafood," she said.

"Very well, I believe it will be served shortly."

She nodded carefully and asked, "So, um..." She laughed nervously and asked, "What's the occasion?"

"Consider this as close to an apology that you'll get. I'm not very big on them," I said, taking a sip of the crisp white wine in my glass.

She took up hers and took a hint of a sip and asked sardonically, "There's nothing in this, right?"

I chuckled and said, "Just wine."

"Okay," she murmured, but she set the glass down and folded her hands in her lap, fidgeting slightly with them, gripping them, and twisting them slightly.

"Tonight, we're meant to have a nice dinner, and then, if you're amenable, we'll take a bit of a walk back to my place. I had them take your car there and park it in my garage."

She bowed her head and smiled, shaking her head, and I could tell it was with some displeasure.

"You really like to be in control of everything, don't you?" she asked.

"It is one of my things, yes," I agreed.

She took a deep, slow breath and let it out between her luscious and perfectly glossed lips and said, "That's bound to drive me crazy."

I chuckled and said, "I fully admit, I enjoy that aspect of things as well."

"Ah-huh."

It was at this point that the door opened once more, and the first course was brought to the table. She said nothing in the presence of the waiter, and I kept silent, too. While I was perfectly comfortable in the silence, I could tell she was not – that she likely held a multitude of burning questions, and I was curious if she was brazen enough to ask.

I picked up one of the steamed mussels and the tiny fork that came with the dish to dig them out of their shell. She watched me as I forked the tender morsel and held it out to her. She reached for the fork, eyes fixed on me. At the subtle rise of my eyebrows, she blushed a light pink and dropped her hand back into her lap, leaning forward like I wanted her to, and parting those lips.

I passed the tidbit between them, and she took the little bite between her teeth, her lips grazing the oyster fork as she drew back and carefully chewed.

I fed myself one and enjoyed the bright burst of citrus and wine with the underlying richness of the mussel itself.

"Why did that feel so obscene?" she asked softly, dabbing at her lips with her napkin.

"Because all I can picture is those beautiful, soft lips wrapped around my cock."

She froze, wide-eyed, staring at me as though I'd just set something on fire. Judging by the creeping blaze of color seeping up her chest and into her cheeks, I perhaps had.

"Why do I get the impression that appeals to you?" I asked with a slight smirk. She turned her head resolutely in another direction and stared at the door, as though half-willing someone to come through it, while the other half contemplated making a break for it. But alas, there was another part of her that kept her rooted to her seat, and that intrigued me more than anything.

I could see the struggle play out in her stiff body language, and I relished it.

"Have another," I murmured. She turned back to me, all wide-eyed and innocent, trying to cope with a myriad of emotions and thoughts. I thoroughly enjoyed the cognitive dissonance playing out in real time before me.

"Are you always so crude?" she asked softly, and yet she took the proffered bite of mollusk I held out to her.

"Oh, you have no idea, Bright Eyes," I told her.

She blinked, mystified at the little pet name, and chewed slowly and thoughtfully. I let her think about it, the rest of the way through the course.

The next course was a traditional Caesar salad, the notes of vinegar intent on cleansing the palate before the main course, which arrived promptly just as we each had taken our last bite of crisp romaine.

She seemed to relax a little as the main course was served. Rockfish stuffed with a shrimp and crab medley with a rice pilaf of exquisite execution, the likes of which would torture my brother, Torment, who was an executive chef.

We ate quietly, and the silence had shifted to something quite pleasant, and considering how I wanted my dessert, I was alright with that.

"Who were those men?" she asked quietly, after taking a fortifying sip of wine. "The ones who came after you..." She didn't need to clarify. I knew who she meant.

"You've probably guessed by now that I'm an Iron Wraith." She jolted with a bit of startlement.

"You?" she asked, and gave a long, slow blink. "I never would have guessed in a million years, actually."

"Ah, excellent," I said and took another bite of my fish. I chewed carefully and slowly, thoughtfully studying her as she silently ran up and down the catalog of implications that the revelation had brought with it. She really had no idea, which just meant I had done well at keeping my mundane, day-to-day business life and my real life separated well enough. That was a good thing.

"I somehow can't picture you as a biker," she said finally, and I laughed decently long and hard at that.

She winced and said, "Don't make fun of me. Clearly, you didn't *want* anyone to know, and I can have a guess or three at why."

"Enlighten me," I said with mirth. "And I would never make fun of you."

"I've heard a rumor or two about the Iron Wraiths operating more like the Mafia rather than a biker gang," she said evenly, but there was a slight tremor in the lilt of her voice that gave her away. She was afraid, and rightly so.

"I suppose with that reaction, now would be a bad time to

mention I'm more than just a member... I'm the vice president of the club."

Her fork clacked against the fine China we dined off when it slipped from her suddenly nerveless fingers.

"You're joking," she said incredulously, and her deep blush returned. If I were a betting man, which I was want to be from time to time, I would bet that it had more to do with anxiety this time rather than any sense of embarrassment or what have you.

"I don't joke about things so serious to me," I told her flatly.

She looked at me with new eyes, and I watched her visibly shrink as she leaned back into her chair and let it catch her.

"Those were some of my club brothers, to answer your question, and now you likely have put two and two together on why I'd rather *not* involve the police in such matters."

"I'd wondered about that," she whispered faintly.

To their credit, my brothers *had* arrived slick-backed to the occasion of cleanup on aisle thirteen. There was no need to advertise the Iron Wraith's presence in such dirty deeds, should anyone happen along at the right place at the wrong time for us. At any rate, that was why she had no idea who we were that night. There were absolutely no clues.

"I believe that should answer the majority of your questions?" I said pointedly, a less-than-subtle hint that I would really rather she not ask any more.

"Yes, um, thank you," she murmured. With a trembling hand, she took up her fork to resume our meal. I expected her to pick at her food or to merely shuffle it around on her plate, but it would seem she hadn't lost her appetite with the new information provided to her.

Her esteem went up a notch in my book for that.

We finished our meal, and I could see other burgeoning questions and queries lighting up her eyes. I waited for a time until she began to shift in her seat before relenting and saying, "Go on, ask. I won't promise you I'll answer, but you can ask."

"Oh, um, I mean... how long?" she asked.

"Since the club's inception," I told her, which I knew was a non-answer, really, being as no one could really know, except for the club itself, how long we had been going on.

"I see," she said, and she looked thoughtful for a minute before finally accepting that at face value.

"You all, um, go way back?"

I smiled then, and nodded, the question evoking nostalgia for the days in our mutual boarding school when it was just me, Syn, and the core group of a few others.

"We do," I said. "Some are newer to the club and came after its creation. But they aren't too far behind, and they're as important to us as the next brother."

"I never understood how any of that was meant to work," she confessed as the door opened and the final course was served, though they only brought the one plate.

They set it down in front of Savannah with a single dessert fork and set a glass of top-shelf bourbon at my place setting. I nodded with appreciation as the staff set about clearing the rest of the dishes and cutlery away, leaving us with just our drinks, the dessert, and the faintly glowing candlelight of the centerpiece.

"You're not having any?" she asked.

"I'm not much one for sweets," I told her.

She looked at the slim slice of New York-style cheesecake, drowning in a bourbon-and-peach-glazed compote, and took up her fork.

"Mm!" She rolled the first bite in her mouth, letting the flavors soak into her being, her eyes slipping shut, and her expression lighting with pleasure.

My lips flickered into a smile of pleasure of my own at just watching the spectacle of her before me.

"That is *amazing*," she said, and her delight was a real and palpable thing.

"Yeah?" I asked, and I couldn't help my grin.

"Mm-hm," she hummed around another bite.

I enjoyed watching her savor every last morsel of the dessert, and she sat back, sighing in satisfaction.

"That was definitely the crown jewel in an otherwise sumptuous meal," she said. "Thank you for that."

"It wasn't hard to guess that peaches are something you like," I told her.

She blushed faintly at that, and said, "Let me guess... my perfume?"

"Indeed," I told her.

She smiled, then a thought occurred to her, and the smile slipped ever so slightly. "So, what happens now?" she asked softly, and my smile grew.

"Now, it's my turn for dessert," I told her, and her solemn blue eyes met mine. I loved watching the uncertainty creep back in.

I snapped my fingers twice, and the door opened. Savannah jumped slightly as three staff members entered the chamber. One took her plate, while another used a candle snuffer to put out the centerpiece.

The third member of staff took the centerpiece away, while the man with the candle snuffer removed the top-most layer of linen, leaving the clean one beneath. All three filed out of the room, the door shut, and the dim light of the crystal chandelier rose ever so slightly to make up for the light that'd just been whisked away. The door closed, and Savannah turned at the snick of the lock being thrown.

"Relax," I told her, and took a large, old-fashioned, antique key from the inside of my breast pocket and set it on the table beside where I'd set my glass.

"It's the privacy I paid for, not a trap," I told her gently.

"What do you want from me?" she asked. I rose from my place, letting the napkin fall from my lap to the floor. I held out my hand, indicating she should rise as well, and she did, standing slowly as I moved deftly between her and her chair. She looked up at me, fearful, as I backed her against the edge of the table.

I brought my lips to hover just before hers and whispered against them, "Relax, I'm not going to hurt you." I was going to tell her to close her eyes, but as luck would have it, I didn't need to. They slid shut of their own volition as her breathing became shallow.

I intentionally stole her breath, touching my lips to hers in a light, chaste kiss, relishing how her body shook and shuddered as an ensuing sigh escaped her chest and brushed my lips with warmth.

I took advantage of that sigh, wrapping a hand tight in the back of her hair. My other hand found her waist, as I stepped into her, trapping her between my body and the edge of the empty table as I strengthened the kiss into something deeper, stronger. A kiss that broke down walls and left her breathless, a whimper of protest humming along my tongue as I passed it between her teeth and stroked along hers, her mouth sweet and tasting of how she smelled. Ripe and full-bodied, like the personification of the sun itself.

Her hands pressed against my chest, briefly, but then their touch lightened, and her initial resistance gave way into the sweetest supplication.

It was about that time I let my hand drift down her back, releasing her tangle of curls to join the other at her waist. I continued to kiss her breathless, as I began to inch the material of her short skirt up her legs until it was in such a way that I could step up my assault on her senses.

I tore my mouth from hers and picked her up, setting her ass on the edge of the table and ordering her, "Lie back." I pressed my palm between her small, but pert tits.

Her blue eyes widened in something like fear, but she obeyed beautifully, lying back with some trepidation.

I skated my hands from her knees, up the outsides of her thighs, and stepped in closer between them.

She sucked in a sharp breath as I tugged at the waistband of her panties and resisted, momentarily, by not lifting her hips as was expected. I gave her a warning look with a slight cocking of my head and a raised eyebrow. She complied, looking as though her heart was in her throat, bracing her arms against the table, and obediently lifting her hips for me. I whisked her panties down her legs, stepping back and working first one side over her spike heels she wore, then the other.

I pulled up her chair and took a seat, scooting in and keeping her knees apart with my shoulders.

"Relax, Bright Eyes, and put your knees here." I draped one over my shoulder, then the other.

She lay back against the table, pressing her hands over her heart, which no doubt thundered in her chest. I took a sip of my bourbon, watching her as her chest heaved with panicked breaths and she squeezed her eyes shut.

She had a beautiful little pussy that was glistening at the slit, and I could only imagine how much she *ached*.

I touched her with a light index finger, gathering the wet from her entrance, slicking it over her clit, and labia, watching that little kernel of nerves jump and begin to engorge itself on her desire to be fucked.

She could deny me with her voice all she wanted, but her body positively screamed otherwise.

I pulled her hips closer to the edge of the table and, with no preamble, plunged my tongue into her wet and waiting cunt, tasting her, teasing at her opening, and thrusting as far as I could inside her.

She tasted remarkable, with notes of honey and musk – nothing overpowering – quite delicate in fact. She tasted clean and pure, and I fucking loved it.

I dragged my tongue from her opening, up her slit, and latched onto her delicate pearl of a clit, sucking and tasting, rolling it around with the tip of my tongue, as she jumped beneath me and my hands tightened on her hips, a silent warning to hold still.

She gasped and covered her mouth with both her hands, and I took it as a personal challenge to see how vocal I could make her. See how far I could push her until she forgot herself and howled her pleasure for me.

I started by slipping my middle finger into her wetness, questing around at the roof of her twat for that slightly ridged patch of pleasure center, just a couple of inches inside her. I found it and curled my finger against it, stroking with the pad against her in a come-hither motion to drive her wild.

I'd given up on teasing her clit in my quest to find it, and I held off on tormenting it further for a bit more, until a gagged little cry came from behind her hands, and I could feel her wet little pussy tighten around my invading finger. It was enough that I had to force my index finger into her alongside its mate.

Her hands flew off her mouth and tangled in the linens at her hips, as she held on. I began my two-pronged attack, teasing her G-spot with my fingers, and swirling my tongue around her clit, until her back arched, and her voice slid from between her lips in a begging whine that rose and fell with her frantic breaths, higher with her exhale, deeper with her panting inhale. It was a harmony of profound pleasure that I lost myself in as I devoted myself fully to her exquisite torment.

I would not relent until she came completely undone, and I was not disappointed. She hit her peak, and wailed, a long peal of siren's song and the sweetest music to my ears as her back arched off the table, and her knees quaked where they lay over my back. Her pussy clenched and released my fingers in a rapid staccato as I used my free arm to hold her down, barring her hips and pressing her into the table as I thrust my fingers now three at a time in her, in and out, prolonging her orgasm and fucking her tight little hole.

I watched her writhe beneath me, watched her come completely undone, and relished the feel of her hands wrapping around my wrist in her futile attempt to pull my hand from her drenched pussy as I worked her mercilessly.

She shuddered, gasped, and let out a little "oh!" of defeat, and I knew she'd had enough.

I stood in front of her, looking down on her, I fully admit, smug as hell. She cracked her eyelids and looked up at me as I sucked my fingers clean, and stroked her leg. The praise left my lips...

"That's a good girl, Bright Eyes. That's a good girl."

Chapter Thirteen

Savannah…

Oh, holy hell. I hadn't expected any of that, and as I lay there, chest heaving, body still twitching from his glorious and not entirely unwelcome assault on it, I couldn't help the suffusion of glow that rose up in me to meet his praise.

I couldn't believe we'd just done that – in a restaurant, no less! I was terrified that someone out there had heard me, but I just couldn't bring myself to worry about it just yet, as he took my hands and helped me to sit up.

"Take your time," he urged.

His cock tented the front of his slacks, and I swallowed hard and tried *very* hard not to look, as much as I tried not to think about how much I really wanted it right this minute. God, how I hoped that he would let it out, and slide it into me – but I was sure that was just the raging hormones thrust up to the surface by the burst of light that was the afterglow settling into my very bones.

"You good?" he asked me quietly, pressing the glass with the remainder of his bourbon into my hand. I swallowed it gratefully, hoping that it would do something, *anything*, to settle my jangling nervous system.

I nodded mutely.

He bent down and picked up my purse and the jeweler's bag with my belongings in it, holding it out to me.

I took them and clutched them to my chest. He bent once more and held up my scrap of panties, making deliberate eye contact with me, before he stuffed them in his pocket.

"The bill and gratuity are paid," he said. "When you're ready, we'll depart."

"And go where?" I asked, breathy.

"For a walk," he said with a slightly cruel smirk. "I don't know about you, but back to my place sounds good. I've only just begun my fun."

"I-I don't know how I feel," I said truthfully, trembling. He braced his hands on either side of my hips and leaned in, his lips by my ear. I could smell myself lightly perfuming his beard, and I *really* didn't know how I felt about that.

"Not what you expected?" he asked softly.

"No," I confessed.

He got closer, and promised with all darkness intended, "It's only just begun and it can and will be so much better."

I swallowed hard, my libido just about throwing a goddamned parade, while my mind quailed from the thought in dismay.

I didn't know if I was prepared to go any further than this with him. The thought positively terrified me, to be completely honest.

I tried to sort through the tangle and static of the sensations running through me, my better judgment, and my innermost dark thoughts and feelings urging me to take the risk.

He already was the best sex I'd ever had, hands down... but the problem I had was that I was completely unsure if I could keep things compartmentalized at *just sex.*

Fuck!

Girl, it's not like you have a choice, I reminded myself and slipped to the floor from the table, with a clack of my heels.

I set aside my purse and the jeweler's bag, and huffed a breath, pulling down my skirt and smoothing it in place, ensuring nothing was hitched or stuck anywhere. Because that was all I would need, was to go downstairs past all those people who may or may not know what we'd been up to up here and give them a show to go along with whatever little audio drama they'd been subjected to over their dinners.

I ran fingers through my curls and huffed an intrepid breath before hanging my purse over my shoulder and taking up the small bag with all the individual little boxes, including the parts of the box that'd contained my watch.

He picked up the ornate classic skeleton key and put the other hand on my back, pushing me a little ahead of him as we went for the door. I stopped and stood aside as he got the key in the old lock and opened it up, a man on the other side stepping aside for us.

He'd been standing guard, I guess, and I blushed furiously and tried like hell not to make any sort of eye contact with anyone as Corbett-fucking-Prescott guided me to the top of the stairs.

I stared resolutely at my feet, watching my footing as we descended and went all the way out through the front door and into the sultry Savannah night.

I swallowed hard and let Corbett take my hand. He led me through the throngs of people waiting outside, along the sidewalk, and to the corner, where we turned to leave the crowd behind.

He slowed his pace and looped my arm through his, resting my hand at his wrist, and covering it with his other hand.

It was an old-fashioned, gentlemanly gesture that I let him perform, even though it felt as though it was just to keep me from pulling away or making a run for it.

We didn't speak on our stroll, and I just followed his lead, hoping that at the end of our walk, I would be allowed to just get in my car and go... although that hope was barely a glimmer on the horizon.

"Are you always so..." I groped for the right word that wouldn't come off too insulting, but he went ahead and said it for me.

"Depraved?" he asked, simply.

"Um, *yes*," I said, and could feel the color creeping up on me as it had so many times since I'd set foot in that private dining room.

"Worse, typically," he said nonchalantly with a one-shouldered shrug. "I would put your hands to any of these garden fences if I could, and bone you where we stood if I thought I could get away with it."

I very nearly swallowed my tongue.

"I would very much so rather *not* catch a public indecency charge or wind up on some sex offender registry, if it's all the same to you."

"Oh, I understand completely," he said. "Modern laws on such things do tend to take the fun out of just about everything."

"You're outrageous." The accusation, or rather condemnation, was out of my mouth before I could stop it.

"Why, thank you," he said with a wicked sort of grin that said he really did take that as a compliment.

Add insufferable, too, I thought to myself, but I didn't exactly want to push my luck by saying it out loud.

"How much farther is it?" I asked quietly, just a little further down the sidewalk.

"Uh, just a block, maybe a block and a half," he said. I used his arm to steady myself and kicked off my shoes, bending to scoop them up to hold in my hand along with my jewelry.

"Surely you don't intend to walk the rest of the way barefoot," he said with an incredulous chuckle.

I shrugged my shoulders. "I've been in these heels all day and my feet are killing me," I said. "It's only a block to a block and a half. We're going slow. I'll watch where I step."

He looked at me as though I had done or said something equally crazy, and I stared back at him, mollified.

"You'll lay me out on a dining room table in the middle of a restaurant to eat my pussy, but me walking the rest of the way to your house *barefoot* is crazy?"

"On these streets? Yes," he said.

"Then give me a piggyback ride," I said boldly.

He laughed at that, and I do mean really laughed and said, "You have some surprises to you, Savannah Kittridge." With zero preamble, he crouched down for me to get on his back.

I laughed and called his bluff, but he picked me up with ease in our nice clothes and just kept heading in that direction.

We were both giggling and laughing until we very nearly wheezed at the way some people smiled and pointed, laughing at our antics. It wasn't much more than a block more, and we were stopping on Charlton Street in front of a fairly non-descript door set into the brick face of the building, a low-hanging porch with wrought iron-work over our heads.

He carefully set me on my feet on the mat out front and took out his keys.

"And they say chivalry is dead," I joked. He smiled slightly and turned the key in the lock.

"Don't expect me to put my jacket into a puddle for you," he said. "My Italian suits are where I draw the line."

"Noted," I said, and he gestured that I should go before him.

I slipped inside, and he stepped in after me, shutting the door and throwing the lock. I didn't know what to do with myself, so I simply stood still and waited for some kind of indication of what he would like. It was awkward, but by the same token, it was his house.

"Dinner was wonderful," I said. "Um, thank you again."

I was trying like hell to say my goodbyes, but he wasn't going to let me out of things that easily. He took my purse and bag from my hands, led me into the living room, switched on a lamp, and set them down on one end of the expensive leather couch.

"You're not getting away that easily," he murmured, and I swallowed hard. "Take off your dress," he said, and the heat in his gaze very nearly burned me.

I pursed my lips, and he cocked his head. My face flamed, and I said, "I'd rather not if it's all the same." I twisted my hands together nervously in front of myself, and he smirked.

"Need a little bit of what I gave you last week to loosen you up?" he asked.

"What? No!"

"Surely you haven't had enough." He arched one brow as though challenging me, and I felt myself straighten.

"There is such a thing as too much of a good thing," I countered.

He chuckled, and it was a dark sound.

"Tell you what... I'll give you some grace and a head start. Go upstairs. I'm sure you remember which room is mine. Take off your dress, take a shower if you'd like, but, Bright Eyes, you're not leaving until I've buried my cock inside you and made you come, screaming my name."

I stood frozen, eyes locked with his, unable to move.

"Those are your choices," he said. "Either get naked right here, right now, or get naked upstairs. Either way, you're getting naked and I'm getting what I want."

He was dead serious, and I thought back to what he'd said at dinner – about it being my choice to make this as pleasant or unpleasant as I wanted. I stood up a little straighter and said, "Give me twenty minutes to freshen up."

"You have ten, now go," he said, looking at his watch.

Oh, shit.

I didn't waste any time. I went upstairs, padding quietly through his home, and feeling like a ghost of myself.

I was torn between two clashing sides of my psyche. On the one side, I wanted to be the girl my family believed in. The good girl. The doting daughter and granddaughter. On the other hand, *Jesus Christ* – this was hot – and I wanted to throw caution to the wind and indulge in everything this wicked man had to offer.

I just didn't know how both facets of my personality could exist in one body... I mean, was that even possible?

I found myself staring into the mirror above his bathroom sink, as I reached behind my hair and undid the clasp behind my neck, holding up my dress. I let it fall to the floor, the silk pooling at my feet, and stared at the ugly, healing bruise that was just starting to fade from purple to that sickly brown with yellow and green.

It was putrid in color, and I hated it. I couldn't wait for it to fade completely.

I swallowed hard, and unclasped the barrette holding up half my hair, and set it aside, letting my hair foam and froth around my face. All I could say is I felt vulnerable, exposed, and I didn't know if I was ready, no matter that my pussy grew wet all over again at the thought of his hands on me.

I braced my hands against the cool marble of the counter around the copper sink, and stared into the bright metal, willing myself not to stress or cry.

His hands, warm at my hips, his lips brushing my shoulder, very nearly had me coming out of my skin! I jumped and made an inarticulate and terrified sound, and his arms slid around my stomach, pulling me back against him.

He'd lost the coat and had rolled his sleeves back over his muscular forearms. I stood, staring at our reflection in the mirror as his eyes searched my face carefully in the looking glass.

"Close your eyes, baby," he muttered against the side of my neck, and I was still scared.

I asked him, "Why?"

"Have I hurt you?" he asked me, raising his eyebrows.

"N-no," the confession stammered. He hadn't physically hurt me, no – honestly, he hadn't emotionally hurt me, either. The things he had done thus far were definitely dubious and questionable... but pain had not been part of the equation.

"Close your eyes," he tried again firmly.

I closed my eyes, and he moved. I could feel his arms drop from around my waist, and he reached into his pocket. My eyes flew open to find him clutching the white satin ribbon from the box my grandmother's watch had been contained in.

"Trust," he urged quietly, and I swallowed hard and closed my eyes again. Everything with him had suddenly become so *tense* and *intense.*

I was normally very good at pretending I was so sure of myself, and in certain arenas, I was very sure of myself! But this... this left me no room for certainty or surety, and I really didn't know what to do with that.

The soft satin with its slightly crisp, scratchy edges was laid over my eyes, and I gripped the counter in front of me until I knew my knuckles mottled red and white without having to see them.

"I want you to listen to the sound of my voice, and I want either a 'yes, sir' or 'no, sir', do I make myself clear?" he asked.

"Yes, sir," I whispered uncertainly. His hands were gentle and warm where he rested them on my shoulders, his thumbs digging ever so slightly into the base of my neck.

"Do you prefer I wear a condom?" he asked.

"Yes, sir," I said, and my throat felt so tight it almost made an audibly clicking sound as I tried to swallow past it.

"I'm going to push you," he whispered in my ear. "I'm going to make you feel things you've never felt before. I'm going to introduce you to a pleasure so fine it may be confused with pain. I'm going to hurt you, not badly, but enough to make you suffer beautifully for me. Can you handle that for me?" he asked.

I know he wanted a yes-or-no answer, but the truth felt more important in this moment. "I don't know, sir..." I breathed.

"Hm..." The noise was so small, and yet so profound as he *listened to me*, and really contemplated what I'd just said. That, in and of itself, sapped some of the fear away and left me feeling both hopeful and grounded.

"This dynamic isn't for the faint of heart, Bright Eyes, so I'm going to go slow tonight. Some night, though? The training wheels are going to come off, and I'm going to scare the living shit out of you.

But I promise, if you're a good girl and you take it all, I'll be the one to kiss away your tears."

His lips touched the side of my neck like the brush of butterfly wings, and I let out a breath I hadn't realized I'd been holding as I'd hung onto every single one of his words.

I *ached* from the dark promise of his words. I knew it was very likely absolutely batshit insane for me to want what he was offering, *but damn did I want it.*

"Does that sound good?" he asked beside my other ear, and I jumped, having not felt him move.

"Yes, sir," I breathed, and I think my lack of hesitation pleased him because I could hear him smile.

"Come with me, Bright Eyes." He turned me carefully in his grasp, and slid his fingertips down my arms, capturing my hands with his and towing me along. I stepped out of the ring of my dress carefully. It probably looked comical to him, but he didn't laugh.

The tile of the bathroom floor was cool against my feet, but with only a step or three, it transitioned to a plush carpet that felt like it went on for days.

He turned me and backed me against the bed, much as he'd backed me against the table at The Olde Pink House, and ordered me gently, "Sit." I sat, and his hands disappeared from mine.

I listened hard, which was honestly harder than it sounds, with the way my heart pounded and the blood swished behind my eardrums with every pulse. I faintly heard the rustle of clothing as he more than likely disrobed, and my anxiety spiked.

Shit. I was doing this! I was really doing this!

"Lie back, try and center yourself on the bed," he ordered. I put my hands down by my hips and pushed myself back, putting my legs up and laying my head on the pillows. I swiped my hands over the velveteen covers and to the edges of the bed, and did my best to scoot over when my hand reached the edge on one side but not the other at first.

"Is this good?" I asked nervously and was met with a noise of disapproval.

"Ah! What did I tell you? The only thing you're to speak right now is 'yes, sir' and 'no, sir', remember?"

I blushed. "Yes, sir..."

"That's your one and only mistake, do you understand? Do it again, and I'll have to suitably punish you."

"Yes, sir," I said, my mouth suddenly dry.

"That's a good girl," he murmured, and the bed dipped at my knee off to one side.

It was silent, for a time, but then his fingertips lightly touched the apex of my thighs, and I jumped.

"You're so beautiful," he murmured. "But I think I'd quite like you helpless..."

I jumped slightly as his weight shifted, and there was a rattle of chain above my head.

"Give me your wrists," he ordered, and I hesitated for a second. He waited me out, and I held out my wrist vaguely in the direction of his voice. He wrapped gentle fingers around it and lifted it over my head, where satin-lined leather wrapped around it. There was a snicking sound as he fed a tongue through the buckle on what had to be a restraint, and he worked to fasten it tightly.

"Give that a tug," he ordered, and I did, my hand catching at the thumb joint and nearly sliding through. He adjusted it a notch and ordered, "Again."

I wasn't going anywhere that time.

He picked up my other hand from where it lay beside me on the bed and did the same thing.

"Do you want the blindfold on, or off, when I put myself inside you?" he asked and followed it up with, "Permission to speak."

"On, please," I murmured, and his hand slapped the outside of my thigh, the crack loud, and the sting immediate. I yelped and bit my bottom lip.

"On, please, what?" he asked.

"On, please, sir," I said breathless with fright.

He rubbed the mark that he was sure to have left and remarked, "Your fair skin pinks up so pretty."

I didn't say anything. I mean, it felt like the right thing to say something like thank you, but I liked to think I was a quick learner.

When I remained quiet, he chuckled lightly and said, "That's my good girl."

I swallowed hard. So, it *had* been a test.

The bed shifted several times as he walked himself up on it and pushed my knees apart to get between them. A moment later, I heard the packaging rip, and him spit a fragment off to the side.

I listened, ears straining, voice likewise straining to remain quiet, as he made himself ready. I listened to the latex strain, and the crisp noise of it rolling down his length, and I could picture him, hard and straining against his slacks after he'd finished making me come at the restaurant.

My breathing picked up, his hands warm as they slid up over my ribs and cupped my small breasts. His fingers pinched my nipples and rolled them, and I bit my lips together, hoping to keep the moan trapped behind them.

I didn't know if that would count as talking – but apparently, it did not, because he sighed out and continued to touch me, his one hand sliding further up my chest, wrapping around my throat, and squeezing. I gasped, afraid, but he didn't cut off my air or anything. Instead, he just pressed me down into the bed and held me in such a way as to let me know I was indeed helpless, and he could indeed do *anything* he wanted to me. I reached for him, and my hands came up short, the chains jolting against whatever held them in place.

He walked back on his knees and wrapped his powerful arms around my thighs, bodily pulling me down the bed. I yelped in surprise as much as fear, as the manacles he had me in stopped short and pulled my arms taut over my head.

"You're going to take every inch of me," he swore, and he slapped his cock against my pussy, spanking my clit with the swollen head.

I captured my bottom lip between my teeth and let my head fall back as he situated himself at my opening. God, I wanted it. I wanted him inside of me *so bad*. I was wet, and my pussy ached to be filled. I was running purely on how turned on I was, but then there was the small part of me that was just screaming, the sound reverberating on the inside of my skull, just in an absolute panic and dread over what a bad idea this was.

"Just breathe," he ordered, and I realized I'd stopped, that I had been holding my breath, every drop of air squeezed from my lungs, and I was waiting on pins and needles so hard that I'd forgotten to draw any back in.

I sucked in a sharp breath, filling my screaming lungs, and that's when he penetrated me. His body invaded mine, sliding into my wetness, stretching me around his not-inconsiderable girth, which just got wider the further he pushed himself into me. My body was more than eager to have him there, my pussy throbbing, and pulling him in, silently begging his cock to quench its thirst, to vanquish this gnawing hunger that'd settled in my womb.

My fucking, God, how long had it been?

I knew the answer with my head, but my heart denied it, crying out that it'd felt like eons since I'd let anyone this close. Oh, how *good* it felt even though it simultaneously felt so wrong, so dangerous.

I instinctively wrapped my legs around his lean hips in a futile bid to create some semblance of a transfer of control, allowing me to slow things down, and put a little distance between our bodies, even though I didn't want to kick him out of me completely.

He twisted his hips in such a way that it rubbed so good inside me that I cried out, and then his hands were at the backs of my knees. I lost my grasp with my legs as he pushed them apart, freeing himself while simultaneously pushing my legs to my chest – folding me like a fucking lawn chair – before letting his weight carry him down on top of me, and thrusting his cock into me brutally deep, where he bumped my cervix and made me cry out with the pain of it.

"I'm driving," he reminded me coolly, as I writhed ineffectively beneath him, gasping and trying to both find the words and fight them from coming out. I breathed through the sensations and scrambled through my thoughts, all the words and things I wanted to say slipping through my fingers like grains of sand until the gleam of what I needed to say caught my mind's eye.

"Yes, sir," I gritted out. He eased up, just enough, and started riding me, pulling out and surging forward with precision, finding that place between too much and not enough, so that he could expertly exploit it. Believe me, it blew my entire worldview on what was just pure, unadulterated sex.

There wasn't anything loving about this. There was no feeling behind this. No sweetness, no caring. This was animalistic, single-minded determination in action, although I couldn't for the life of me figure out what the end goal was supposed to be.

It wasn't hate-fucking – there was no hatred involved. It was clinical, precise, and cold on an emotional level, which upped the ante on other things – dirty, raunchy, and darkly decadent among those things.

I focused on breathing. I focused on enduring, and somehow, some way, I found myself stumbling through the weeds and out into a stream of purest fucking pleasure. The kind of pleasure that cut like a razor and revealed the complex layers of one's psyche.

At some point, I simply switched off, stopped thinking, and just gave myself over to the feeling of his warm body over top of mine, of the punishing rhythm, of the feel of his cock scouring the inside of my walls and igniting a fire in me I didn't think was possible.

I wanted so desperately to touch him. I wanted so badly to pull his mouth to mine and have him kiss me. I desperately missed the reassurance of lips on mine, of soft touches, and of the magic of connection. Eventually, I managed to let those things go, and just gave myself over to the feeling of touch, and the sound of his breathing as he crushed me to the bed, and moaned his own pleasure that he took from me into my ear.

A glow of pride suffused me at that sound, and it was a rush for me, knowing that he was enjoying himself so thoroughly. Still, I couldn't help but realize that the stripped-down and empty hollow center of my being was just everything about the overwhelmingness of my entire situation, with him pulling back from my shore.

It wasn't leaving me. It was regrouping, and as everything rushed back in, crashing into my shore in a cacophony of mess and hurt, desire and friction. It was as though he had stripped me completely bare to the bone of everything that had made me, *me,* and now it was all crashing into me at once.

A lightning bolt of pleasure forked out from where our bodies met at our groins. It licked along the inside of my being with flame – scorching me finely, the tongues of electricity curling around my tight nipples, and fizzling out through my limbs in a spectacular spray of sparks as his body and the motions it made completely unmade me, pulling me apart like a tornado going through a trailer park, and leaving inestimable damage and wreckage behind.

It was one of those moments in your life that you knew you were changed and that there was no going back to who you used to be, and *that* was terrifying.

Chapter Fourteen

Corvus...

I needed to immediately switch gears. She lay trembling beneath me and had taken everything I'd demanded of her body beautifully. But be that as it may, her soul was pointedly in distress. She couldn't catch her breath, and it wasn't lost on me that she was sobbing. Though I didn't feel as though I'd broken her completely, she was definitely in need of some repair.

I hadn't banked on shifting her completely off her foundation, but I was definitely getting a sense that was what had just happened. God, she'd felt incredible, and the sight of her blindfolded and chained to my bed, powerless and as tame as a new kitten, had fucking done so many outstanding things for me.

I had ravaged her, thoroughly and completely, and though I knew she'd come, and that I'd made her come undone, her fear had spiked at the same time, and now she lay shattered and vulnerable beneath me.

I lay over her, smoothing her hair back from her face, the blindfold beginning to stain, the satin turning from white to gray, and her makeup transferring and bleeding through with her tears.

"Shhh," I soothed, and kissed her lips lightly. "Let it out," I urged. "I've got you, Bright Eyes. You feel whatever you need to feel."

The permission made her gasp and pause in her trembling. It was anyone's guess whether she would collect herself or fall apart completely.

I unshackled her wrists, and her arms came down to hide herself from my sight. There was a part of me that was swamped with immense guilt.

Too much, too quick, I surmised, and I captured her face between my hands, pushing the blindfold up out of the way, pulling her to me, and burying her face into my shoulder. Kissing the side of her head, I breathed into her ear, "Take your time. Take as long as you need to." And I meant it.

She dissolved into a flood of tears, and I could only admit to myself my folly. She wasn't at all who I'd thought her to be. I had thought she was just another rich girl, used to these sorts of head games, guarded, stronger than steel – but this? This was something else, something completely unexpected. I had one of two choices – stop now, let her go, and hope that she didn't breathe a word of this to anyone, or sink my claws deeper, hold on to her even tighter, and take my time figuring her out and what made her tick.

As she trembled finely against me, sobbing into my shoulder, my cock softening inside her and the condom both, I had to admit to myself that the mystery that was Savannah Kittridge was thoroughly under my skin. Option one was a nonstarter.

There was only one way to go, and that was to *keep* going, albeit more cautiously than I had moved up until this point. Clearly, Savannah wasn't just another pretty face with an icy-cold heart, even if she had played the part so very convincingly up until this point when it came to our mutual business practices.

This? On a personal level? It was such an unexpected and completely different animal, but no less intriguing to me.

I was a man of my word and did what I promised her. I held her and kissed her forehead. When she looked up at me in hopeless confusion, I kissed first one eye, then the other, kissing away her tears, the salt of them still on my lips when I pressed them to hers, grateful to an extent that she wasn't so distressed as to not let me in.

Her lips parted, and I slipped my tongue past mine to taste her bottom lip and see if she would be amenable to something deeper between us at the moment, or if I had well and truly scared her off.

I found myself hoping against hope that I hadn't, and my heart fell when she hesitated. I fully expected a rejection, but then at the last moment, when I was about to withdraw from her, her hand fluttered to the side of my face with the kiss of a butterfly's wing, and she parted her lips to let me in, meeting my tongue with a tentative touch of hers.

I kissed her with reassurance and captured her hand with mine, where it touched the side of my face, pulling my lips from hers to turn them into her palm and kiss her with reverence there. I breathed deep her perfume, no doubt daubed on the inside of her wrist, and my senses were filled with bright light and sun-ripened peaches.

It suited her more than I could have thought.

I looked into her somber blue eyes and murmured to her, "Stay right where you are, Bright Eyes. I'm going to draw us a bath."

She swallowed hard and searched my face as I reached between our joined bodies to hold the condom on myself so I could withdraw from her. She sucked in a breath and shuddered beneath me as I pulled from her. I pushed up, getting off the bed and stripping the rubber from my flaccid cock, tossing it in the waste basket tucked between the bed and the nightstand.

I went into the bathroom and started the bath, testing the water to make sure it was neither too hot nor too cold.

She appeared in the doorway a moment later, hugging herself, hiding herself from me, and said, "I need to use the bathroom."

"Take your time," I moved past her and shut her inside. It wasn't long until the toilet flushed, and I gave her just a moment before I slipped back in, letting the door swing wide.

She stood before the mirror, her dress halfway up her legs, and I went to her, hands on her hips, pushing it back down, taking it from her hands.

"You're okay," I breathed in her ear. "You're not going anywhere but the circle of my arms, tonight."

"I don't know how to feel," she confessed, her confused gaze meeting mine over her shoulder in the silvered glass above my sink.

"I know," I murmured. "We've got nothing but time for you to sort that out." I drew her back from the sink, palming her hair clip, and led her to the bath.

"Is that too hot?" I asked.

She left my arms to sink to the edge of the clawfoot tub and stuck her hand in the water as it flowed.

"No, sir," she said. I smiled and kneeled down in front of her, gathering her hands in mine.

"Playtime is over for tonight, missy." I brought them to my lips and kissed her fingers. "Get in the tub."

She was sweetly obedient, getting into the tub, standing, and swishing her feet in the water to get used to the heat. I got in with her and got down first.

Fucking hot! I didn't make a face or jump or any of that nonsense, though. I simply parted my legs and gave her hands a gentle tug to come join me. She turned and got to her knees in front of me, sucking in a breath as the water rose and she waited, growing used to the heat before uncurling her legs and sitting back against me.

"Mm." She made a short noise as I curled my arms around her and caged her gently within my legs.

"Lean back," I urged. "That's it. There you go." I kept my tone gentle, and she didn't protest. She just sank back against me, as I held my hands out of the water on the edges of the tub. The water was creeping, and I asked her, "Sit up just a bit?"

She did, and I wiggled to sit up just a little straighter. I gathered her hair, her clasp between my lips, as I twisted it into a ponytail, and kept twisting until I could put it up and fasten it out of harm's way.

She sat very still for me, and I sank back down and pulled her back against me. When the time was right, and the steaming water had reached the peak amount we needed for a nice, long, hot soak, I used my foot to turn it off – first one faucet, then the other, as quickly as I could.

The rushing water ceased, and a silence crept into the bathroom.

"Better?" I asked after a time, her arms layered over mine, where I hugged her around the middle.

"I don't know," she said haltingly.

"Talk to me," I murmured and kissed her behind her ear. She sighed out with the little touch, and yet remained stiff in my arms.

"It's been a long time since I was with anyone," she confessed.

I had kind of figured that part out, but I still lied and simply came back with, "Oh?"

She made a rude noise, somewhere between a scoff and a snort, and said, "Don't play with me. I'm not going to run and scream abuse or anything. I think I'm more shaken because I..."

"Liked it?" I hazarded.

"Parts of it, yes."

"It's important you tell me what you liked and what you didn't like," I told her.

She was quiet. I didn't think she would speak, that she was shutting down and wouldn't share, but she surprised me. Though she was halting in her speech at the beginning, waffling back and forth on whether she *should*, she did the brave thing and ultimately did share.

"I liked it, at the restaurant, even though that was way out of my comfort zone," she said. "I've never done anything like that in a public setting."

I chuckled a little darkly and gently reminded her, "It wasn't exactly public."

"No, I know no one could *see* us... but they definitely heard things."

I chuckled again and said, "I concede the point."

"What else did you like?" I asked when she was quiet for too long.

She swallowed hard and said, "I liked the blindfold, and your rules... but I..."

I waited her out. "I didn't like that I couldn't touch you," she said. "It made everything feel so sterile and – and impersonal."

The complaint was a valid one and a point I could concede as well, however, that was by design. I didn't precisely want her to catch feelings – nor did I want to fall victim to any, either.

"I see," I hedged. "You would rather be loved than fucked?"

She sighed wearily. "Loved?" she scoffed. "I don't see that happening. I think *respected* is a better word. I don't mind doing dirty things, but I like to be able to participate. That just... it felt..."

"Defiling?" I supplied.

"Yes," she whispered, and I could feel her hurt, almost palpably.

"I see." I held her a little tighter and rested my lips on her shoulder, breathing her in, thinking furiously.

"I rather like defiling you," I confessed, and she made a brittle little tittering sound that I think was supposed to be a laugh but fell woefully short of the mark.

"I didn't mind the defiling at The Olde Pink House," she murmured. "But this was... different. I don't know why or how, but it was and it felt..."

"Gross?" I supplied.

"I was going to say 'icky' but that felt childish," she said. "Gross seems too strong a word, but yeah... gross will do."

"Hmm." I was thoughtful.

"What are you thinking?" she asked softly after a time.

"I was thinking that I do so very much enjoy playing with you and your body, and that I would very much like to continue to do so. I like playing on the dark side. I like to be in control, but there's clearly a fine line between that and being overbearing. That was a line that was crossed with you, tonight."

She sat with me, long and thoughtful in her pause as she soaked up what I said.

"One of my kinks is very much coercion. I love to coerce the reluctant, but judging by your reaction to round two, I may have missed the mark on consensual non-consent and sailed into much darker territory. A state of being I abhor, and would never want to be."

I was deeply concerned by this point. That was exactly what had happened.

"I don't know what to say," she said finally. "I never expected to want anything like this, but..." she thought for a time. "I've never had anyone do to me what you do to me. I like it, but it terrifies me in some ways. I-I just think the being tied up this time was too much too soon?"

"You give me grace that I am wholly undeserving of," I told her, and it was true. I could hear her in real time trying to diminish or minimize the trauma I'd dealt her, but I wasn't deserving of a free pass.

On the contrary, I was well aware that there was absolutely no way in which I could even begin to make this kind of faux pas up to her. I said as much without confessing to any criminal culpability, even though I was well aware that, should she want to pursue it, she more than could.

She swallowed hard and rolled her head back along my shoulder to look up at me with those bright and innocent eyes of hers. I was quickly learning it was just who she was, and wasn't a ploy at all – which was admittedly hard as hell to fathom with how she swum with the sharks as though she was one of us out in the real estate world.

A sheep in wolf's clothing, if you will.

I gazed down into those twin blue pools, and she said, "I'm not looking for a relationship. I really, honestly, and truly would rather focus on other, more important things to me right now."

"I'm not looking for anything close to a relationship, either. Just some debauchery and a good time in my own dark little fantasy world."

The confession was an easy one to make, and one hundred percent true.

"I have definitely enjoyed more than I haven't," she said carefully, and pointedly wouldn't look at me, a blush creeping up what I could see of her chest.

"Perhaps a different sort of deal is in order," I suggested.

"Great sex, pushing boundaries, no strings attached?" she asked.

"Sounds good to me," I said.

"You don't get to push me around or pull one over on me during business hours. Business is kept strictly separate from... from whatever this is," she said.

"One caveat," I proposed. "You piss me off enough, I get to punish you however I see fit during one of our little dalliances."

"I don't know if I like the sound of that," she said uneasily.

"Okay," I negotiated. "When I say 'pissed off,' it's all lowercase letters. If you genuinely anger me to the point that it's all in capital letters, or I see red, we shout it out behind closed doors and nothing happens until you're comfortable that I'm merely irritated and ready for funishment and not to really hand out any punishment."

"Did you just say funishment?" she asked, and she very nearly giggled.

I grinned. "Yeah, you like it?" I asked.

"Yeah, I actually kind of do. I think that's exactly what it is... round two, as you put it, didn't come off as funishment for me. It felt too cold, and like you were genuinely wanting to punish me with sex."

"No, not at all." I cuddled her close and genuinely felt bad for a flicker of a moment. "Genuinely, I just want what you want – to have fun, and explore – no strings attached."

"Okay," she whispered. "Thank you for taking the time to clear that up."

I smiled to myself, and she shifted a bit and said, "I really should go home tonight."

"Not tonight," I argued. "I want to make sure you're alright."

"I'm fine," she said.

"Then I selfishly just want a beautiful woman in my bed tonight," I countered.

She laughed and shook her head, saying, "You don't have to do that."

"Do what?" I asked. I was genuinely confused as to what she was getting at.

"Keep calling me beautiful. It's sufficient enough to just say you want a woman in your bed tonight. You don't have to butter me up like that. I'm just fine with... I don't know if we can even call it 'friends with benefits', to be honest. I thought you hated me."

I laughed then, and I couldn't help myself. One, she was in fact, *gorgeous*, and two, hate was a rather strong word.

"You're beyond beautiful," I said, and she snorted. "As for hating you? The only thing I hate about you is – well, there are two things really. That you best me more often than not at the real estate game, and that God-awful, thick-as-fuck, corn-pone, country-bumpkin accent you use. It makes you sound dumb, and you are *not* dumb."

She giggled at me and said, "Believe it or not, that *is* my natural accent. This one is the fake one. I learned to stop using it in college, and then figured out it was one of my greatest assets once I graduated. Go figure."

"That thick-as-hell accent is not your natural accent. I mean it. Talk normal for me."

She cleared her throat and said, "Why? What do you want me to say?" Sure enough, the accent was real, but not nearly as souped up as she used on clients. It was somewhere between her, I didn't know, customer service voice and the clean, clear American accent she code-switched to when she was just Savannah, and not Savvy Savanna.

"See, now that's not nearly the same as what you use on a daily. You can talk to me just like that all you want," I told her, and I meant it. "You don't need any of that shit. The makeup, the designer clothes... although I do like many of the things you wear. That dress tonight was choice."

She was silent for a time, cupping her hands and bringing them to her face, scrubbing them.

"What are you doing?" I asked.

"I just realized I cried most of this off, and I likely look dreadful!" I laughed then and picked up a washcloth from the little side table beside the bath and put it in her hands.

"Thank you," she said, and worked at getting the makeup off her face, which I had absolutely no problem with.

We stayed in the bath, not really doing much more talking, merely soaking up the warmth of the bath and one another's company. There came a time when I felt pruned enough that I asked, "Ready to get out?"

She sleepily murmured back, "Yes."

She got up at my gentle prodding, and I helped myself up by bracing on the edge of the tub. I wrapped her up in one of the lush bath sheets I kept in here, rubbing her briskly through the thick fibers.

"You fuss too much," she complained.

I chuckled and countered with, "Let me. I certainly owe it to you."

She got out and handed me a towel, and I stepped out onto the bathmat and dried myself. She went to the mirror and took down her hair, shaking it out and setting the clip aside.

I went to her and asked quietly, "Would you like one of my shirts to sleep in?"

"Would you mind?" she asked, meeting my gaze in the mirror.

"Not at all," I said, and I went into the bedroom and took up the light blue shirt I'd been wearing earlier at dinner. I held it open to her, and she shrugged into it, letting the towel slip to the floor beneath it as she quickly buttoned it down the front.

I stood behind her and rolled back the sleeves for her while she did, making her laugh and giggle.

She turned around, looked up at me, and asked me gravely, "Why do you want me to stay?"

I answered her truthfully. "I sleep better with someone in my bed. I like the warmth and the softness. Call me a pussy or a weak-ass motherfucker if you want, but it's true." I shrugged. "Still, I don't let just anyone into my bed. Usually, if I bring a woman home, I use the apartment above the carriage house and let them think that's my place."

I didn't know why I told her that. I probably shouldn't have, but she was an exception to my rules in more than a few ways.

She looked up at me and asked, "No shit?"

I tipped her chin just a little bit more and whispered, "No shit," against her lips before I brushed mine against them.

"Huh." She covered one foot with the other and looked positively adorable, fresh-faced, and in my shirt.

"Bedtime," I told her, and turned her about and marched her back into the bedroom. I pulled back the blankets and let her crawl in first, joining her and tucking her against me. She lay her head on my shoulder in the dark of the room, and it was nice.

Chapter Fifteen

Savannah…

I lay awake in the dark for a long time, thinking about everything. Corbett wasn't what I thought he was, but there was still so much about him that I didn't understand. Still, after how he had cuddled me in the bath and talked through everything, I could only come to one conclusion.

He genuinely felt bad about what I guess we had dubbed "round two" from tonight, and that we had both so wildly misunderstood one another. I could see it now that my act had become entirely too real to him, and that he genuinely had no clue that I wasn't elite in any way, nor that I didn't come from rich stock.

On the one hand, I was proud of myself that things got as far as they did before I'd given myself away. On the other hand, I was low-key afraid that he would start prying and out me to the rest of Savannah's elite as a huckster and a fraud.

I hoped not.

I would keep his secrets if he would keep mine.

Yes, the second round had been super overwhelming and had left me wrapped around the proverbial axle, but I had to confess, I'd still enjoyed facets of it. Now that we had a better understanding, I didn't feel so off-center or insecure.

No-strings-attached fun.

I'd never really done casual sex, but to get more of the utter damned ecstasy I'd felt on that dining room table, I was willing to give it a whirl.

You only live once, I thought to myself, and I sighed deeply.

"You're thinking awfully hard." Corbett nuzzled behind my ear and kissed me lightly, the sensation sending a sweep of goose flesh down my arm and along my back.

"I have a lot to think about," I murmured.

"Having second thoughts?" he asked, cuddling me closer, pulling me back into him.

"No," I said, and I was a little surprised, but not that I meant it.

"Then what is there to think about so hard?" he asked.

"I've... I've never done casual sex before," I confessed, and I blushed.

"Ah." He sounded like he understood, then followed up with a curious, "Really?"

"Really." I turned in his embrace to face him, tucking the arm toward the mattress between us, the other I laid over his trim waist.

He turned onto his back and pulled me in, so that I lay my head on his chest and shoulder, and slid his arm closest to me under me to hold me.

I closed my eyes and listened to the sound of his beating heart, and it was his turn to sigh.

"How is it I've been the one to introduce you to so many things?" he asked, and I had to chuckle then.

"I guess I've lived a sheltered life," I murmured.

"Intriguing." He sounded thoughtful then, and I fully expected the prying to begin any moment.

Instead, he slid me off him onto my back and leaned over the top of me.

"They say practice makes perfect," he whispered in my ear, and then his mouth was over mine, and *this time*, I could touch him. I cradled his face between my hands as our lips met, and tongues danced, and he lay over the top of me, pressing his erection to the apex of my thighs, rubbing it against my pussy lips, but not penetrating. No, he teased me, humping me in that way that made you want to scream and beg for him to put himself inside you.

I whimpered into his mouth. He unbuttoned his shirt that I wore, parting the material and moving the onslaught of his mouth to my right breast, kneading it with his hand, sucking on the tight little bud of my nipple, and grasping it between his teeth, pulling it away from me with a heat in his molten gaze that left no illusion that he could hurt me, and badly, but he was being kind.

That look stole my breath away and made my pussy clench with need.

I had no notion as to why I was the way I was, in that it turned me on so *fucking* much.

He moved to my other breast, giving it equal treatment, and I gasped, tangling my fingers in his hair, and pushing him down my body. I wanted that mouth on my clit. I wanted him inside me anyway that I could get. Fingers, cock, tongue, I didn't care as long as he made me feel good to the point that the thoughts sank into the oblivion of dark pleasure that he brought me.

Round three was no less intense than round one or round two, but he took his time more with arousing me – his hands exploring as much as his mouth, his lips leaving bits of fire in their wake. He pressed them lightly to my skin, his breath warm and just as enticing, fogging the rest of my senses as much as my sense of touch.

I expected his hair to be stiff with gel, given how he had it slicked back, but it wasn't. Instead, he used some sort of pomade that left it feeling somewhere between velvet and silk. Likewise, his beard was conditioned, which I found out when I gently grasped his face between my hands to drag his lips to mine.

Kissing him was unique.

I'd never kissed someone I had disliked so immensely before –

and it was a strange sort of cognitive dissonance. Like in the front of my head, I knew that I shouldn't be so accommodating or even *want* to put my lips to his, but then there was the part of me that sank into the kiss gratefully. A part of me that yearned for his hands on my skin and his body over mine, and to feel so…

I didn't know what to call it.

Safe? It certainly felt *good*, but safe didn't seem to be the right word at all. It was another bit of cognitive dissonance. I suppose thrilling was a better word. As though I played with fire, or that I sat in some big cat's enclosure. It was like petting a wolf, or having a bird of prey perched above me, talons digging ever so softly into tender flesh.

I was well aware he could hurt me. Maybe even that he wanted to hurt me – but deep down I knew I could trust that he wouldn't.

Dangerous… it was a dangerous thrill being in Corbett Prescott's bed, and even though it was exhilarating, it was also frightening and a myriad of other things, not all of them good.

Still, I felt like Eve tasting the poison fruit the way he kissed me, capturing my bottom lip between his teeth and biting down just enough to let me feel the sharpness of his teeth, relenting only when I gasped.

I swear he sipped at the fear on that slight exhalation of breath, and in doing so seemed to draw a strength or resolve from it, his body overtaking mine, and pressing me back into the mattress and mound of pillows behind my head.

I felt the hard length of his body press against mine, velvet-wrapped iron, as he teased my pussy lips apart and slid up and down my sex, rubbing against my clit.

I moaned into his mouth, a begging, whimpering sound, and I was surprised to find that I positively *ached* for him to ride me, to put his length inside me, and to drive me into the softness beneath me.

I just wanted to touch him while he did it.

He tore his mouth from mine and reached into the bedside table to get a condom. I boldly played with my pussy, biting my bottom lip between my teeth as I watched him tear open the foil packet to roll the latex down his hard length – and my *God* did this man have a beautiful penis.

Seriously, it was a work of art the way it pulsed and throbbed against his stomach as he brought the rubber to its head, weeping precum at its tip. He deftly rolled the condom down his length and made sure it was snug at its base before allowing himself to fall forward over the top of me; one hand bracing over my shoulder, the other guiding his thick cock to my entrance.

I moved my hand and rolled my hips up off the bed in offering to him, even as his mouth captured mine once again. It was almost too perfect the way his body met mine, and he slid into it.

I twined my arms around him, and my legs followed suit, wrapping around his narrow hips that fit more than perfectly between my own as he surged into me with a groan that tasted like excellence against my tongue.

He delved his arms beneath me and held me close as he worked himself in and out of me, rotating his hips just so as our mutual breaths deepened and dragged the passion from the hidden depths of our being. For the first time since entering into this *arrangement*, I felt a spark of real connection.

I held onto him and nurtured that spark into a lick of flame even as he licked along my bottom lip and kissed along my jaw.

I threw back my head with a throaty gasp and surrendered myself to his touch, my hands roaming over his warm skin in light strokes and butterfly touches, marveling at the feel of him against me.

He kissed my jaw and found his way behind my ear, breathing me in deeply, before attacking the sweet spot on the side of my neck with lips and teeth, in playful little nips that sent goosebumps cascading down the opposite side of my body.

He gave his hips a thrust and a sort of wiggle, and *holy shit*... "Oh, my God, there! Right there!" My voice was breathy, and thin, and I hardly recognized it.

He chuckled darkly against the side of my throat and pitched a rhythm that was pure, sweet torture in every way. Exquisite, beautiful, and breathtaking was how my body responded to it. I held onto him, almost half overwhelmed by the sensations, and all I could really do was surrender to them, to him, and *let go* – which for me? Lord, was that hard to do, but I managed.

The reward for my surrender was the sweetest, sharpest pleasure that weighed down my womb and grew exponentially with his every deliberate movement. He switched sides, and the burst of sensation from his lips meeting that sensitive spot on the side of my neck pushed me over the edge. The light building inside of me thrusts me off the cliff and out over to the abyss.

I felt like I was falling, falling, falling, the waves of warm pleasure sweeping through me as the world fell away from around me and left bursts of color and fireworks going off against the inside of my eyelids, even as he cried out, moaning, as my body pulsed around his.

He sat up, driving into me harder, his hand braced against my chest below my throat, fingers splayed, holding me down to the bed, his eyes a molten whiskey staring down at me with such a possessive ire, it raised entirely different gooseflesh along my body as he drove into me, taking his own pleasure, certainly, but more than that, it kept mine going.

The gentle wind blowing over and through me picked up into a gale, a maelstrom that battered me without as much as within, and set off yet another orgasm.

I found both of my hands had wrapped themselves around the wrist that had me pinned to his bed, but I didn't try to pull his hand away. It was an almost comforting weight against my body, holding me in place, grounding me as I swear parts of me were torn away in the storm of sensation he created.

His wicked grin belied that he knew *exactly* what he was doing to me, and that he gladly, almost gleefully, fed off me like some kind of vampire.

I closed my eyes and shuddered beneath him. He called out

wordlessly, losing his steady pace, shoving into me almost painfully hard, as his own orgasm overtook him.

His hand lifted, replaced with his body, as he lay over the top of me and pressed his lips to mine, and I kissed him back fervently.

"God, you're so good," he muttered into my ear, and I couldn't help my smile, shyly hiding my face and my lips against his shoulder and the side of his neck.

"You did all the work," I murmured in a light protest, and he chuckled, gathering me close and vaulting over my one leg to lie beside me and pull me into his arms. He tucked my head beneath his chin, and I put my ear over his heart, listening to it thunder against the inside of his ribs.

"Agree to disagree," he murmured, and my lips twitched lightly into a smile.

I didn't remember anything after that.

I think I was too exhausted and that I fell asleep. Lord knows, I needed it.

The next morning, I woke to light streaming through the bedroom window. I winced, groaning, and turned onto my stomach, sliding an arm across the crisp sheets to find the bed empty beside me.

I frowned and opened my eyes to a crisp fold of white paper on the pillow next to mine.

Had work to do. Make yourself something to eat. I'll check the kitchen, so, don't disappoint me. Call you for the next round soon.

-Corvus

I rolled my eyes and set the stiff and fancy stationery aside, breathing in deep and exhaling the cobwebs and dust of sleep and the dreaming away.

He wasn't the only one who had work to do today. I'd just been smarter about my scheduling and didn't have anything until two o'clock this afternoon.

I checked my watch, and it was only a little after ten in the morning. Plenty of time to go home, get cleaned up, have something to eat, and deal with hair and makeup – but honestly, only if I left now.

I didn't want to fix myself something here while he wasn't home. It just felt weird – so I got up, got dressed, picked up my bag of cleaned and maintained jewelry on my way out, and headed out to the garage beneath the carriage house.

I hit the switch to open up the garage, pulled my car out carefully into the street, got out, whisked myself to the switch, and hit it to close, ducking out and getting back in my car as quickly as possible.

I headed home and spent a luxurious amount of time under the hot shower spray before my stomach, protesting loudly enough at its neglect, made me get out.

After drying off and wrapping up in my robe, hair in a towel turban atop my head, I went to the kitchen and fixed myself a salad with all the good things. Torn chicken from a rotisserie I'd picked up from the store, a bed of dark leafy greens, slices of apples, dried cranberries, crumbles of goat cheese, a smattering of walnuts, and a light and bright vinaigrette to top everything off.

I settled on my couch and munched happily away at my lunch while I scrolled through emails on my phone.

Corbett Prescott: You didn't fix yourself something before you left, did you?

I rolled my eyes, snapped a picture of my salad, and sent it to him.

Corbett Prescott: That's not breakfast, and that's not my place.

I giggled and shot back... ***What? You going to punish me?***

I watched the dots bounce.

Corbett Prescott: Since you asked so nicely, I think I will. Be at the following address tonight at eight-thirty.

The address he sent wasn't one I was familiar with, and so I looked it up.

It was outside Bonaventure Cemetery, down the road from the funeral home, across the street, and down some from the cemetery's gift shop.

I sent back, ***I'll see what I can do about that.***

He sent back the grinning purple demon emoji, and I had to laugh.

I finished my salad, turned on some music, and spent the rest of my time getting ready with full hair and makeup, and an outfit for the day.

I decided to wear what had been professionally cleaned and got into the bag I'd brought in that Corbett had given me the night before.

There was one box too many, I realized, even counting the one my grandmother's watch had been in.

I opened it and gasped.

Inside was a necklace I'd never seen before. It was gold and had a beautiful oval-shaped stone that was a blue that matched my eyes. I couldn't tell if it was a sapphire, topaz, or something else, but it was certainly made all the more vivid by the pure white surrounding diamonds.

I swallowed hard, took a picture of it, and sent it to Corbett with just one piece of punctuation...

?

My phone remained maddeningly silent, and I got no return text.

I looked down at what I was wearing, which happened to be a thrifted Neiman Marcus linen dress. I put on the necklace and looked in the mirror above the bathroom sink.

God, it was probably the most expensive thing in this shabby, rundown joint.

I swallowed hard and stared at myself for a long time in the mirror.

It definitely helped sell the illusion that I was meant to be among the elite, but the cognitive dissonance was real, staring at the expensive bauble around my neck in the mirror that was rusting and the backing was blackened and peeling from around its edges.

It was beautiful, though, and the way it matched my eyes near perfectly did something to draw the gaze to them and to it, just making everything about looking at me... I didn't know. It made me look cohesive, and as the Lady Chablis would say, "*stinkin' mother-fuckin' rich*" – which *was* what I was going for, so I definitely couldn't complain.

I heaved a sigh and said to my reflection, another thing the Lady Chablis would say, "Two tears in a bucket – mother *fuck* it."

I gathered the things I would need for the day out in my living room – laptop, expensive leather briefcase to hold it, and my purse, phone, and keys.

The briefcase had been a gift from my younger brother when I'd graduated from college. He had worked hard, all summer long, doing odd jobs for two summers to make sure he had enough to afford it and the shipping. It was Italian, handcrafted. Just *beautiful* workmanship with a lifetime guarantee. If anything broke, any seam came unraveled, or anything like that when it came to the manufacture of it, I could send it back to them at no charge, and it would be repaired or replaced for free.

I felt a pang of longing to go home and see my family as I slung it up onto my shoulder before picking up my Coach bag I'd thrifted and paid more than I'd paid for the bag itself to have it cleaned and repaired – but *worth it*.

Still far cheaper than it would have been to buy new.

I left my little rental, went to the garage to get my Jag out, and headed into Savannah and the office to meet with my client to get a better idea of what they were looking for.

It was a good meeting, and as I'd been instructed by Corbett, I put in another call to the Swede who shall not be named and acted like I was valiantly trying to reach him for the property he'd wanted, warning that it was apt to go quickly if he didn't act.

It was a dark storm cloud that hung over my head – the knowing, the waiting, the hoping and praying I could pull it off with whoever came looking for him, that the lie wouldn't show on my face or in my eyes.

I sat back in my desk chair and sighed. I still had a few hours before heading to the address that Corbett had sent.

I was hungry again, and decided that there was no time like the present to take a little "me" time, have an early supper, and get my nails done.

I called in my assistant, Fabian, and let him know I was taking the rest of the day off for nails and an early dinner before I had a personal meeting, and he almost immediately perked up.

"Girl, I am in need of a manicure, and I have *got* to *know* – who is taking up all your time lately?"

I stopped what I was doing – shuffling paperwork and my laptop into my briefcase – and looked up at him.

"I plead the fifth," I said after a long pause in which I considered very carefully what I should and should not say.

It was like chumming the water to his shark's nose for gossip.

"Right," he declared. "I'll get my murse!" I always cracked a smile when he said that. He carried a purse like any one of the girls, but refused to call it that. He called it an m-u-r-s-e for man-purse. I rolled my eyes and finished gathering my things.

It wasn't too often that we got our nails done together, but it wasn't unheard of either.

Nails, yes, I thought to myself. *Dinner, no.*

I really did want some time to myself before I went to the unknown address out near the cemetery.

"I'll drive," I told him. "Then drop you off at your place."

"It's a deal, sweetheart. I have a date myself tonight."

I smiled, shook my head, and said, "Mine's not a *date.* It's an arrangement, and no, I won't say anything more than that."

"You're killing me, doll," he complained, but held the office door open for me so I could step out. He followed after me, and as I already had my keys at the ready, I locked the door behind us. He pulled up the alarm system on his phone and armed it as we walked down the hall to the elevator to the garage.

Fabian had been my introduction to the Grand Empress of Savannah, the original Doll herself, the Lady Chablis. First by way of the movie, *Midnight in the Garden of Good and Evil,* and then by way of some of her performances that had been recorded when she'd MC'ed at a few of the local clubs.

He'd known her when she was alive, and I was sorry I'd missed her. She'd died of pneumonia in 2016 and would, as far as many in the scene here in Savannah were concerned, always be *the Grand Empress* of Savannah.

Fabian chattered away, taking wild stabs in the dark as to who my new infatuation was, to which I gently, but firmly, corrected him by saying that it was no infatuation. I was just freeing up my wings a bit, and it was just some NSA fun.

That just put Fabian onto the scent even more. He was a bloodhound about it, determined to figure out just who I was fucking, which was hilarious and also none of his business.

I left him pouting on his doorstep a little over an hour later with a sharp but polite admonishment to drop it, even though I knew it was killing him.

Honestly, though, I didn't want him to think less of me for fucking Corbett Prescott. Especially after we had spent as much time as we had bagging on what a pain in the ass the man was.

I took myself to a quiet little Irish Pub for dinner and relaxed with a glass of wine and my thoughts as I dined.

I had no idea where I was going, and I expected that if I asked, I wouldn't get a straight answer from him. More than likely, he would say something bold-faced and pointed, like I would go where he told me to when he told me to do it, which, as much as that annoyed me, it also thrilled me.

I stared at the picture of the necklace I wore, and the question mark beneath it. The text had been marked as read – so he'd seen it, and had chosen not to respond to the message.

Insufferable, I thought to myself, and it certainly wouldn't be the first nor the last time I thought of it where he was concerned.

I wondered about the note I'd left abandoned in his bed that morning. He'd signed it *Corvus*, which I didn't know what that meant. I Googled the word.

Corvus is a widely distributed genus of passerine birds ranging from medium-sized to large-sized in the family Corvidae. It includes species commonly known as crows, ravens, and rooks.

So, it meant, crow... or raven... or rook – whatever that was. I wondered if I'd ever encountered a rook before, which led me down a whole different rabbit hole of Googling images to see if I had.

Apparently not. It was a bird specific to Scandinavia, Northern Europe, and Siberia, and I guess it was just like a crow with a few differences.

Hmm...

It was an odd thing to be called, and I wondered why he'd chosen it.

My dinner was wonderful, and I took my time with it. It was a wonderful fisherman's pie – a flaky top crust layered over a ramekin filled with a delightful white-wine-and tarragon-infused medley of different fish.

It paired delightfully with the crisp white wine I was drinking and put a bit of rose into my cheeks.

I waited and rested, well satiated and a touch tipsy from the one glass.

I wasn't much of a drinker, so I kept to myself, on my phone, and paid my tab and tipped well so I wouldn't be chased from my seat while it was still too soon for me to get behind the wheel.

After about forty-five minutes and a glass of water, I was feeling well enough to make the short drive to the mystery address in my phone.

Curiosity killed the cat, I thought as I pulled down the Spanish Moss-draped road that led to Bonaventure Cemetery. As I hit my turn signal to turn into the lot my GPS told me was the one, I eyed the building with some trepidation.

Satisfaction brought it back. I thought of the next line of the children's rhyme as I turned into the lot and took a fortifying breath.

The building was two to three stories tall and painted a deep, midnight blue – the Iron Wraith's logo painted larger than life on the outside, the draped skull with its glowing green eyes and matching scythes behind it ominously looking down on the parking lot.

I didn't know what I had expected, but somehow, pulling into the lot of the most notorious motorcycle gang in Savannah hadn't been it.

Chapter Sixteen

Corvus…

"Well, that's new." I looked up at the monitor in the corner behind the bar, its screen split six ways. Revenant had made the dry comment, but he didn't mean anything by it. He was just bringing the presence of what, to the rest of the club, amounted to an outsider and thus an unknown quantity.

"She's mine," I said with conviction, and Rev turned from the monitor to look at me, curiously.

"The real estate lady from last week?" he asked.

"Word sure does get around," I said, and though I probably sounded disgruntled, I wasn't. I didn't care how much the boys talked about business, like clean up on aisle thirteen. What I worried about was whether their faith or trust in me was shaken.

"Just the facts, man. A few got a little nervous, but I ain't one of 'em," he said and took a drink from his bottle of microbrew. I threw him some chin in acknowledgment for having my back.

"Appreciate it," I said.

"You going to go down and get her?" he asked, his attention back on the monitor as she took some halting steps across the cracked asphalt of our parking area out front for visitors and cages.

"Nope," I said and took another drink of my beer. "Let's see how she does finding her way up here on her own."

"Specter's down there," he said dryly.

I grinned.

"Even better," I muttered.

"Bets on if he'll give her hell?" he asked.

"Pfft, that's a given," I said. "The real bet is if she'll fold like cheap origami or if she'll give him hell back."

Rev turned back to me with a slow grin and said, "So, that's why."

I raised an eyebrow and said, "So, that's why, *what?*"

"You lose interest entirely too quick if they aren't a challenge," he said.

I rolled my eyes.

"It's not like that," I said.

"Isn't it?" he asked.

I frowned. "Okay, maybe it's exactly like that—" I said, but then I stopped myself and leaned forward, swatting his arm and pointing up. She'd made it through the open garage door and was looking up and around. Specter was already heading down the stairs to intercept her.

"Yo!" We heard him through the door, and the cadence of his heavy boots descending the metal scaffolding-style steps to the landing before they turned to finish their way down to the garage.

We couldn't hear what she said in return, but we saw her lips move on the monitor.

The burst of laughter out of Specter didn't surprise us. The guy could be a real asshole – but none of us minded too much. He tended to keep the tourists and lookie-loos out of the club, which suited us just fine.

"She's gonna fold," Rev said.

I chuckled and said, "Five bucks she doesn't."

She said something back to Specter, and Rev pulled a hundred out of his pocket and put it on the bar. I matched him, and Specter got in her face. She stood her ground, and when he reached out to grab her face, she batted his hand away and called out with a voice raised and clear, somewhere between iron and steel, "Corbett, come get this mongrel out of my face, please?"

I slapped my hand on the bar and slid the two hundreds my way as Rev chuckled and shook his head.

"She's got a brass pair of ovaries. Surprise, surprise," he said, and I winked at him, went out onto the catwalk, and leaned on the railing.

"Let her up, Specter. She's with me."

He muttered something at Savannah, catching her by her arm as she made to pass him. She stared up at him with stubborn pride and jerked her arm out of his grasp as she ascended the stairs past him. He winked at me behind her back, and I raised an eyebrow and shot him an amused look when she took her eyes off me to hold on to the stair rail and watch her step coming up the metal grating in her heels.

I met her at the top of the stairs and took her hand lightly, glimpsing the necklace I'd bought her and she'd inquired about by text.

I buried my hand in the back of her hair and pulled her to me, covering her mouth with mine, and she responded beautifully, practically melting into me.

Her tongue touched mine, and it was a burst of sensation, like sweet sunshine filling my mouth and surging through the rest of me, setting me aglow with all the colors of the sunset. We kissed on the steps in front of my brother, and I felt wholly possessive of her. It was intoxicating as it was dangerous.

I wasn't exactly known for catching feelings, and to be honest, I would rather keep it that way. Feelings complicated things, made them messy and unpredictable. I didn't like that feeling. That feeling of falling and of being out of control. I preferred my heart tame and, in my breast, rather than flying wild and fancy free.

I'd done that once, and I'd paid a steep price when I'd found I'd just been... well... when I hadn't mattered at all, really.

Savannah drew back, and I let her, her blue eyes wild with excitement and her smile an echo of the one I kept firmly off my face.

"Well, hello to you, too," she purred, and I couldn't help but chuckle.

My eyes wandered back to the pendant I had gifted her, and I couldn't decide if the blue of the stone made her eyes that much brighter, or if it was her eyes that made the stone glow. I touched the hollow of her throat where it rested and let a pleased smile slip.

It was stunning against her sun-kissed skin.

"I don't know what to say," she murmured.

"How about 'thank you?'" I suggested.

She smiled wryly and said, "Thank you, but I'd like to know why."

"Come with me." I changed the subject and guided her toward the bar and caught Specter looking up at us with a strange sort of intensity. Well, not *me*, but Savannah.

"Revenant, this is Savannah. Savannah, this is Rev." I made a short introduction and said, "You met Specter on the stairs."

"Pleasure to meet you," Savannah said to Revenant, and held out her hand to shake his. He grasped hers and brought it to his lips, brushing her knuckles lightly with his lips.

"Pleasure's all mine, for sure," he said, and she giggled.

Rev was the brother who looked a lot like that actor, Daniel Craig. We loved his James Bond flicks the best, but he really was great in all he did – even that flop, *Cowboys vs. Aliens.* Still, the more folks likened Rev to Bond, the more he just sort of adopted that air of mystery. His greeting with Savannah was just one more thing that came off as cheesy as fuck to me because it was so a thing that Bond would do.

Rev may be drowning in pussy galore – but this pussy was *mine.* I let him know it by gathering Savannah into my side.

Savannah remarked about Rev being a lot nicer than Specter, and he and I shared a laugh.

"Specter has a chip on his shoulder," Rev said. "Don't mind him."

"Agreed," I said.

"Good to know," she murmured.

I asked her, "What's your poison?"

She turned to look at the bar and laughed, saying, "I prefer fruity and girly. Afraid I'm just apt to be made fun of if I ordered what I usually do when it comes to cocktails."

I chuckled at that and said, "We've got wine, beer, cider, some hard seltzers..."

She heaved a sigh and said, "With the day I've had, a cocktail is where it's at, honestly."

"Prospect!" Rev bellowed, and Savannah jumped in the circle of my arms at the unexpected noise.

Spooky appeared from one of the bathrooms he'd been cleaning and stripped off the blue gloves he had on.

"Yes, sir?" He looked expectantly to Rev.

"Make the lady a drink. Whatever she wants," he said.

Spook went behind the bar, tossed the gloves, and reached for a glass. Both Rev and I shouted at him at the same time, "*Wash your hands*!"

He immediately diverted to the bar sink without touching anything, hit the soap dispenser to load a hand with soap, then flicked on the sink with the other hand.

"What'll it be?" he called back over his shoulder at Savannah, who looked amused, but did her best to hide her smile behind her hand.

"A Georgia Peach, please," she called just as he cut the water and shook out his hands. He picked up a bar towel to dry them off.

"Uhhhh..." He didn't know what it was.

Before he could ask, Rev was already there, snapping at him, "Look it up! There's a whole ass cocktail book right next to you!"

He picked up the bar's copy of *The Ultimate Bar Book* and at least had the brains to go to the index to look for it.

"Uh, the only thing in here is a *Georgia Julep*. Is that the same thing?"

She laughed and said, "No, juleps have mint, and I'm not a fan of mint in my drinks. A Georgia Peach is simple – one ounce *Peach Schnapps*, one ounce *White Rum*, stir in orange juice, and give it a float of cranberry."

"Oh, shit, I can do that," he said. "Tor would probably make it better, but I can give it a go."

"Tor?" she asked, looking up at me curiously.

"Torment. He's an executive chef. Anything he touches when it comes to food or drink winds up magic, so Spooky here isn't wrong," I explained.

"Ah," she nodded. I guided her to a seat at the bar and helped her up. I took the one next to her, keeping myself between her and Rev while Spooky busied himself making her drink behind the bar.

"So, why here?" she asked me as Spook set her drink in front of her and set a fresh beer in front of me.

"Fuck off," I told him when he looked at me expectantly.

"Rude!" Savannah protested on his behalf.

"It's part of it," Spooky said with a half-assed laugh and a shrug of his shoulder as he did what I told him and fucked off back to cleaning the shitter.

Savannah gave me a reproachful look, and she wore the disapproval well on her lovely face. So much so, it *almost* moved me, but not this time.

"So, what was so important you just *had* to have me here?" she asked, taking a sip of her drink.

"You didn't do what I told you to do this morning," I said casually, and her eyes lit up with a darker, almost salacious light when she caught on.

"Oh? And remind me, what was it I was supposed to do?"

I smiled as she played the game *with me* this time, but I couldn't tell if she knew or was genuinely stumped over what transgression she may or may not have made, and so I clued her in.

"I told you to make yourself some breakfast at my place, and you didn't," I said as I reached out and cupped her fair cheek, running my thumb over her luscious bottom lip.

"The whole idea of fixing something for myself in your kitchen without you there was *weird*," she complained.

"I don't care if it's weird or not," I gently scolded her. "I care that you were fed."

I let her sit with that for a moment or three, and she swallowed hard, tried to hide behind her drink as she took several more sips.

"I don't understand," she said finally.

I cocked my head, and it struck me... "Are you not used to anyone insisting you take care of yourself?"

"I mean, not really," she said. "I live alone."

Interesting...

"Come on." I touched her elbow and slid my hand to hers, grasping her fingertips. She slipped from her barstool. I stood from mine and guided her around the bar and back downstairs, taking the room beside the bathrooms. It had a couch, a side table, and not much else. It was a small room, with a single window overlooking the garage, the venetian blinds lowered.

I turned on the recessed overhead lights and dimmed them with the wall switch just inside the door. Satisfied that the blinds were shut tight, I closed and locked the door behind us, closing us in to the intimate space, which had, once upon a time, been an office.

"What do you want?" she asked, and a little apprehension filtered into her voice.

"You didn't want to fill your mouth in my kitchen, so I figured it was only fair to fill your mouth with my cock as punishment." I unzipped and pulled my aching boner out of my pants and underwear, taking a seat on the couch. I put my arms along the back of it and spread my knees enough for her to kneel between them if she chose that option, rather than climb onto the couch beside me to do it.

I didn't care how she got it done, just that she did it.

Obediently, she took a step toward me and went to her knees on the thin office carpet between my feet.

Her hand was soft and her grip firm, just the way I liked, as she jacked me. When she went to suck me, it was like her inner vixen knew what to do and came out to play. I didn't know, maybe it was the setting, or the fact we'd already fucked a few times. Maybe it was just that we were finally on the same page, but a sort of darkness filled her bright blue eyes, and she started by licking me, balls to tip, with the flat of her velvet tongue. And combined with that look?

Fuck me – yes, please!

I tilted my head back, closed my eyes, and let go of the stress of the day. Let go of the office politics and club politics, dropped the weight of my responsibilities, and homed in on the here and now. On the feel of her soft pink mouth enveloping my dick, of her lips snug around my shaft, at the barest teasing graze of her pearly whites, here and there, as she swallowed me practically whole.

She gagged and drew back quickly, and I opened one eye and checked on her. Her cheeks were stained red with embarrassment at her little slip-up, but she was a trouper and got herself back on track quickly.

It was a fight between watching her and closing my eyes and losing myself to the feel of her. I went back and forth between the two, my respirations deepening and picking up their pace as she worked magic with her mouth.

Fuck, I could get used to this. She was quickly becoming an addiction, and I wasn't sure how to feel about that.

What's more, and what was more dangerous, was that I actually cared. I was genuinely miffed at her that she hadn't eaten breakfast that morning – and I was even more surprised to find I was miffed at myself for not staying to make sure she'd eat.

God, she worked magic on me with that mouth of hers, though – the pressure, the cadence of her bobbing blonde curls, the way she sucked and licked – Goddamn, I couldn't get enough.

I held back her hair so I could watch her beautiful face, her eyes closed in concentration, an almost peaceful look upon her elf-like features, as she went down on me, carefully taking me past her gag reflex. Watching her almost did as much as the feel of me in her mouth. It was like time stopped, and we were outside of its constant march forward. If it'd been raining outside, we would have been able to step between drops suspended in the air.

I'd only had that sensation once or twice in my life – the whole time-stopping thing – and this, by far, was the most intense. I didn't want her to stop. I didn't want to rejoin the flow of time and be forced to go back to the grind of club and work life. I wanted it to stay stopped with my dick buried in her perfect mouth for as long as she'd have me, which by my body's reckoning wouldn't be much longer now.

I felt that familiar tingle at the base of my spine, my balls drawing up tight as I stood at that precipice, tipping forward, suspended for entirely too long on that moment before taking the plunge off the cliff into the crystalline warm waters of satisfaction.

I warned her, barely in time, "I'm gonna come!" She just redoubled her efforts, quickening her pace, and taking me to the back of her throat, swallowing everything I had to give her expertly.

She had a hidden talent for this... one I would definitely exploit for myself in the future. I was suddenly glad there were times when Savvy Savannah had a smart mouth. It would give me plenty of excuses to fill it.

I mean, it's not like I didn't have any interest in returning the favor. She was sweet as a summer peach and tasted like sunshine herself.

She sat back on her heels, blushing faintly, and running a fingertip at the edge of her lips to neaten up any smudged lipstick. She was beautiful, her blonde hair faintly mussed from where I'd held it back from her face to watch her.

"Get up here," I ordered, and she clambered a bit awkwardly to her feet. She stepped close, and I reached up under her skirt and whisked her panties down her legs.

"Whoa." She covered herself, down there, with an uneasy laugh, and gripped the light and flowy material of her dress.

"Come here." I had her step out of the scrap of lace and satin and pulled her down into my lap. Her dress's skirt was between us, which was annoying, but not what I was after quite yet. I captured the back of her neck with my hand and dragged her mouth to mine, kissing her soundly. The way she relaxed against me and fell into the kiss was *amazing,* and as soon as my cock recovered and got with it, stiffening up again, I just had to be inside her.

She melded the front of her body to mine beautifully, her mouth soft against my own, tongues dancing. It was unique to have her taller than me from our respective positions on the couch, and I couldn't say I disliked it.

She rubbed herself against me, and she was already hot and wet, causing my excitement to rise. I thrust my hips beneath her, causing a delicious friction that did nothing to whet either of our sexual appetites. Despite having just gotten off literally moments before, I was ravenous and needed to be inside of her *now*.

Thankfully, my cock got with it, and I was already starting to grow hard again. I wrapped my arms around her, and guided her up onto her knees so things had a chance to line up. When she came back down, it was more than perfect, and I unintentionally slid right in – no barriers, which I *hadn't* intended. I was a man of my word after all, but both of us needed a moment at the unexpected contact.

She felt so phenomenally *good,* I couldn't deny wanting to savor the moment and linger a little longer. I froze, and she froze, and our gazes met.

"I have a condom in my pocket, I didn't mean to—" I wasn't exactly apologizing, but rather was still trying to at least explain myself when she did the hottest thing imaginable.

"Fuck it," she said and rolled her hips, her mouth crashing down over mine.

Well, alright then!

Part of me knew it was potentially a bad idea, but I was wholly in the moment and couldn't stop myself if I wanted to, which was jarring all on its own when I prided myself so much on my near limitless self-control.

I guess she'd just found my limit.

She rode me, and it was a thing of beauty – the way she leaned tall, gathering her hair and holding it off her neck, sweat lightly dewing her skin in a light wash over her decolletage.

It was hot in here. The airflow from the system wasn't quite doing what it was supposed to in the small room. Either that, or the heat rising between us couldn't be contained.

Shit, I didn't care. My hands were on her hips, encouraging her rise and fall, her back-and-forth, and the way she came down and *rolled* those hips?

Goddamn.

It was as though she'd found her inner siren, and it was hot as hell.

She went until her legs trembled with fatigue from the unfamiliar workout. When she began to falter in her rhythm, when both of us were maddeningly high and about to make that shining plunge, I leaned forward and wrapped my arms around her, thrusting up into her wet heat with a near brutal pace. The friction growing, her panting breathy cries reaching a sweet crescendo, both of us shuddered with a mutual completion of our satisfaction.

I couldn't even begin to explain how fucking good it felt to fill her pulsating twat with my essence.

Fuck it felt good. Too fucking good, and also, too fucking real.

"Shit, I shouldn't have done that," I said, gasping as she folded into me and I held her close.

"I'm on a shot," she gasped out. "God, that felt so good."

"Won't happen again," I grunted, and smoothed a hand down her back.

"Mm," was her non-committal reply.

We sat quietly, my cock softening and slipping out of her, a rush of our combined love pooling between us a little uncomfortably.

"We need to clean up." I grabbed a wad of tissues from the end table beside the couch and shoved them into her hand, gathering her skirt up out of the way so she could get up the worst of it.

We both laughed a little uncomfortably at the initial cleanup, and I took the soggy Kleenex from her and tossed it in the wastebasket under the table, satisfied when I heard the light rumple of the grocery bag that lined it.

She got off me, and I tucked myself back in, even as she sat beside me on the couch and pulled her dress down over her knees, hugging them to her.

"You good?" I inquired.

"What? Yeah! I've just... never done anything quite so... ah... public."

"Public?" I looked around the sealed-off room, and she laughed a little uncomfortably and said, "I mean, there are other people around, in like the building... You know what? Never mind." She covered her flaming face with her hands, and I chuckled.

"You're not very experienced, are you?" I asked gently and sat down next to her.

She shook her head and looked up at me, mortified.

"Don't worry... I think I like that about you," I said. "You're just full of surprises."

"Thank you?" she murmured, and I could tell she was definitely at a loss for words.

"Come with me. We can do a little better on getting ourselves together and presentable in the bathrooms right next door before rejoining the others." I held down a hand to her, and she took it, standing with a bit of a groan, reaching down to step her other ankle out of her panties, which had gotten hung up on her heel and had been swiftly abandoned.

Panties in one hand, my hand in the other, I unlocked the door and ducked my head outside.

"Coast is clear," I said with a wink, and drew her out into the garage and over to one of the single-occupancy restroom doors. I dragged it open, glad the prospect had already been down here and guided her in.

"Be right next door," I said and shut her in. I heard the lock latch and went over to take care of myself in the next one over.

Chapter Seventeen

Savannah...

What in the fuck was that? I thought to myself, leaning heavily against the door and taking in my relatively stunned and shattered appearance in the mirror above the sink.

My pussy still throbbed faintly with all the good feels, but *holy shit* – I had never been so... *I didn't even know what,* as I'd been in that room just minutes ago.

I used the toilet and sat for several moments in a sort of post-sex haze of wonder at my wanton behavior.

I hadn't been entirely comfortable blowing him, but if it was one thing I had had a lot of practice at? It was blowjobs. I'd only had one partner before Corbett, and that was back in high school, before college. And while we'd *ahem,* sealed the deal before I'd gone off to college, it'd only been one or two times before the distance had been too much for him and he'd cheated. And... well... I'd been more than a little busy with getting my degree and building my little life here in Savannah to spend much time in the dating pool.

Plus, nowadays, guys weren't interested in any kind of relationship, which bothered me. They just wanted sex. While Corbett

Prescott was much the same in that regard, there was at least one thing I appreciated about him. He didn't mince words, throw mixed signals, or lie about it. He had been very clear from the get-go on what he wanted and how he wanted it, and I could at least appreciate that.

I mean, the man, for all of his arrogance and pushy behavior, knew precisely how to set me off, and there was something… I didn't know… *comforting* to not have the burden put on me for everything all the time. His weird alpha maleness wasn't degrading, even if it was demanding of me, and the payoff?

Well, let's just say I have never been wetter or felt as free as I did under his control – which was weird, I know. I mean, wasn't that weird?

I cleaned myself up as best I could in the small bathroom with what was at hand and donned my panties. I refreshed my makeup and finger-combed my hair into some semblance of less wildness and more professionalism. When I opened the door, Corbett was leaning against the wall beside it, scrolling on his phone through what looked like a group text exchange.

"Hey," he said, giving me a once-over and smiling slightly. Butterflies took off in my stomach at the sight of that little smile, and never had I ever even thought about this man in that way before all of this.

"Hey," I said and drew the word out on a sigh. I needed a minute. I needed some space. It was as though the world had tipped on its axis a bit, and I didn't know what to make of it.

Overwhelmed was a good word for it.

"I really hate to do this, but I've got to go," I lied. "Work calls."

I hoped he bought it. His whiskey-colored gaze roved my face and lingered with enough prolonged eye contact that it made me want to squirm, but I held perfectly still.

"I understand," he said. "I'll walk you to your car."

I put on a bright smile and said, "Thanks!"

We struck out in the direction of the parking lot.

"You, okay?" he asked me once we cleared the door and stepped into the evening sundown. It was still barely light out here, which meant I really had spent no time at all here, but lord, it had felt like the entire world had stopped for us when we'd been in that room together.

"I'm good!" I said quickly. "More than good, actually."

I reached out and slid a hand up the lapel of his leather jacket beneath the colorful patched vest he wore over it, the patches stained with wear and road grime.

"I call, you answer," he reminded me, and tipped my chin so gently to bring his lips down to mine.

He kissed me, and it was so sweet, almost like a little reward for a job well done.

"Am I forgiven then?" I asked quietly, and what I hoped was playfully.

He smiled and said, "Oh yeah. That was a *very* good girl."

I couldn't help it. I laughed at that and rolled my eyes, even as the praise showered me in unexpected, internalized tingles.

"I'll call you later tonight and check on you," he said.

"I'll answer," I said, and opened my car door and got in.

He closed my door for me and stepped back, raking a hand through his hair, back from his face.

I smiled and started my Jag. He watched me pull out of the parking lot, and I shivered.

Wow, that had been intense.

Wow, wow, wow!

I drove home, my day thoroughly done, and arrived just after full dark. I completed my ritual of pulling into the garage, closing things up, carrying my purse, briefcase, tumbler, and juggling my keys to my front door.

I let myself into my house and shut the world out, sighing as I dropped my stuff inside the door, holding onto just my tumbler as I didn't want any of the contents to spill.

"Well, that was intense," I said to no one and nothing in particular. I heaved a sigh and turned, locking the door behind me before switching on a light.

I stepped out of the mess I'd made of my entryway and went right in to strip and shower.

Yeah, the dress needed to go into my dry-cleaning pile – for sure – and I flushed with embarrassment thinking about how the place might judge me for the stains that were clearly dried on it.

Woof. My mind raced as I stepped into the shower. I was still stressed about if and when the cops would come knocking over Hal Lindstrom... but at the same time... I didn't think I regretted what happened one bit.

Was I still off-kilter and trying to learn how this whole new dynamic worked with Corbett? Yes... But I was also trying to work through how something so binding could also feel so freeing!

The cognitive dissonance was real, and it was really uncomfy. I couldn't say exactly where my mental health was at with all that was going on. I mean, a lot had happened in a very short amount of time, and I just couldn't seem to process fast enough.

I scrubbed my face free of makeup and my hair free of product and just stood for an inordinate amount of time under the hot shower spray and thought myself in circles.

There really wasn't much for me to do in this dynamic except, honestly, pick up the phone when he called... which, thus far, hadn't been difficult.

I got into my coziest pair of pajamas and put on a robe, taking myself to the kitchen to make a hot cup of tea. I turned on the fireplace ambiance while the electric kettle heated, trying to decide whether I was in the mood for a movie or to read.

The answer was, I wanted to go home – back to the farm where I felt grounded and centered and more like myself than I did anywhere else.

The truth of the matter was this was all a sham, and I was pretending to be brave and sucking it up on a daily to wheel and deal, all in a bid to save my very favorite home. And as if that wasn't stressful enough? No, I had a murder to cover up and was at Corbett Prescott's beck and call – which, honestly, though frustrating, wasn't *all* bad. It was just... a lot.

I didn't have the concentration to read a book, and so television it was. I snuggled into my couch under my fluffy throw, and wrapped my hands around a warm mug of tea, trying to forget my circumstances lately, and no, it didn't come anywhere close to working.

A WEEK OR TWO PASSED, and Corbett was a little busier than usual, so despite phone calls here and there that were mostly business related, I had a bit of a reprieve which put me back on track.

That is until Savannah PD showed up in my office asking questions about Hal Lindstrom. I lied my way through the interview, convincingly I hoped. He'd shown up to the showing a little late, but not significantly. He'd come from dinner, he'd said. I'd noticed alcohol on his breath, and he appeared to be slightly inebriated, but in good spirits. No, he hadn't driven there – he'd taken a car. He had made an offer on the house. Yes, I thought it was weird that he just stopped answering the phone and didn't return any calls. Yes, I'd been worried. No, I didn't think it was my responsibility to call the police when he failed to answer his phone. Maybe he had buyer's remorse or any other number of possibilities. I'd seen similar in real estate before. People could be flaky, but it was so few and far between that it was still odd.

They thanked me for my time and left, no closer to figuring out what'd happened to Hal, but thankfully seemingly none the wiser that I had anything to do with it. Still, my heart hammered in my chest, and as soon as the office door closed, I sagged in my seat. My eyes drifted to the window that certainly wasn't there for any kind of view, but did let in natural light.

My phone buzzed and I jumped, quickly picking it up to see a message from Corbett.

How did you do?

I looked around my office, which I know was stupid, but...

To what are you referring? I asked.

You know what. Meet me tonight. My place. 8 o'clock.

I sighed and had to frown.

What if I'm too tired? It sounded lame, even to me, but I'd already hit send.

I call, you answer. I frowned and texted back – but, of course, I got no response. I hated that he knew I would show up – how could I not? My curiosity was already killing me. *How did he know?* Literally, how did he know the police had been here? Was he stalking me?

Of course he was, I thought to myself. *It was stupid of you to think he wouldn't.*

The whole thing threw me into such a tailspin, but I couldn't cancel the rest of my day, even if I wanted to.

I wondered if he knew my schedule somehow, too. Because there was no reason I had to miss the appointed hour, and in fact, his place *was* closest to my last appointment for the day, conveniently so.

"Two tears in a bucket, mother fuck it," I muttered, and I gathered my wits, shoving all else to the side to finish out my day.

I arrived at his place at seven thirty, and I hoped that I was early enough that it would catch him off guard and annoy him somehow.

Instead, I pulled onto his street, and the garage was already up and waiting for me to pull in under his carriage house.

For some reason, today, it sort of ground my gears that he always seemed to be ahead of me. The police presence looming in my office earlier scared me more than a little.

I walked across his courtyard, my heels clacking smartly over the bricks, and caught sight of him in the kitchen through the French doors. He had his sleeves rolled back over his forearms, and his collar was open at the throat. What's more, he had on an apron and was running a knife through some herbs on a cutting board. I froze, taking it in.

He looked up at me and stuck his thumb in his mouth, and I swallowed hard. He sucked something off it and jerked his head to indicate I should let myself in. I entered the kitchen and closed the door behind me.

"How did what go?" I demanded, and I wanted him to be crystal clear that he meant the cops being in my office.

"With the detectives," he said, not even bothering to deny it.

"Are you stalking me now?" I demanded, crossing my arms over my stomach. He gave me a lopsided and almost sinister grin.

"I'm keeping tabs," he answered.

I rolled my eyes and threw up my hands.

"Honestly, I have no idea if they believed a word that came out of my mouth or not. You probably know how these things go."

He chuckled, tossed the herbs into whatever he was sautéing, and gave the contents of the pan a flip or two to mix things up. The room was fragrant with white wine and a familiar, if not readily identifiable, smell.

"Sit," he ordered, gesturing to the little table at the end of his kitchen, which was set for two.

"What if I can't stay?" I asked. I knew I was being petulant, but this was really rubbing me the wrong way for some reason.

"It wasn't a request, Savannah. *Sit.*"

I huffed a sigh at his incorrigibility and went and sat. He came over and poured a glass of white.

"It's a good vintage," he promised. "Try to relax a little. Catch me up. What did they ask?"

I wrinkled my nose, took a sip, and gave him the rundown, just as though I was ticking off problems an inspector had found making his rounds on a property.

Every once in a while, as he moved about the kitchen, he would ask me, "And your answer?" I would tell him, apprehensive, and blessedly, all he would do was nod and say nothing, but I kind of got the gist that no news was better than bad news. I mean, he wasn't ripping my head off for any of my answers, and they were pretty much verbatim what he had told me to tell them if they had come knocking.

He set a plate of linguini and clams in front of me, and said, "You did good."

I rolled my eyes and said, "Well, thank you for that! Whatever would I do without your brilliant insight?"

He snorted and said, "You're a salty little thing today. You need to learn to relax."

My shoulders sagged in utter frustration, and I said, "Killing people may just be another Tuesday for you, but it most certainly isn't for *me*. Honestly, I'm scared to death."

"Don't be," he said starkly, and pinned me with his gaze.

He brought over his own plate and set it down before pulling off his apron and hanging it on the back of his chair.

"Eat," he ordered gently.

"I'm not used to this," I said quietly, staring down at the food, which looked and smelled lovely, but *lord*, my stomach was in knots. How could he possibly expect me to eat at a time like this?

His hand covered mine, where it rested listlessly on the table, and I jolted, meeting his inscrutable gaze with mine.

"I know it's a lot. I know it's overwhelming. It does get easier with time, and the best thing you can do for yourself right now is to eat, try to relax, and get a good night's sleep. Just keep doing what you're doing with your daily routine."

"I understand, but I don't know how. How do you do it?" I asked mollified.

"Just keep calm and carry on," he said as though it was as simple as that… and I thought about it. Maybe it was? Maybe it was literally just as simple as that. I mean, wasn't that what I'd been doing essentially this whole time since first coming to Savannah?

"Take a deep breath," he ordered, and I did, mimicking him as he pantomimed doing likewise in a slightly exaggerated fashion.

"Good, good…" he murmured. "Now eat your dinner."

I speared some of the Caesar salad on a smaller plate at the top of my place setting with the salad fork that'd been set out.

"Mm!" I perked up a little in surprise.

"Yeah, that's not a salad kit." He smiled a little, and it was almost... bashful?

"No?" I asked. "You made this yourself?"

"I mean, it's probably not as good as Torment makes it, but it *is* his recipe... so..."

"I don't think I've met him," I said, and he shook his head.

"You haven't, yet."

"Were the three at...?" I faltered, letting the question hang between us.

"They were, and you'll meet them eventually," he said. "Just play it cool, like you haven't before, unless they broach the subject. Understand?"

"Yes, but who were they?" I pressed.

"Does it matter?" he asked, and it was with an earnest stare.

"I mean, I guess, not really..." I mumbled, speared some more salad on my fork, and he sighed.

"Your curiosity is rather insatiable, you know that?" he asked, but it wasn't rude. "Curiosity killed the cat," he said gently, and I cocked my head.

"I thought that just the other day," I said. "Truly... but you know the next line?" He shook his head.

"I didn't know there was a next line."

"There is," I said. "'*Satisfaction brought it back.*'"

He chuckled and nodded. "Touché."

"So..." I smiled a little wryly, and he shook his head.

"Relentless."

"I mean, if I'm the cat, I have nine lives, so '*you only live once*' is out the window."

He laughed then, and I couldn't help but smile. His laugh was rich and robust, and I liked it when it was genuine.

"Fair, Kitten. Fair. But you don't want to use them up too quickly, so best let this one lie for now. You'll meet them sooner or later."

"How many are there?" I asked. "Or is that off-limits too?"

He said, "Thirteen. If you count the prospect, fourteen, but he's not exactly one of us, per se. Not yet anyway."

"How does that work?" I asked.

"So full of questions," he admonished, but it was jovially. He looked me over and said, "This is something I *can* answer and should – so here goes."

He took a deep breath before launching into it. "Once upon a time, the core of us all went to the same boarding school. We were a bunch of dumbass rich kids displaced or pretty much disowned from our families and stuck somewhere off to the sidelines to grow out of being inconveniences to the family lines. At least, that's what it felt like anyway. Synister was sort of our de facto leader when it came to school. We all just sort of fell in under him."

He paused, letting memories wash over him, and I could tell by how the muscle in his jaw ticked that they weren't particularly fond ones. I didn't think that had much to do with Synister or his classmates, but rather his family, which the Prescotts were *old* money here in Savannah. Like clear lineage dating all the way back to the Oglethorpe days. Fresh off the boat and ready to colonize the Americas from England.

"Syn and I became fast friends, and the rest just sort of found themselves in our gravitational pull. You know how it is." He shrugged, and I simply pursed my lips and nodded, continuing to eat and listen because... no. I absolutely didn't know how it was. I mean, I had a bit of an inkling, I guess. My family was firmly middle class, which made my brother and me pretty much the upper echelon in our respective schools, but we didn't let the fact that our family owned the farm where most of the other kids' parents worked go to our heads. Our parents raised us humble and, lord, I wouldn't want to disappoint Nana or Pop-Pop.

The type of dynamic Corbett spoke of was... I mean, I could feel the *Cruel Intentions* kind of vibe from it, but I didn't think that was necessarily *real*. That was just a movie... but I guess in some places and on some tiers above even my family's, it was as real as it got. I mean, I knew that coming here and working my ass off and faking it until I made it had risks, but... this? All of this? Being complicit in a murder and watching how casually these men covered it up and just went back to business as usual was intense, and beyond anything I thought it could be.

It was definitely too late to tell the truth of my origins now, though. I was afraid that if I did, well, it might just be the thing to make *me* disappear too, which I did not want to do.

"Before we knew it, we grew to become enough in numbers that we formed the Iron Wraiths. At first, it was a sort of rich-kids' school secret society sort of thing. But as we got older and ended up in the same shop class, we all fell in love with motorcycles at the same time, and things sort of just naturally evolved from there.

"It became a rite of passage when we each hit eighteen to get our first bikes, go for our motorcycle endorsements, and thus be grandfathered into the club.

"Certainly not how most motorcycle clubs formed, but we were like, '*fuck it*,' it was our club, we could form and do things how we wanted.

"Some of us went to college, some of us went to war, some of us got into family businesses, or got the startup money from family to go do our own thing. Some of us were successful, some of us weren't, and some of us got caught up in drugs or what have you and struggled along the way. But you know what none of us ever did?" he asked.

I shook my head silently because I couldn't fathom.

"We never gave up on each other."

His gaze was intense, the way it bored into mine, and we sat perfectly still, the weight of the moment settling onto our shoulders and sinking into our beings.

He was telling me something without coming right out and saying it, and his message was crystal fucking clear.

The men of the Iron Wraiths were his ride-or-die friends. More than friends, more than family, if there was such a thing.

"Ever hear the proverb '*blood is thicker than water?*'" he asked.

"Yes, but I know that's not the whole thing. Something about covenant or something, something," I said.

He smiled and he said, "*The blood of the covenant is thicker than the water of the womb,*" he quoted.

I nodded.

"They're your covenant," I murmured.

He nodded slowly. "They're indeed my covenant, and I need you to never forget it," he said.

I nodded carefully.

"I won't," I breathed.

"Good girl," he murmured, and I felt my breath catch in my throat.

"You know, there's something else about this little dynamic between you and me," he said, motioning between us with a forkful of pasta before taking it into his mouth.

"What's that?" I asked, as my curiosity had once again been sparked.

"My sources with the police tell me that you did fantastic today," he said. "The police one hundred percent believe you."

My eyebrows went up.

"You maybe could have led with that," I said, and he laughed again, that rich and boisterous sound.

"What would the fun in that be?" he asked.

"I'm beginning to think you love to torment me," I said with a soft smile, because honestly, there was no beginning. I was just being charitable, throwing that in there.

I took a bite of my pasta then, now that it'd properly had time to cool and the salad was done. For real, though, that was by far the best Caesar I had ever eaten. A perfect balance between salty, the bite of lemon juice, married with all the other flavors, and the cool, crisp romaine was to die for.

He chuckled at that and shook his head. "Be grateful you got me and not Torment. That's more his speed, and he's a million times worse than me."

"You know, you're not exactly doing much to really sell me on wanting to be around these guys." I arched a brow, and he laughed at that, lightly this time.

"I'm not trying to," he said. "These guys are my brothers. I'm not saying they aren't assholes – most of us are, and with gusto – but we're more than that, too. On that, you'll just have to see for yourself, given time. You don't have to like them, you just have to tolerate them. Because hard line, they aren't going anywhere."

"I get that," I said softly. "I suppose that makes me disposable?" I ventured, knowing that I was more than likely going to hurt my own feelings by even asking.

"Not at all," he said, reaching out and stroking my cheek lightly with his thumb. "I don't ever want to hear you say that about yourself again, either. We clear?"

I swallowed hard and nodded, unable to look him in the eye.

"I'm serious," he said, catching my chin and forcing me to look at him. His eyes were the softest I'd ever seen them when he looked at me, and it rendered me speechless. The sincerity in them had me feeling like I somehow lived in the upside-down. There wasn't any other description for it.

"You growing soft on me?" I asked.

His smile was a cutting one, and he let me go, ordering me with a false, playful sense of sternness, "Eat your dinner." I took another bite, snickering around it.

"Wouldn't dare risk that punishment again," I said, rolling my eyes, and he smirked.

"Tonight's not about punishment, Kitten," he said. "It's about reward."

"There goes my curiosity again," I murmured, and he smiled genuinely this time.

"Finish your supper, and then see what I have in store."

"Mm." I nodded and relished the delicate buttery wine sauce with its slightly searing bite of garlic and lemon, which complemented the salad. The whole meal was a perfect balance, if a little heavy being pasta, but I could cheat every once in a while.

The meal concluded with us throwing playful little barbs at one another, and things felt... almost like they were achieving a sort of normal between us.

I liked it.

"What are you doing?" he asked when I got up, my dishes in hand.

"Taking my dishes to the sink to wash them," I said.

"No way." He grasped my wrist lightly. "I've got it. It can wait until later."

I shook my head. "I'll help you. It'll take no time at all. My mother would be horrified if I left dishes in the sink for any length of time."

He cocked his head curiously and took the plates from me, but he didn't argue, surprisingly enough. He just gathered his and took them to the sink to rinse.

I went over, my heels clacking on the expensive slate tiles of his kitchen floor – which was a bold choice. One dropped pot or pan was apt to shatter one or many if it struck just right.

I opened the dishwasher, and he rinsed and I loaded. It was nice in a quiet, domestic sort of way – and I appreciated getting it done. I hated clutter as much as my mother, and apparently as much as he did.

When the final dish had been loaded, and the last lid had been put on a container for leftovers, I sighed contentedly.

He gave the sound a wry little smile as he opened the fridge to put the last container of leftovers away.

"I abhor clutter he said."

"What a coincidence," I murmured. "So do I."

He pulled me into his arms and kissed my forehead.

"Thank you for the help," he murmured. "It was nice."

"Of course," I said.

We stood like that for a little while, lost in each other's eyes, and I honestly didn't know what to make of it. It certainly didn't feel anything like *no strings attached*, but then again, I'd never done anything like it before and wasn't sure how that all worked. I guess I was still learning.

"Now onto your reward," he murmured and drew me along with him to the bottom of the stairs.

"I thought dinner *was* the reward," I said softly.

He shook his head lightly, eyes locked on mine, and said, "Dinner was because you needed to eat dinner."

I laughed lightly at that and said, "Well, it certainly was a treat and very good, so thank you."

"You're welcome," he said at the top of the stairs, and then he turned me around and marched me ahead of him into the soft golden glow of his bathroom.

It was hot in here, but that was because of the multitude of glittering candles along counters and on a low stool at the foot of the tub. The amber glow warm and inviting.

He kneeled at my feet and took up my heel, slipping my shoe off one foot and then the other.

I wore a khaki wide-leg pants set and a cream satin blouse, the outfit simple and tasteful for a real estate setting. I tried my best to dress in warm neutral colors for showings so that the house could be the star of the show. Plus, I just didn't go for a lot of brights – it just wasn't in my wheelhouse to be ostentatious.

I steadied myself on Corbett's shoulder and let him take my other shoe off.

"Wait right here, don't move a muscle," he ordered.

I nodded, mute, curious as to what all of this was about.

He ran the tap, fingertips in the flow of water until he was satisfied with the temperature, then added a stopper to the tub before drizzling some potion from a cut-crystal bottle into the bottom.

An explosion of bright peach scent filled the bathroom, with something lightly floral underneath, enhancing the rich smell of what I considered sunshine as it crept to the ceiling, raised on the golden candlelight.

"That smells amazing," I complimented.

He smiled and came back over to me, turning me to face the mirror so I could see myself, then standing behind me, and eyeing my reflection with an intensity that bordered on frightening.

He gathered up my long hair and pulled the simple comb, holding it back from my face from just behind and high up by my temple.

"You have a way about you, you know? Elegant and old-fashioned. I like it."

I blushed faintly at the praise as he continued to gather and twist my hair. There was a claw clip, a faux tortoiseshell, sitting on the edge of the sink in front of me. He took it up, holding it between his lips as he put some final twists in my hair using both hands, scraping some errant strands back from my face before quickly taking the clip from his mouth and pinning it in a pile at the back of my head.

I stared at ourselves in the mirror and couldn't help but think that in another life, with a different set of attitudes, we would have fit, like two puzzle pieces meant to nest together. Not only that, but we could have been a powerful couple and run our own little empire.

Corbett Prescott may be an asshole, and a control freak – but I was starting to find that he had a softer side, something kept secret and viewed as a vulnerability. It was as though these sweet moments between us, when he spoiled and held me, were something he had always wished for but had never received, and that made my heart squeeze and flutter with a broken little ache for him in my chest.

"What is all of this?" I asked curiously, after finding my voice. He nuzzled behind my ear and pressed a light kiss there, which made me shudder. He smiled as he reached in front of me and plucked the button through its hole at my collar.

"Just relax for me," he whispered, and his voice took on that timbre that just made me want to melt.

"Okay." I decided to trust him, as he took his time undressing me, kissing me, and running his warm hands over my skin as he swept the cloth away and the tub filled.

I had some idea of what was in store, but not really. With the food still warm in my belly and the carbohydrates starting to make me a bit sleepy, I was indeed beginning to relax, and the bath with its mound of fragrant bubbles building... well, let's just say I felt due for a treat and that looked downright divine.

Chapter Eighteen

Corvus...

I'd like to think that things like this weren't in my nature, except that it secretly was. I loved to take care of my woman, and I had – once upon a time, but she had been the *wrong* woman who had taken advantage and strayed, making a total fool out of me. I wasn't apt to make the same mistake twice, but I couldn't deny that there was something different about Savannah.

From the first time she was in this tub, my hands buried in her hair as I made certain any bit of the crime scene we'd left behind was off her – I could tell, and I was positively *itching* to do things properly for her since that night. She'd been so good back at the club a couple of weeks back that I had been truly frustrated that life and business had gotten in my way of this most just reward.

I undressed her and helped her into the tub. She gasped at the heat of the water, and I know – it was definitely a touch too hot, but I wanted it that way. I wanted the heat of the water to sink into her very bones and work loose the tension she seemed to always carry in her back and shoulders.

"Relax," I ordered her. "I'll be right back."

"Okay," she murmured, leaning back against the end of the tub. "I don't think that will be a problem."

I chuckled and left, going back into my bedroom to change.

I had my phone silenced, but I couldn't stop myself from checking it at least once. The group text was slightly active, but it wasn't anything that needed my attention, so I set it down and vowed not to pick it up again.

Syn knew I was... *indisposed* this evening, and said he had it in hand, and I believed him. I just couldn't cede my control over anything for even a moment. I was well aware it was a "me" problem, but it wasn't actually problematic for me, and thus I felt no need to change it.

A sort of *"if it ain't broke, don't fix it"* mentality, if you will.

I changed out of my suit from the day and opted for comfort, putting on a fresh undershirt in my signature color, black, of course, and a comfortable pair of black lounge pants.

I checked the bedside table, set up for the next phase in helping Savannah to relax, and lit the mild candle that would melt into a lovely massage oil and balm.

It'd been a long time for me, rewarding a woman in this way. I still wasn't sure how to feel about it, other than fulfilling the driving *want* to do it.

I was wrestling with a lot of feelings when it came to Savannah Kittridge – she was a divine puzzle, a challenge, and I was enjoying playing with her and figuring her out. I was also trying to figure out why she seemed to press so many of my buttons. She flipped so many of my switches back to the 'on' position. Switches so long dormant they were covered in a layer of dust and cobwebs.

I wish I could say it bothered me, but what truly bothered me the most was the fact that it *didn't*...

I swore off anything serious with any woman years ago, and I was determined to keep this the same – but I had to admit, what she'd done to please me the most over the last couple of weeks, was what she *hadn't* done! Which was that she hadn't seen anyone else.

She hadn't gone on any dates or hooked up, and the way she rebuffed Specter's advance on the staircase had stung him to the point that even he wouldn't admit what she'd said.

I ran my fingers through the flame of the massage candle and huffed a slightly conflicted sigh before clenching my fists and banging them together one on top of the other in a fidget before taking myself back into the bathroom.

The tub was filling nicely, with her long, graceful neck and shoulders the only things above the mounds of bubbles.

"Where's the waterline under there?" I asked, taking a seat on the low stool up by her head.

"It's almost ready to be shut off, but not quite," she answered, blowing a bit of the heavenly scented foam off her hand and into the mountain in front of her.

I chuckled, and she rolled her head back to smile up at me with those bright blue eyes of hers, and I shook my head.

"You're adorable." The compliment slipped out of my mouth before I even knew I was going to make it.

Her smile brightened, and she turned, rolling in the tub to cross her arms on the back of the tub and look at me, resting her chin on them. I was struck by a thought and so asked, "You like to swim?"

She looked curiously at me for a moment and said, "How did you know?"

"You're a natural in that position. Looks like you've done a lot of chatting at the edge of a pool."

She smiled then and said, "My brother and I spent a lot of summers in the pool at my grandparents. I did swim meet in high school and partway through college."

"Did you now?" I asked.

"Mm-hm. Won State in the 200-meter butterfly my senior year. I just couldn't keep up with the sport and academics in college, and for me, the grades were more important than the athletics, so I dropped it midway through my junior year. I miss it, but I don't regret the decision. There were so many talented girls and even some Olympic hopefuls, and I just wasn't in it to win it like they were."

"I get that. I was on the swim team in the boarding school I talked about."

"Oh?" She raised an eyebrow like she was surprised we had such a thing in common.

I nodded. "Freestyle and water polo."

"Water polo?" She giggled. "I can't imagine you in the stupid little helmets." I laughed and nodded.

"Ah, yeah – might even have a photo or two downstairs of it."

"Oh, this I've *got* to see," she proclaimed, and I shook my head.

"Some things are better left buried."

She giggled and turned around, leaning against the back of the tub with a lingering sigh.

"I love this tub," she confessed. "And it was kind of a week – bad inspection on one place and just—"

I drew her head back, a hand under her chin, and stood just long enough to smack a kiss on her lips and another on her forehead on my way back down into my seat as she giggled.

"You're supposed to relax, that includes *not* talking about work or getting yourself worked up over what stresses you out."

She turned and leaned her chin back on her arms to look up at me.

"That doesn't leave me much to talk about," she said.

"Then don't talk," I said, raising a brow. "Sit right for me, please."

She gave an adorable little pout but righted herself in the tub. I laced fingers and bent my hands back, thrusting them out from my chest to a satisfying crackle through my knuckles. I put my hands on her shoulders; her hair piled off them and her neck, and worked my fingertips and thumbs in deep. She gasped, then let out a groan.

"This is just the appetizer," I said gently, and she breathed out a gentle breath and practically turned to putty in my hands.

I concentrated on my thumbs, pressing at the base of her skull where I knew tension was sure to hide, and started with a gentle pressure, increasing until she whimpered, then backing off just slowly enough until she relaxed under my hands. I kept it there for a count of thirteen – just an arbitrary number that I happened to like, considering the rest of the world didn't.

At the mark of thirteen, I dragged my thumbs down alongside either side of her spine and, keeping the pressure on, glided against her damp skin over her shoulders, pressing into her traps as I went, letting my fingertips find the hollows above her collarbone and carefully hooking them there so I could keep applying steady pressure.

She turned her head this way, then that, and the bones gave a satisfying pop that I both felt and heard.

"Damn, that sounded like it felt good," I said.

She laughed a little and said, "You have *no* idea."

"When was the last time you had a massage?" I asked her.

She was quiet and finally said softly, "Never, really. At least not a professional one. As for something like this..." she pondered.

"If you have to think about it, it's been far too long," I whispered into her ear and she nodded carefully, barely perceptibly.

"When was your last relationship?" I asked.

"End of high school. Beginning of college. Yours?"

"Hmm." I thought about the last time I would have classified anything as a *relationship*, and honestly, my thoughts went back to Courtney. Which was boarding school... she was one of the girls. While the school was co-ed, the dorms remained segregated, but that didn't stop us from finding ways around it and getting it on, on the regular.

"If you have to think about it," she said softly. "It's probably been too long."

I laughed at that and said, "Touché, Kitten."

"Why do you ask?" she wondered aloud, and I sort of froze a little, dismissing it out of hand with a light shrug, which I'm sure she felt through my hands on her shoulders.

"Curiosity," I murmured.

"So, you have multiple lives, too?" she quipped, and I chuckled.

"You only live once, as far as I'm concerned."

"Hmm, so don't believe in the hereafter, or reincarnation?" she asked.

"No," I said simply.

"What do you think happens when we die, then?"

I worked my hands into her tense muscles gently and said, "I believe that's it. We're just snuffed out. Like turning off a television set – no power, no sleep mode, just... gone. Lights out, the end."

She took in a shuddering breath and said, "That's sort of sad, isn't it?"

I shrugged again, "Not so much sad as the practical reality, really. It just is what it is."

Her knees came up, and she hugged them, her shoulders gently pulling from my hands as she said quietly, "It sounds... lonely. I'd much rather believe there's someone or something waiting on the other side for me."

"What, like heaven?" I asked.

She laid her temple atop one knee and looked back at me.

"I don't know if I believe in heaven or hell, per se," she said. "Just... it'd be nice to think there's something waiting on the other side. Your family or friends who have gone before you. I just... I don't think anyone should die and then just cease to exist. That's not fair."

"Life isn't fair," I reminded her gently. "Death is even less so..." I trailed off, not really wanting to bring the mood down any further.

Inevitably, she asked, "What do you think happened to him?"

"Who?" I asked, carefully.

"The man you killed..." She was very still and very quiet now, her chin resting atop her knees. I trailed fingertips in the water and suds behind her and down her back in wet lines and sighed as I thought about it.

"I think he just stopped being," I said. "Lights went out, and nobody's home – but I'm sure if there is such a thing as Hell, or whatever, he's roasting in it. He hurt you, and that is unforgivable," I cleared my throat. "Likewise, if he was so cavalier in hurting *you*, a well-connected professional in your field, I have to imagine he's hurt others before you. You don't get that bold unless you've gotten away with it before."

She sat up, and turned in the bath again, holding onto the edge of the tub and half-hiding her mouth behind her hands, her blue eyes sincere and cautious as she asked me; "Speaking from some sort of experience?"

I cocked my head, considered her, and decided to be honest.

"I would never touch a woman that way; that's not my style. Dubious consent is fun to play with, such as in your case... but outright forcing a woman? That's disgusting. Hitting and hurting? That shows a lack of restraint. I am a man, not a dog; I can't say the same for the rest of my gender."

"I can't exactly say my gender is all sunshine and roses, either," she murmured. "Nobody's perfect."

I smiled faintly and held down my hand to her. She took it, and I murmured, "Let's get you out of that bath before you turn into a prune."

She laughed, and nodded, letting me help her to her feet. I picked up a towel out of the towel warmer I had set up nearby and wrapped her in it, helping her over the edge and onto the bathmat.

"Thank you. That was lovely," she whispered and I smiled at her and rubbed her arms through the warm terrycloth of the bath sheet I'd wrapped her in.

"Oh, I was just getting started," I said, and I led her in the direction of the bedroom.

Chapter Nineteen

Savannah…

Corbett led me by the fingertips toward the bedroom, which I just now realized was similarly lit with a golden glow as the bathroom had been, but the light from the bedroom was several times less than the flickering candlelight of the bath.

In here, it was cooler, and fewer candles were lit.

The dark wrapped around us, making things more intimate somehow, as he guided me to his side of the bed, closest to the door.

"I still have a ton of paperwork," I protested, and he gathered me to him lightly and said, "Not tonight you don't."

"Corbett," I tried to argue.

"Ah!" he cut me off, giving me a stern look. "In the morning, Savannah. It will be there in the morning."

I gave him a petulant look and he smiled, genuinely, and while he was so damn handsome when he was oh, so, serious, but when he smiled at me like this? My heart swelled and gave an irregular little flutter against the inside of my ribs and I swear my knees went weak.

"Lie down on your stomach," he ordered gently, and he tugged the towel from my grasp at my chest.

I let him have it and hated how my cheeks flushed with embarrassment like he hadn't already seen me naked several times and been inside me in just about every way to make a preacher faint on Sunday.

"Lie down on your stomach," he murmured, running two fingertips from the hollow of my throat down between my breasts.

A heat curled low in my belly, as I crawled up onto his side of the bed and lay down, delving my arms beneath the pillow as I turned my head toward the nightstand and the glowing set of candles there.

One of them was a single wick in an aluminum tin, the label turned so I couldn't quite read it. It smelled wonderful, though. Like honey and a light hint of vanilla.

He straddled the backs of my thighs and scooted down to about my knees, but kept himself off me by kneeling to either side of me in the plush bed. He rubbed his hands together briskly, the sound a tantalizing one, then picked up the candle in the tin and tipped it over my back.

I tensed, expecting it to burn, but a pleasant hot oil was delivered in delightful little rivulets down my spine and drips across my shoulders to his dark little chuckle.

"Relax, it's made for this," he said, and he set the tin with its cheerful little flame back down on the dark bedside table.

His hands pressed into my skin, seeking below the layers of tissue and finding and teasing at the knots of tension there, his thumbs working deep, and in even little circles, the pressure mounting until the knot gave with a little pop, and he was able to glide through the area with little to no effort at all.

I closed my eyes and groaned into the pillow as he worked through some of the lighter and smaller nuisance knots and lumps in my muscles, working them slowly into submission.

I lay helpless under his touch as he teased every bit of tension out of me, and yet, no matter how hard I tried to get it to quiet, my mind raced.

I questioned everything... *why was he doing all of this?* It didn't feel like this was what was supposed to be *no-strings-attached fun*. It felt very much like we were tethered, a thin line of spider silk betwixt our souls. I had yet to identify if that thin line of gossamer was some kind of a trauma bond, or if it was something more... something lighter... something, dare I say it? *Good.*

"Relax," he ordered gently and I realized I had stiffened up under his touch. "What are you thinking about?" he asked after I had relaxed my muscle groups one by one.

"That this doesn't feel like *no-strings-attached fun,*" I confessed.

He chuckled lightly and said, "I don't want anything from you," he said.

"Now how is that, exactly?" my tone was chiding.

He laughed, "Touché, once again, Kitten." He was silent, almost meditative for a time and I shifted so I could look at him. He tapped my nose with his index finger and ordered me sharply, "*Relax.*"

"You know you don't have to do all of this if you want sex, you know..." I said and I couldn't readily identify why, but I was getting mildly upset.

"Of course I don't," he said. "I'm doing this because I want to – not because I feel obligated to. I do what I want," he said the last simply as though it should explain everything but quite honestly, it explained *nothing* and just left me that much more confused.

I turned over onto my back and he sighed, a long-suffering sound and cocked his head.

"Don't," he warned and I raised my eyebrows.

"Don't what?" I asked.

"Don't ruin it by starting a bunch of shit," he said.

I felt my brows crush down into a frown and said, "I'm not trying to start anything, Corbett – I'm just trying to understand..."

"Understand what?" he asked.

"Why you're being so nice to me..."

I fell quiet, because once I'd said it out loud, it sounded... lame. Stupid. *Desperate.*

He sighed and reached out a hand, curving it around the back of my neck and smoothing a thumb along my cheek. His whiskey-colored eyes searched mine, and he had such a look of tender concentration on his face.

"Because you've done well, despite so many hard things lately. Because you deserve the reward for all the shit you've put up with. I'm not an easy man to—" He shook his head and said, "I'm not an easy man to get along with, and you've done admirably in keeping your cool and sticking things out. The least I can do is spoil you just a little."

I thought about it and lay still beneath him. He kept up on his knees, and rested his hands atop his thighs and I thought, and not for the first time, that as arrogant and irritating as Corbett Prescott could be – he was a *gorgeous* man.

I swallowed hard and said, "I don't really know what to do with the kinder, gentler Corbett Prescott."

He smiled then, and said, "How about Corvus?" he asked. "Corbett feels like a shell. A costume I wear."

"Corvus..." I murmured and it was my turn to cock my head like the curious bird the name came from.

"Why did you choose that name?" I asked.

"Turn back over, let me touch you, and I'll tell you."

I stared at him, wary for a moment, but then complied. I hated how unreadable his face was to me.

He pressed hands into my lower back and slid them up to my shoulders, pressing deep, my back giving a series of satisfied pops as he dropped his weight onto me. One hand slid down my body in a deep caress, the other came up and his hand captured my chin.

He murmured next to my ear, "If you just want to keep it to fucking, I can do that..." and his hand that wasn't holding my chin fast, delved in between my body and the bed, his fingertips aiming for and finding my clit effortlessly.

I kicked, and struggled and he laughed.

Of course, my efforts were ineffectual. He had me, whether I liked it or not. What did it say about me that I *liked* it?

He pulled back on my chin, my back arching, my pelvis thrust into his hand and the mattress below as he rubbed at my clit. I pressed hands against the bed for lack of anything better to do with them, and whimpered when he pulled just a little too much and my abdominals stretched painfully.

He didn't let up.

If anything, the small sound of pain heightened things for him and he redoubled his efforts with his fingers slicking through my wetness, to get me to rise rapidly.

I panted, knowing he wouldn't relent until I came, and *God* why did that turn me on that much more?

"That's it, Kitten. Come for me, baby," he growled and I whined, the pleasure coiling low in my belly like a snake, waiting to strike. I was on that sharp precipice for far too long, until with a wiggle of my hips, grinding down against his hand, I hit that spark and the snake struck, and I was coming with wave after euphoric wave of pleasure slamming through my veins.

I panted, and he lowered me to the bed, and massaged my back, stroking over my skin lightly as the poison took hold and I swallowed my fear and accepted that Corvus was a drug, and like most drugs, he was highly addictive and I was hooked.

I shuddered helplessly beneath him as he chuckled darkly above me and I realized that I was wholly in his thrall.

Did he scare the shit out of me?

Yes.

Could I trust him?

In the bedroom? Absolutely. Out of it? Not as far as I could throw him... and that was the crux of things, wasn't it?

My heart ached with a sudden loss and loneliness even though the man was right here.

The words escaped my lips before I could stop them as though all sort of filter had been removed from between my thoughts and my mouth: "Dammit, I love what you do to me. At the same time? I hate it."

He laughed at that, and then it was as though *his* thoughts caught up to the weight and the meaning behind my words.

"This is just sex, Savannah. Don't get attached," he warned.

"No, I know..." I said faintly, and I hadn't even been thinking along those lines... *was he*?

Impossible, I thought to myself.

That begged the question, though... *was I?* Was I catching feelings for him? I mean, the sex was incredible... the best sex of my life! But honestly, this whatever it was between us was toxic as hell. What lunatic in their right mind would want this full time?

Which was a funny thought as his thumbs pressed deep into my lower back, near my hips, just absolutely *sending me* and making me yip with that pain that oh, once I got through it, I knew I would feel *so much better*.

"Really?" he asked. "There?"

"I sit a lot!" I complained and he chuckled.

"Too hard?" he asked.

"Harder!" I gasped, and he laughed then.

"A woman after my own heart," his tone was dry and I turned to look up at him as best I could from my prone and captured state beneath him and I pointedly threw his own words back at him. "This is just sex, Corbett – don't get – AIIE!" He pressed in that spicy spot that sent an electric pain lancing from my butt and hip, midway down to my knee and without thinking, I kicked up. My heel tapped him right in his butt from the way he was sitting on me.

"Oh! Achievement unlocked!" I cried, and I tapped him in the butt again with my heel. "I can finally say I kicked your ass."

"Oh, really?" he demanded, and he sat back fully on my thighs and *mercilessly* tickled me.

I shrieked, and wriggled, and fought but to no avail – not with the way he held me down; and as much as I *loathed* being tickled, I loved that he did it and that I felt safe – even knowing he would push boundaries.

When he'd deemed that I'd had enough, and I lay beneath him

gasping, giggling, and spent, he lay atop me, cuddling me, cozy, laughing and gasping with me and it was in that moment that I knew, it was too late for me.

That I loved this Corbett Prescott – *Corvus* – whatever he wished to be called. This version of him? The playful, sweet, and considerate version? I loved him and being with him and I knew that I would put up with all manner of Hell from the asshole version of him just for these moments... and I also knew in my heart of hearts that *that* wasn't healthy, or good, at all.

Still. I didn't know if I could help myself.

Chapter Twenty

Corvus…

"Well, well, well… look at what the cat *finally* dragged in…" Specter stood up from the billiard's table after taking his shot. I rolled my eyes and stopped at the bar. Spooky didn't even ask – just popped the top on one of my favorite beers and handed it over. I rose the bottle in an absentminded salute in his direction and he gave me a half-assed little grin of appreciation for the acknowledgment.

"Fuck, I take a timeout for one night and it's like you girls couldn't live without me," I shot back and Synister chuckled from where he sat back on a bar stool, eyeing the table, his hands wrapped around a cue as he calculated.

"You've been spending a lot of time with this one," he said.

"Just getting my dick wet," I lied. I could taste it like the bitter tang of heated, acrid metal on my tongue just saying it. I felt a pang of actual fucking *guilt* just phrasing it that way… because I knew better. I knew just how much Savannah was starting to mean to me.

It had started out all fun, games, and cruel intentions… but the more layers I peeled away from her, the more of a mystery she presented.

She was turning out to be one of a kind, and she was hiding something – and hiding it *well* from *me* might I add.

She wasn't all she appeared to be and was exceedingly private. I'd realized it over the intervening weeks since I'd first captured her that almost all of her *Savvy Savannah Davenport* persona was one hundred percent Bona fide bullshit, and though I'd asked and tried to get to her history she was sealed as tight as a clam freshly dug out of the sand and I couldn't help but wonder if she held a pearl in there.

In fact, I could almost feel that she did.

I just didn't know why she tried so hard to hide it.

The more interaction that I'd had with her, both in our working and private lives, the more she stoked my curiosity... and I couldn't help but feel it was a dangerous game that we played because I had sworn to myself; *never again.*

"Come with me," Syn said, rising and putting his cue onto the table.

I blinked and checked that he meant me and not Specter, and he did. I followed him into the chapel, and set my beer on the coaster at the boardroom table, taking my seat at his right hand in the conference chair. He took his seat and leaned back in it, swiveling to face me.

"Things are different," he said without preamble. "*This one* is *different,*" he cocked his head, his dark eyes studying me. "Bring her in."

I shook my head and said, "I don't think that's a good idea."

"I didn't think I was asking," he shot back plainly.

I breathed in deep and let it out slow.

"I thought so," he murmured. "You don't want to bring her here with the rest of the guys on a Friday or Saturday night because you don't want to claim her – but you don't want any of the others to make a move on her, do you?"

"Get the fuck out of my head," I muttered.

"Can't," he said plaintively. "We've known each other too long for that shit."

I smiled, but it didn't hold any mirth.

"I'm still figuring her out," I said and he raised his eyebrows.

"I beg your finest fucking pardon?" he said.

"She saw you kill a man, saw Requiem, Grim, *and Reaper's* faces – and you're still *figuring her out*?" he was sitting up now, and at full attention.

"Relax," I told him. "I'm not worried about that part when it comes to her *at all*. She's got her own secrets. Is hiding something. I'm just enjoying the hunt and the mystery."

Synister scoffed.

"Clearly your judgment is impaired with this bitch—"

"Don't call her that," I said sharply. "She's not just some hanger on club slut walking through the door. She's different."

Synister dropped back in his seat and said carefully, "You haven't defended a woman's name like that since..."

I raised my hand and said, "Don't say it." My expression felt like I just sucked on a lemon. I washed the bitter taste of memory down with a healthy swig of my beer.

"I don't want to talk about Courtney. That was years ago and I'm over it."

Synister looked amused by that. "It was almost twenty years ago, maybe even twenty-five and it was basically *high school* and you're *still* not over it. That's part of why you have your fuckin' name. A crow never forgets and they hold grudges for generations."

"Yeah, yeah, yeah... I know."

"I'ma need you to bring her in. See how she handles one of our parties."

I sighed, and asked, "You just want to get her measure, yeah?"

He grinned. "Among other things."

"She's been here once already," I tried and he shook his head.

"On a fuckin' Tuesday – when practically no one was here and to blow you downstairs. I know."

"Specter or Revenant?" I scowled.

"Who do you think?" he demanded.

"Fuckin' Specter," I grumbled.

He shrugged, "She pissed him off."

I smiled at that and said, "I'll just bet she did. Reject one of his crude advances?"

"Yeah," he grinned and we shared a laugh.

"I can never tell if he's trying to be serious with that shit or not," I said.

"Me either – he has to know it ain't going to work."

"You'd think," I agreed.

"Split the difference?" I asked.

"I'm listening," he said, one brow raised.

"Dinner at the Manse," I said.

"Sounds like a formal introduction to me..." he trailed off and I shook my head.

"It's not like that – she's legit just my latest plaything."

"Bullshit," he said. "Stop playin' in my face, brother. You dropped everything for her a few weeks back, brought her by when it was light on traffic to test her loyalty – albeit lightly, you've never had Requiem look into or track a plaything before, and you let her into your place not the carriage house apartment." He ticked each item off on his fingertips.

"I barely have a finger left over on this hand for how differently you've treated her than any other and I'm not hearing a *why* of it."

"Why?" I asked. "Let's try because I've never blown a motherfucker's head off in front of any playmates before her." He raised a thumb.

"Bingo!" he declared with a gusty sigh. "She's been different from the word *go* – and the sooner you stop lying to yourself about it the better. This one is different; why?"

I swiped a hand over my face and beard and sighed.

"I don't *know*," I confessed finally. "I'm still trying to figure that shit out for myself."

"Well, you better figure it out quick and fuck her on the dining room table like I did Madisyn or you *know* someone else is going to make a play – them's the rules."

I nodded, "I know the fucking rules – I helped you come up with them, remember?" I smirked, "Besides, I already took her out The Olde Pink House and spread her on the dining room table and ate her pussy for dessert, does that count?"

He laughed and slapped the table, and shook his head – "No witnesses, so fuck *no* it doesn't count."

My face lost its slow smile and I said, "She *is* different..."

Synister's amusement evaporated and he nodded, "You ain't telling me nothing I didn't already know," he said. "Real deal?" he asked.

I shrugged miserably and said, "I don't know. As close to it as I've come across since Courtney, anyway."

He was quiet for a time and finally said, "She *wasn't* the real deal – not even close, Cor. You've always known that."

I nodded.

I'd been all-in with Courtney. Would have let her dog walk me on a fuckin' leash if she'd liked... and Savannah was absolutely *nothing* like her.

If anything, Savannah was light to Courtney's dark in every way possible... maybe that was the difference. I told Synister as much.

"She's everything Courtney is *not*," I said. "With an air of mystery that's damn near irresistible."

"Spill, brother. I'm listening..." he said.

So, I did. I told him everything that I knew. How her vibe in real estate was just about as cold, cutthroat, and as calculating as mine and how that had been the first thing to attract me – even though it'd pissed me the fuck off because nine times out of ten when I got to witness it, it was being used *against* me, and easily six times out of those ten she won the bone of contention.

How I'd had myself convinced for a long time that I'd hated everything about her – and how honestly now, after having her in my bed, right where I'd wanted her, I was realizing it wasn't hate at all. It was anger – mostly at myself for being attracted in the first place. For making me feel something, for invoking the desire I had suppressed for so long and for doing it so fucking effortlessly.

About how I'd gone too far the first time we'd fucked with the perverted games and how I'd been able to see the heartbreak and devastation in her brought blue eyes when the blindfold had come off and pretty much all because she hadn't been able to touch me with the way I'd had her shackled. About how I'd been swamped with actual *guilt* for the first time in a long time.

I spilled, because Synister *was* my brother of the covenant more than any other fucking brother we had in the club. He was my best friend, and my confidant, and the closest thing I had to a motherfucking priest and I knew he would fuckin' die before he told another single soul any of this shit.

"Conclusion?" he asked when I'd spilled my literal guts across the table.

"I don't know if she's the real deal, but she's the closest thing to it that I've ever come across and I'm just not ready to risk parading her in front of the brothers to have them pick her apart – because I know that's what you motherfuckers will do."

Synister nodded, "You're goddamn right we will – we almost lost you to the depression that Courtney caused when she cheated, brother. You damn well better expect that each and every one of us is going to test anyone you come even close to that depth or level with. We'll not see you break that bad a second time."

"I have no intention of allowing myself to break like that again," I said. "I know it was fucked up."

Synister shook his head, "Nothing fucked up about feeling that hard and that deep for someone. We all just wished that Courtney could have been a better person than she was for you."

He looked thoughtful and said, "This one's different – for sure, so yeah, we'll split the difference. Dinner at the Manse. Thursday night.

Most of the boys'll be there but more importantly there's a game so Specter *won't*. He already shot his shot and lost."

I shook my head and said, "it's a wonder he gets any pussy at all with his attitude."

Synister shrugged. "He is who he is, just like you are who you are."

I nodded, "True that."

I took out my phone and texted Savannah: ***Synister would like an audience. Thursday night at*** – I checked with Syn.

"Thursday night, what time?"

"Seven o'clock sharp," he said.

I backtracked on the text, took out the "at" and finished it off with ***Thursday night. I'll pick you up at your office at 6:30. This is one of those times that I call and you answer, Bright Eyes. No argument, please.***

I sent it.

We sat and chit chatted, waiting for the rest of the boys to filter in for our weekly church meeting, and I felt a lot better for having offloaded what was on my mind to Syn.

My phone buzzed in my hand, just as I was about to drop it in the bag for the prospect to take before we got started.

I'm free was the only thing on the screen under the notification heading, so I dropped it in the bag and let him take it.

"That was easier than I anticipated," I told Syn and he nodded, catching my drift that we were on for Thursday night.

The meeting was called to order shortly thereafter, and I wondered what Savannah was doing in that moment...

Chapter Twenty-One

Savannah...

"Shit! Shit! Shit!" I grabbed the nearest thing which happened to be a trash can and stuck it under the steady drip coming from my bedroom ceiling. "Goddamnit!" I muttered with a gusty sigh, as the steady rough downpour outside was thrust into the trees outside and lashed the glass of the high window in here.

It was just a passing thunderstorm, but it was *coming down* hard enough that the leak had started again.

I rose my phone to take a picture for the useless landlord when a text came through.

Synister would like an audience. Thursday night. I'll pick you up at your office at 6:30. This is one of those times that I call and you answer, Bright Eyes. No argument, please.

"Just fucking great," I mumbled, and I checked my calendar right then and there. Would wonders never cease? I was open. I quickly took the time to block it off before Fabian had the chance to schedule anything and with a gusty sigh, got back to taking pictures and texting the slumlord.

Then, and only then, did I text Corvus back.

I'm free. I sent, then thought about it a moment or two and nibbling my bottom lip, I texted again.

Any way I can stay at your place tonight?

The leak was just oh-so-conveniently over my bed. So, it was either that, or I was sleeping on my couch.

I didn't get a reply, and I sighed out harshly.

I shouldn't have asked... I really... "Dammit," I muttered and I shook my head.

If he didn't get back to me by the time I was ready to turn in, then the couch it was.

I went into the living room and curled up under my throw, the little heater going in the fireplace and I turned on the television. I was on my laptop when a loud crack of thunder sounded, and then everything went out.

"Son of a bitch!" I screamed at the moldy ceiling. The glow from my laptop screen the only thing illuminating my darkened living room.

I checked and made sure it was alright and didn't take a hit from a power surge, even though I kept it plugged in to a surge protector. Satisfied it was still in working order – just stuck with no internet, which I needed, I took up my phone, and used its flashlight to go check the small breaker box in the bedroom, hoping against hope that it was just a flipped breaker and the power wasn't *out*, out.

No such fucking luck.

I sighed and lit my three-wick candle. It was dark by now, and the little light it gave off made things seem a little less ominous.

I cuddled on my couch under the throw, and must have nodded off – because it was super dark, the candle barely doing anything against it anymore when I sat up sharply.

I didn't know what'd woken me, and so I sat still, ears straining, listening intently. A rapping came at my front door, and I leaped to my feet.

I swear to God, if the lazy-ass fucking slumlord deigned to answer any single one of my texts or complaints about this place and he showed up to fix it *in the middle of the night*, I was going to lose my shit! Considering nobody even knew where I lived, it was the only thought to enter my brain as to who would be knocking at my door – I checked my watch, at nearly *midnight* on a Tuesday fucking night!

I ripped open the door and immediately quailed as it wasn't my diminutive landlord standing on my stoop, but *Corvus*.

"How did you find me?" I blurted, and he cocked his head.

He looked past me and looked down at me.

"You got somebody in there?" he demanded.

"What? No!" I cried. "What are you even doing here?"

"I missed your text about crashing at my place. You didn't answer your phone so I used the tracking software I have on it to find you."

"You *bugged my phone?*" I demanded, aghast.

"Technically it was the club's phone before it was yours, and no – it's not like I've been listening to you or your phone calls. It just has GPS tracking software on it. What's going on? You *live* here?"

He took a step off the sagging porch and looked up and around.

"My power went out," I said unhappily, trying to come to grips with the whole being tracked thing.

"Let me in, Savannah," he said gravely, and I huffed a breath and stood aside. He brushed past me and froze just inside my apartment.

"What's that dripping, the sink?" he asked as I shut the door on the darkened neighborhood and the cool night air.

"My bedroom roof," I said unhappily.

"The fuck is going on here?" he demanded.

"*Don't*," I said sharply.

"No, I want answers. This place is a shithole, Savannah. How long have you lived here like this?"

"Since I moved here," I said defensively. "And it is not. I did most of the inside myself."

"Baby, we're in real estate. Be so for fucking real right now! You can polish a turd, but it's still just a turd at the end of the day. I highly doubt this place would *even* pass inspection!"

"It's what I can afford! Alright! What would you know about it?" I demanded.

"Everything, if you would let me in and tell me," he said quietly, and I jerked back as though I'd been slapped.

Ouch.

"It's just *sex*, Corbett. Don't pretend now that you want something with me other than that!" I snapped.

He looked... hurt.

"I deserved that," he said, and he sniffed. He looked around and tried a light switch. Power was still down.

He raked a hand back through his hair which was as messy as I'd ever seen it, and moved like a storm cloud through the house. It was then that I realized he wasn't dressed like I normally saw him, in one of his expensive suits.

No, this wasn't Corbett, this was Corvus... and he looked every inch the badass biker from the boots that thudded dully against my cement floor, to the rugged jeans and leather chaps on his legs. He wore a zipped up thick leather biker jacket, and the Iron Wraith's vest over that and it made me back against the wall, leaning heavily on it because *Lord!* The man was *fine.*

He turned to look at me and shook his head. "What is this?" he asked. "You do as well if not better than me at the real estate game. You should be making money in the fucking *millions*. Is old man Beauregard holding out on you? What?" he demanded.

"No! No, it's not like that," I said unhappily, and I scrubbed my face with my hands.

"Then what is it?" he asked.

"You first," I said stalling for time. "Why Corvus?"

"My laugh, for one—" he said. "My ability to hold a grudge for another."

I frowned at him.

"I love your laugh," I said and his eyebrows went up in the dim golden light.

"Stop stalling," he ordered.

"My family is in deep with the IRS," I said. "Every bit of extra is going to Uncle Sam to keep the family home and to take care of my grandma. She has memory issues, dementia. She needs round-the-clock care and my mom can't do *everything* as much as she would like to."

He stood, hands flexing in and out of fists.

"Throw some shit together. You're coming home with me," he said.

"Seriously?" I blinked.

"Pack a bag, Kitten. Before I change my mind."

I gave a haughty and somewhat incredulous laugh and crossed my arms.

"I knew this would happen," I said bitterly.

"What?" he demanded.

"That you would look at me differently if you knew I didn't come from money," I said.

He nodded slowly and said, "You're right. I respect you more – now pack some shit. I'm not leaving you here."

I stood frozen, and he looked at me, his expression harsh and yet inscrutable.

It was then that any argument I could have made became an entirely moot point, because with a loud groan and a crack, I swear the whole little house shuddered and we both stood staring at each other wide-eyed and confused.

I went in the direction of the sound, which had come from my bedroom, and the smell of mold, mildew, and rot shoved me back a half a pace and right into the wall of Corvus' chest as he was right behind me.

"Holy fuck," he muttered, and I stared wide-eyed at the collapsed ceiling, old insulation and gross water pouring onto my bed and the floor.

"Son of a *bitch!*" I screamed, and I doubled over with the force of it, even as Corvus pulled me back out of the doorway and shoved me in the direction of the living room.

"You don't know if there's asbestos," he said and I covered my face with my hands and tried like hell to *breathe.*

"I can't do this," I said, shaking my head.

He gripped me by my shoulders and said, "You can. You're not alone. Let me help you."

I sniffed and stared at him, which there barely was an "up" when we were both standing. He was only a couple of inches taller than me. Still, the way he held such a commanding presence, it felt like so much more than that.

"Get your shit together for work. I'll try and rescue some shit out of your closet and drawers."

He pulled out his phone and called someone, putting it between his ear and his shoulder as he marched into my room.

I stood there and blinked for several seconds, before I got moving.

Laptop, briefcase, keys, purse, and phone. I silently repeated the checklist in my head as I gathered the items from their various places around the house.

Corvus came out of my room and hung up his phone, shoving it into his back pocket. He had a bunch of my things on hangars, and my overnight bag in his other hand.

"Where's your car?" he asked.

"Jag is in the garage," I said tiredly, and he nodded.

"Put some shoes on. It's muddy out there and there's no telling what tetanus is lurking and waiting to happen."

"Shit," I grumbled. I slipped on some ballet flats and belted my cozy robe tight. I followed him out into the night, and unlatched and wrestled the old garage door up. He looked stunned as I keyed open my trunk. We sort of just unceremoniously dumped everything into it, he shut the lid, and knocked on it twice.

"Follow me to my place," he said.

"Who did you call?" I asked.

"Nobody you need to concern yourself with," he said. "Let's go."

I watched him trail out to the front of the drive and climb aboard his motorcycle.

I sighed and went and got into the Jag, backing it out slowly and carefully turning it around in the soft mud and earth of the yard.

I pulled out carefully past him, and he fell in behind me, before zipping out in front of me to lead the way.

It'd stopped raining, but everything out here was still unpleasantly... moist. The air hanging thick with humidity, and with the plunging night temperatures, a mist rose from the pavement in places. I followed Corvus into the city, and it wasn't long until we pulled into the garage under his carriage house apartment.

Well, he pulled *through* his garage, parking the motorcycle in the courtyard like he so often did when I arrived.

I shut off the Jag and carefully got out, going to the trunk to get my work stuff at the very least.

"Come on," he urged, and took me by my elbow and led me into his place through the back French doors off the kitchen.

"Where do you want me?" I asked wearily.

"My room," he said. "We do need to talk, though..."

"Yeah, I guess we do," I murmured unhappily.

He came to me then, and smoothed hands over my shoulders and down to my elbows, cupping them through my pajamas and robe.

"I'm not upset with you," he said and I snorted.

"Liar," I muttered.

"Disappointed, maybe. Definitely upset you've been living like that and that your ceiling just collapsed – but I'm not upset *with you*. It's an important distinction to make, Kitten."

"Don't," I said softly. "Not with the pet names, not with the pretenses – not tonight," I sniffed, and felt the weight of my own disappointment settle onto my shoulders. I wasn't disappointed in him, but rather myself at the moment.

That I'd been caught out. Discovered for the absolute fraud that I was.

I reached up and rubbed my forehead and he pulled me into his chest, wrapping his arms around me.

"Talk to me," he said, and it was the first time I think I'd ever heard him beg. He didn't order me. He didn't command or demand it of me. His tone held genuine pleading. He was begging me.

I think that, more than anything, made me lose it and start to cry.

"Okay, or cry it out. I'm good with that too," he said and he hugged me close and I laughed, the sound broken by a bubble of sob escaping me at the same time; but I couldn't help that.

I got over myself as quickly as I could, and he showed some extraordinary patience, leading me into the library as he had that first night, and sitting me in the overstuffed chair, switching on the reading lamp.

He went over to the liquor cart in the corner and poured me a drink, bringing it over and holding it out to me.

I gave him a withering look, and he gave me an amused one back, taking a healthy swallow of the liquor in the glass, and then holding it out to me once more.

I took it and sniffed.

Brandy by the smell of it.

I sipped tentatively.

He hooked a booted foot into the leg of a nearby ottoman and pulled it over, taking a seat on it in front of me and resting his forearms on his knees, lacing his fingers between them and looking up at me expectantly.

"Story time," he said. "Take it from the top."

I swallowed hard and explained, "My family is a farming family from South Carolina."

I sniffed and took another light but steadying sip of the brandy in the glass and huffed a breath.

"The farm was my grandparents' pride and joy – their whole life. Something like three or four generations of my dad's dad go all the way back on that land. My grandfather ran the farm, my grandmother the kitchen. Then my dad took over and my mom too, and then grandpa got sick. He was gone pretty quickly, and it was my senior year of high school. Things were going alright, but then it became apparent that grandma couldn't keep up. She was forgetting and so my mom and dad fully took over."

Dad didn't want to tell us, but I guess things had been tight for a lot of years, and grandpa had fallen behind on the taxes. We had to come up with a way to pay those back taxes and we couldn't afford lawyers or any of that shit. So I went into real estate, sort of faking it until I made it, you know?"

He listened, and I fell quiet, not really sure what to say after that.

"You can't fake the things you've done in this field, Bright Eyes," he said quietly. "That was all you, Kitten. All you." He sighed.

"I don't know if that's supposed to be a compliment or..."

"It's just the truth. You're skilled and smart as fuck to have made it this far. Money doesn't mean a fucking thing. You're not at all what I expected."

His eyes met mine, and I downed the rest of what was in the glass and held it out to him. He took it, tapping his fingertips against the glass as he considered me.

"So, you're not mad or disgusted?"

He shook his head slowly.

"No, definitely I'm neither of those things. A little shocked, maybe – definitely in some awe that you've pulled this off this long. Nobody else knows but me?"

"Fabian... a little... but not really," I shrugged.

"How much were you paying for that place?" he asked.

"Six-fifty a month, all included."

He snorted and said, "Hell of a deal, but that place still wasn't worth that much."

I shook my head.

"No, I know. My dad and I did our best, but it was definitely just lipstick on a pig." I sighed and leaned back in the chair.

"Go to bed," he said, lacing his fingers between mine and giving me a gentle tug to get me on my feet.

"What about you?" I asked.

"I got a few more phone calls to make, and a couple of emails to send. I'll be right up."

"I'll figure something out as soon as I can," I promised and he shook his head.

"Tomorrow, worry about that shit tomorrow." I looked at my watch.

"You mean later today."

He nodded.

"Yeah. That."

"Thank you," I whispered, and he stood up and hooked fingers behind my neck, caressing my cheek with his thumb. He pulled my forehead to his lips and kissed me there before letting me go.

"Bed. Now."

I smiled a little wanly and said, "Yes, sir," and took myself to the bottom of his steps leading up to the second floor.

I could hear him pour himself a drink when I was but a third of the way up.

Chapter Twenty-Two

Corvus...

Tonight, I learned... I don't know why, but the phrase kept turning in my head.

Tonight, I learned... tonight, I learned, tonight, I learned... that Savannah Kittridge had one hell of a secret, and that she was damn good at keeping them.

A lot of pieces had suddenly fallen into place for me. For one, how something about her had always screamed disingenuous and fake – but to be honest, while I'd clocked that, I never in a million years would clock that she wasn't from *money*. Oh, sure, her family farm was multi-generational, but there wasn't a whole lot of money to be had in farming. Most every farmer out there was one or two failed crops away from total fucking disaster and her grandfather's handling of things was something I understood all too well.

How many foreclosures had I myself snapped up, paid to have flipped, and sold for a pretty profit over the years?

Shit, I bet there were foreign investors lined up around the block practically salivating over her family's holdings, waiting with bated breath for them to fail and for the IRS to seize their shit and put it up for auction.

Likewise, I bet my last dollar that Savannah was killing herself when if she'd only hired a tax attorney, she likely would be paying peanuts on the dollar to clear the tax debt. The IRS had a good way of scaring the shit out of people to get their money, and that was what a good tax attorney was for.

I sent an email to one I knew to get an idea of what could be done, loosely describing the situation, then I sat back with my drink and stared into space for I don't know how long while the wheels turned in my brain on what to do with Savannah.

I wasn't prepared to live with anyone. A night here or there was just about all I could stand, and while it was true that I admired her more, not less, for having come from modest means and literally self-making her money in the real estate market, her deceit in order to shortcut the line gave me some pause.

Not that I cared that it was unscrupulous. I could honestly give a fuck about that part. If you weren't playing dirty, then you just plain weren't playing to win – no what bothered me about it was simply that she had the capacity for that kind of deceit and had slid right by even my keen senses.

If she could lie so easily and readily about something like that... what else could and would she lie about?

Fucking Courtney, I thought to myself.

My mistrust really had more to do with her than with Savannah at all.

"Oh, the tangled webs we weave," I muttered, and checked the time.

It was nearly three a.m.

I got up and shrugged out of my jacket and cut, hanging them in the nearby coat closet down here. I took off my chaps and hung them, too. I liked to keep an orderly house. I took off my boots and left them in the bottom of the closet before I padded upstairs in my socks.

She was angelic, her hands tucked beneath her cheek as she slept.

She'd left the bedside lamp on my side of the bet lit for me, and I didn't know how to feel about that. It was kind... and that was one of the things that I think had been one of her tells. She was far too kind and selfless to come from money.

Like I said, pieces were starting to fit for me, and the image they created was *vastly* different from the image I had built up in my head of who Savannah actually was.

I undressed quietly and slipped nude between the sheets. I just didn't have it in me to dig out anything to wear, and besides that, she was too beautiful to pass up in the morning if our arrangement could hold – which if anything, tonight's little revelation had supplied me with yet more leverage to keep it in place.

I just suddenly didn't know if I had the guts or the heart to play the game as I had been all this time.

I lay down facing her and watched her sleep. She looked troubled, even in her slumber, a fine wrinkle developed between her eyebrows, just above the bridge of her perfect nose.

I'd had her all wrong, and I do mean *all wrong*... but then there was a part of me that wondered, *had I*?

She had to have lied somehow, some way, on her application to get under old man Beauregard... but everything after that? She struck me as a 'by the book' sort. I think the lesson had been learned by watching her family's folly on that.

I smoothed some of her long hair out of her face, tucking it behind her ear, and she reached for me in her sleep, cuddling into me as though desperate for my touch, and while it *should* have bothered me it didn't. I was surprised, in fact, how desperate I was for *hers*.

I held her close, her body warm against mine, and closed my eyes.

Sleep caught up to me much too quickly, an indication that I was far more stressed out about her situation that I should have been.

Dawn was a glimmer on the horizon, just starting to lighten the room when I woke from a dream where Savannah and I walked in a cemetery at night. Hands had reached up from the graves and snatched her from me, screaming as she was pulled into the dirt.

My eyes snapped open, and I looked down. I had somehow wound up on my back, my sleepy bright-eyed kitten practically draped over me, her head on my shoulder and chest, her leg over both of mine, one arm tucked against my body and the other draped over my waist, just above – *dangerously* close to where my boner tented the sheet.

She wore a cute little satin shorts and tankini sleep set in a peach edged with cream lace that left little if nothing at all to my imagination. I took a deep, deep, breath and my nose was tickled by her peachy scent and I closed my eyes as a sort of peace I hadn't felt in some time washed over me.

I swallowed hard, and shifted slightly, trying not to wake her, but no dice. She clutched onto me harder and whimpered her wordless complaint and I had to chuckle.

"Time to wake up then, Bright Eyes." I murmured the words into her hair and kissed the top of her head.

She dragged in a shuddering breath and stretched beside me, popping her neck and groaning.

"What time is it?" she whispered without even opening her eyes.

"Early," I murmured and she looked up at me, sleepily.

"I need my clothes," she muttered unhappily. "I need to go to work."

"We need to talk first," I chided.

"I know..." she sounded so dejected.

"You can't go back to that place," I said and she sighed.

"I know that, too..."

"Oh, I made sure of it," I said. "You asked who I called last night? It was to leave a message at the county inspector's office about the place. Pretty sure it'll be condemned."

She pushed up off me and reoriented herself, crossing her arms over my chest and leaning on me pinning me down, as if it would stop me from throwing her off me if need be.

"Why would you do that?" she demanded.

"It was a slum living condition, and I wouldn't have done it if I didn't already have a plan," he said.

"Enlighten me, oh wise master," she said, tone laden with sarcasm. "Where am I going to find *anything* in this city even *close* to that low that isn't some kind of slum?"

"Easy. I have a whole apartment above my carriage house – you can have it, and what's more you can stay as long as you'd like for nothing."

She stared at me, stunned, and asked, "You want me to be your live-in – what? Hooker? Escort? What would you even call that? In the apartment you keep to trick women into thinking that's where you actually live so they don't bother you at home?"

I grimaced and said, "Remembered that part, did you?"

"How in the Hell did you expect me to forget it, Corvus?" she demanded.

"Look, I know that I'm just supposed to be here for a good time and not for a long time or whatever, but that would change things for me, in a big way, can't you see that?"

She closed her eyes as I buried my hand in her thick luxurious hair and tucked it behind her ear, teasing behind it with my fingertips in a light little scratch or tickle as though she really were a kitten and not a very beautiful woman lying semi-irate across my chest.

She batted my hand away with a faint smile on her lips and snapped, "Stop that!" rather unconvincingly which brought a smile to my lips.

"As for the *other* thing, consider it my gesture of good will that I contacted one of the best tax attorneys that I know on your family's behalf. He'll be looking into things hopefully sometime today to see if he can't ease the payment burden. You shouldn't be paying that much monthly; their expectations are more than a little high."

She made a small sound of protest; "They actually *aren't*

expecting what I've been sending them – I've been doing that all on my own to clear the board as soon as possible. It's worth it to me, a little pain in the short run in order to clear the debt faster."

"Well, hopefully we can get the overall amount reduced, spare you some of the drama."

"I don't get it," she said. "Why are you..?"

I pulled her face to mine and kissed her, turning her onto her back, and showing just how easy it was for me to overtake her. She made a blurted sound of something that was halfway between surprise and protest, but I'd done enough talking, and I wanted her.

She put her hands against my chest, and stopped me with her eyes. I stayed above her, holding myself up effortlessly, but that wouldn't last forever.

"This is really huge," she said. "Can't you see that?"

I cocked my head and said, "I see the pros and cons, Savannah. Don't think I don't."

"Give me a pro," she said raising her eyebrows and I dropped my hips and ground my erection into her.

"Pro: with you just steps away, I can have you whenever I want, and likewise you can have me whenever you'd like. It certainly makes the sex easier."

"Con," she said, "What if I'm not in the mood?" I arched a brow considering her hips were moving unbidden, and she was pretty much humping me right back, just the thin material of her cute little shorts and whatever panties she wore beneath in our way.

"Pro, I can keep an eye on you, and it's much safer here. Also pro, you have your own space and I have mine."

"Con, you can kick me out whenever you'd like, and I'm completely at the mercy of your whims and bad moods." I could see the fear that that was just what would happen flash in her eyes and I eased myself down and kissed her gently.

"I'll draw up a contract," I murmured. "Would you like six months, or a year?"

"You're serious?" she reared back, smashing her head into the pillows to look at me.

"I take care of what's mine, Bright Eyes," I said to her, and the look on my face was a solemn one.

"What happened to *'just sex'* and *'don't get attached?'*" she demanded.

"I only have one answer for that," I said with a small grin. "You're a witch, and you've bewitched me."

She choked on a laugh, and we stared at one another for a long time. Both of us burst out laughing at the absurdity of it all.

She pulled me in and we kissed, and a joy that I thought had been long dead burst in my chest and sent sparks through my veins.

She pulled her shorts and panties down, wriggling beguilingly beneath me, and I didn't hesitate. I folded her back knees, to chest and got myself inside her, groaning at how tight and how wet she was to take me.

"Condom!" she gasped and I pulled out.

"Shit, right! I'm sorry, I just got caught up." I reached into the drawer and got one, and while I got it on, she got out of her clothes and we clashed, coming together like two weather systems and it was *electric.*

I held her tight, and moved with a purpose and a surety and was rewarded with her arms twinging around my neck, and her legs around my hips. She forced my head to hers, her fingers tangling and gripping my hair as she kissed me fiercely, and I returned the kiss with everything that I had to give her.

I was desperately trying to hold on to my heart, but her soft hands and even softer little moans were doing a damn good job at chipping through the layer of ice around it.

What wasn't to love about her, now that all pretenses had been stripped away? She was beautiful, not just in looks, but in heart, mind, and soul. Try as I might to not get sucked in, it was difficult. Impossible even. She was tenderhearted and her touch drove me wild, her scent had me drowning in her, and the way she kissed me?

It was with a desperation borne of a need to be loved, and *fuck* I was trying so hard not to go down that road again for myself.

She was the first woman to ever even come close since... *fuck!* Her body squeezed down on my cock and I found it hard to thrust as hard and as evenly as I had before. She was close —so close —and I was fighting to hold off by this point. The pleasure was a deep pool of warmth, spilling over and through me, mounting higher and higher, threatening to spill over the careful dam I'd built around my heart in this rising tide of emotion that I just couldn't fucking ignore if I'd wanted to.

I couldn't believe what I'd walked into last night. I'd thought she'd lived in the big house that Requiem had sent me pictures of. Not the small, falling apart shed outbuilding behind the equally crumbling and sagging garage.

I gripped twin fistfuls of her hair and pulled her head back, driving into her roughly, as my possessive nature reared its ugly head. She cried out, and dug nails into my shoulders and upper arms and I welcomed the sharp, sweet bite of them.

"Fuck, yeah, baby girl. Come for me," I ordered her in a low growl and I smiled at the feral whining cry that emanated from her as she bucked against me, slipping one hand between us to worry at her clit to make my desire a reality.

I fucking *loved* watching her come apart for me, and this time was no exception. She shuddered, crying out, her pussy rhythmically gripping and releasing me and it was all I needed. I felt that hyper quick build and the crescendo was pure fucking *magic* as I throbbed, my cock jettisoning my release into the condom I wore, hot and sticky, making things unimaginably slick and I wanted that feeling to last for fucking ever, so I didn't stop – I couldn't, thrusting in and out of her at a slower and more sedate pace. Dragging things out for as long as I could until we both found ourselves limp and glowing in each other's arms.

We lingered, languishing in the afterglow of the sweet torture that was our intense morning fuck, and she asked me, her voice trembling finely with a fear of letting it out into the ether, "Would it be so terrible? To love me, and be only with me?"

I kissed her forehead and sighed, holding her close, treading carefully with my words...

"No, it's not," I said carefully. "It's not at all..."

I don't know if she caught it, what I was telling her, and she hugged me tightly and I her, but I couldn't bring myself to say it out loud. Not yet, and I felt like the biggest fucking coward for leaving it there, vague, and vaguely impersonal at that.

She deserved better than that from me. I just wasn't ready to do it.

Chapter Twenty-Three

Savannah...

"Savannah!" I jumped, and looked up from where I had been staring at my laptop screen, frozen, without really *seeing* it.

"I'm sorry," I shook my head. "What is it?"

Fabian looked *genuinely* concerned for me.

"Girl, what is *wrong* with you today? This isn't like you." He took the seat across from my desk, crossing his legs and putting his notepad in his lap, snapping its leather folio shut and staring at me pointedly and I could see the come-to-Jesus meeting was nigh, even if Jesus wasn't the religious figure in our case, per se; but more like some cute-as-hell little Cuban gay boy ready to serve up some sangria for the *chisme* about to be served to our little get-together... That's gossip, for the uninformed.

I sighed and sat back in my chair, and searched Fabian's face.

"Corbett Prescott," I said and I worried over his reaction to the name.

"What's he done this time?" he asked, and he snapped his folio back open and I took that to mean he thought I was ten million miles away over *work*...

I shook my head.

"The man I've been... *seeing*... is Corbett Prescott."

Fabian gasped and leaned forward, putting both hands flat on my desk and whispering harshly, "Girl, shut the front door!" he looked at me aghast.

I squeezed my eyes shut and said, "I know, I know! Just, one thing led to another and now here we are and, oh Fabian – I'm afraid I actually really *like* him. Like, *like*, like him, and I don't know where to go from here."

"*How?*" he asked, and he still hadn't picked his jaw up from off the floor.

"Just one thing led to another and, you know... we ended up..." I rolled my eyes and gave him a pointed look and said, "*You know.*" His eyebrows went up. "It was all supposed to be just some no-strings-attached fun, but believe it or not, he's really not what he seems and we really just misunderstood each other and then this morning—"

He gasped. "*This morning?*" he demanded. "We're staying out late on *school* nights now?" he leaned back in his seat and crossed his arms over his chest and I rolled my eyes.

"My power went out at my place from the severe thunder storm, and my bedroom ceiling sprang a leak and then my bedroom ceiling *collapsed* and now I'm supposed to move into the apartment above his carriage house just until I can figure something out and anyway, this morning we had sex, and I asked him if it would be such a terrible thing, him and I together and all he said was '*no, it's not*,' but then he got all distant and cold as we got ready for work and I think I fucked up and now I don't really know what to do about it, and I'm afraid things are going to be so awkward living so close together and that's not really what's all consuming my brain – it's that I *really* want to be a part of his life and I want him to be part of mine and it came out of nowhere and I feel so stupid, but I can't help how I feel and—"

"Savannah!" he barked and I snapped my mouth shut. He tsked, sighed, and shook his head.

"Girl, I take my eyes off you for a *second* and you get in bed with Corbett-fucking-*Prescott?*"

He looked at me pitying for a second, and then sighed and said – "I mean, if he were gay, I would have already tried; let's face it, the man is gorgeous, but he's also an *asshole* and Bright Eyes, you deserve *much* better than that."

I smiled faintly, I couldn't help it, and said, "That's what he calls me, too."

"Oh." Fabian looked dubious and then said, *"Oh!"* like it meant something.

"What?" I asked.

"Oh, Girl – pet names and I have to ask, were those his *exact words?* 'No, it's not' or did he say 'No, it *wouldn't*'?"

I played with the necklace that Corvus had given me, and said, "Trust me, I've been playing those words over and over in my head since he told me this morning, he said 'no, it's not'; why?"

"It may be nothing. It may be something..." he looked thoughtful.

"What, Fabian? What could it possibly mean?" I hated how desperate I sounded.

"It could mean, either A, he has it just as bad for you as you do for him but he's got commitment issues. Or, B, he really loves the sex but doesn't feel the same way about you that you do about him, at all – from the sounds of it and the lack of past tense... I want to lean toward option A, but honey, I don't know that I would get my hopes up."

I sat back in my seat and rubbed my forehead as much to hide from him as to try and ease the burgeoning headache I was giving myself, worrying myself sick over the whole situation which was honestly stupid.

"Why do feelings have to be so hard?" I complained.

"I ask myself the same question, too..." he said. "Now moving past the whole Corbett Prescott bombshell – your ceiling collapsed? What's that about?"

In for a penny, in for a pound... I thought to myself.

"About that..." I said, reluctant to get into *all* of my business all at once; but honestly, Fabian was the only one I felt like I could talk to about any of it. I'd done a pretty good job of isolating myself out of pure ambition since moving here – part of that was out of necessity. I had lied like a rug on my resume to get my foot in the door here a little over a year ago just to get the chance to prove myself.

I had – don't get me wrong – but I actually *liked* Mr. Beauregard and my other coworkers here, and I didn't want to devastate them.

"Nope!" Fabian stood. "It sounds like you've got it handled, and honestly, I think I can handle only so much in one afternoon or you're liable to send me into all sorts of airs and graces. Speaking of... you're clear to leave early if you need to go handle things at your place. I can't imagine..."

"Thank you, I know there's an all-hands staff meeting—" Fabian held up his hand and retrieved his folio from the floor.

"I will send your most sincere regrets at your inability to attend, and I will take copious notes. That *is* what I'm here for, after all – but you owe me drinks and a whole lot of explaining by Friday, if you please."

He gave me a baleful look and I had to laugh.

"It's a deal. I have a thing on Thursday night..."

"A thing, or a date with a certain competitor?" he asked.

"That," I said biting my bottom lip.

"Your secret is safe with me," he said and I breathed a little easier.

"Thanks."

"I want *all* the *chisme*, though – I mean it."

"You've got yourself a deal," I said meekly.

"And I mean *all* the dirty details," he sang over his shoulder as he exited my office and I felt myself turn beet red as the door softly thumped closed.

"I don't know if I want to go *that* far," I muttered to myself, thinking about this morning and the way he'd held me down with his body and by my hair as he thrust into me with absolutely no mercy.

I was more than a little surprised to find I liked it rough…

I sighed and packed up my briefcase.

I had to go and see what was salvageable out of my place and what was a total goner.

Honestly, I was worried about seeing it in the bright light of day. It was bound to be worse than what I'd glimpsed in the dark the night before.

I pulled into the driveway to a whole circus out front. The county and city inspectors' vehicles, a box truck, several motorcycles, and my landlord.

I put the Jag into park and got out.

My landlord glared at me, but the inspectors were keeping him so busy he could do no more than that.

I slunk across the yard and to my door to see several bikers taping up boxes of my belongings, the prospect, Spooky, straightening up from one and saying, "Hey, there you are. Corvus called, said you needed some help… so uh, here we are… helping."

One of the other bikers guffawed and said, "Prospect, shut the fuck up."

"Rude!" I blurted, and all of them cracked up like I'd said the funniest thing.

I scowled at the one who'd spoken last and he threw up his chin in greeting, "I'm Fear, that's Requiem, and pretty sure Reaper's in your bedroom going through your underwear drawer. It's kind of his thing. Grim ought to be in there with him. Hangman's the one out in the back of the truck."

A man with his back to me, stuck up a hand and waved from over by my mock fireplace.

"Oh, I didn't even see him outside," I turned around and sure enough, a bearded man was coming in my front door.

"You Savannah?" he asked.

"I am," I said. "Um, nice to meet you."

"You, too. We got this handled, if you have shit you have to do," Fear said and I turned back around.

"Actually, this is all I have to do for the rest of my day... I had no idea you'd be here."

"Corvus is a control freak like that," Requiem said, standing up and turning around.

"Oh," I didn't say anything beyond the sound of recognition. He'd been the one Corvus had been talking to, at the top of the stairs the night that... well, the night that Hal Lindstrom had been, *ah hem*, disappeared...

He gave me a silent but intense look and I nodded faintly, my hand on my chest as I glanced toward my bedroom doorway, which had a thick sheet of plastic hanging over it.

"How bad is it?" I asked.

"Bad," Hangman said flatly. "Your bed's a goner – I wouldn't trust it after being soaked with whatever toxic mold soup came pouring out of your ceiling. Other than it, everything else seems salvageable. We already got the dresser and nightstands in the truck, Grim and Reap were just finishing up boxing your things from the closet and the dresser. You got a shit ton of shoes."

"Also, probably Reaper's thing..." Fear mused out loud and I tried not to snort.

"Is it safe to go in there?" I asked.

"I wouldn't," Requiem said. "The boys have respirators on just in case. Handy things you find in a funeral home."

"I'm sorry?" I said confused.

The plastic sheet was pulled aside and the other two men from the Lindstrom showing stepped out. I recognized the one by his round blue hippy glasses and the other by his dark hair.

"Grim, Reaper, meet Savannah," Fear said.

"Yeah, we heard," the one with the dark hair said from behind his mask, "and fuck you, for the panty and shoe comments."

Frear laughed and gave Grim the finger, and Grim gave it right back. Reaper was holding a couple of boxes and staring at me rather pointedly, so I suddenly had doubts about whether Fear had actually been joking about the whole panty-sniffing, shoe-obsession thing. Reaper just gave off a creepy, intense vibe. The one that would make a woman suddenly cross the street if she saw him coming down the sidewalk at her.

I swallowed hard and asked, "So what can I do?"

"Nothing," almost all of them chorused at once. Spooky had moved into my kitchen and was boxing up my things.

"That hardly seems alright," I said and couldn't help but blush.

"You want to do something, take some of these boxes in your car and head on over to the fuck studio – er, I mean your new place," Fear said.

"Smooth, real smooth," Grim said and he sounded genuinely irritated with him. I mean, if looks could kill. I swallowed uncomfortably and said, "It's alright... I uh... I kind of already knew that part of the apartment's history. Corvus already told me."

The guys all exchanged a look at that, and all I could really do was stand there and flame with the awkwardness of the moment.

"Why don't Reap and I carry some of these out to your car for you and you can, uh, head on over," Grim suggested. I nodded quickly and couldn't make eye contact and said, "Um, sure."

I went back out, Grim and Reaper in tow, each carrying boxes from my bedroom to the back seat of the Jag.

"You're in heels," Grim observed.

"What?" I looked down. "Oh, yeah... I came straight from work."

"One of us should go with you," he looked to Reaper who nodded.

"Oh, no, that's okay, really," I said with a nervous laugh.

"I insist," Reaper said, his voice quiet, reserved, and sort of unexpected. I gathered he didn't talk much and that Grim did most of the talking for him.

"Cool, you go, I'll stay, we'll be there with the truck and the rest of this... stuff, as soon as we can."

"It's okay," I said with a little laugh. "Most of it *is* cheap shit that I rescued off the curb and re-did myself or bought from a bargain basement website or whatever. Plus swearing never did bother me much."

"Well alright then," Grim said. "For curb rescues, you did a great job."

"Thanks," I said.

"Reap's going with you to unload for you, and help with whatever you need. He doesn't talk much, but he's a good guy. Loyal like a motherfucker."

Reaper and I exchanged a look and he gave a slight nod.

"Okay," I said with an uneasy laugh.

My final thought as we both climbed into the Jag was, *what was I getting myself into?*

Chapter Twenty-Four

Corvus...

"What happened to the moving company I hired?" I demanded.

"Uh, yeah – we canceled that. Figured we'd save you a few bones," Fear said.

"What the fuck are you all up to?" I demanded.

"Nothing much – just feeling her out. She's kind of a timid little thing."

"She's almost as tall as I am," I said. "Save me your bullshit."

"She may be as tall as you are, but one stiff breeze she's liable to blow away. Seriously, I like mine with a little meat on their bones. What's it like to fuck a twig?"

"Oh, shut up," I grated, and Fear laughed on the other end of the line.

"Where is she now?" I demanded.

"With Reaper, headed on back over to your place and the re-established fuck studio. Torment should be there already; he's stocking her fridge."

"Seriously?" I demanded.

"You let her go with Reaper?"

"Hey, that was Grim's idea."

"Who else is at my place?" I demanded.

"Uh, nobody that I know of."

"Jesus Christ, Reaper and Torment," I pinched the bridge of my nose and took a steadying breath in and let it out slowly.

"Relax," Fear said. "I Reaper's been on a short leash since that thing with Hangman's girl, and Torment... you know what? On second thought, you might want to get over there."

"Fear, I swear to God," he laughed and hung up. He was good at that, the fucker – sowing fear and watching the chaos unfold. I shook my head with a small smile and looked at my calendar.

I wasn't really all that worried, to be honest. Reaper had a deep respect for women who were still breathing, and honestly when it came to Torment, it was all about what kind of mood he was in. I figured that if there was ever an introduction to the deep end of the pool and it was sink or swim, Fear had set up a perfect opportunity for Savannah to learn and to learn fast.

I just hoped that Tor *wasn't* in one of his moods – he could put the *cruel* in *cruel intentions* and pull some fucked up shit. He loved to watch a motherfucker squirm. Just as long as that fucker wasn't my Savannah, we'd be cool.

I had too much to do today, and I was stretched like a rubber band. I was irritated with Synister – this had him all over it. He'd likely seen the charge to the moving company and had gotten into things. That's what I got for having each other as backups on accounts.

I'd deal with that later – tonight I was meeting with Luca Di Maritzi over a rather nice Italian dinner to talk business. Mostly about using some of his warehouses as pop-up underground fight locations. So... underworld real estate bargaining, which just so happened to be my niche and thus I was required to appear.

I got through the rest of my day as a mundane before I switched gears into full club life, even if I wore an Armani suit. I took the Porche, because riding in an Armani suit would have been idiotic and I didn't have time to go change… not that biker wear was appropriate for Luciano's. Far from it.

Still, it was intriguing, this prospect… the Italians had actually reached out to *us*, which meant we were certainly going places when it came to our underworld dealings… still; it was an interesting and potentially volatile cocktail as they *did* butt heads with the Colombians from time to time.

It gave Syn and I some pause, wondering if they were trying to butter us up to turn on Castañeda and his boys, which we had no interest in doing. Not unless the Italians had a very sweet offer indeed to make us. Castañeda and the Colombians were our main cash cow. We did the odd street deal here and there with the local gangs, but there was nothing like the Colombian's money; so long as the supply chain didn't dry up from Parris Island anytime soon.

Of course, it'd been America's prerogative since something like the early 1970s to destabilize South America, and nothing about that had really changed; thus, I didn't perceive that being a problem anytime soon.

Luciano's was a small, but fine dining experience. You wouldn't find your typical tourist fare here. Jacket and tie required, hats off before you even stepped through the door – an elegant sign out front stating the rules clearly. It wasn't one of those places you walked into in your summer shorts, flip-flops, political tees and a baseball cap being loud and obnoxious about your First Amendment rights to free speech or whatever.

That was liable to get you a swift escort out into the back alley for an even swifter and unimaginably brutal lesson in how free speech doesn't equal freedom from consequences by the rather large and intimidating Italian men in the corner booth reading the newspaper and chewing on toothpicks. Seated with them was a familiar pair of faces,

Death and peeking out and around looking my direction was Shade. Death inclined his head ever so slightly, and I threw him some barely perceptible chin. The guy reading the newspaper beside him barely glanced in my direction, but that glance was enough to take it *all* in.

Yes. It was *that* kind of establishment, and a relatively new addition to Savannah at that; the neighborhood it inhabited near the water, but also newly gentrified causing an already strained housing market to become completely unbearable for the lower and what was left of the rapidly shrinking middle class.

Which was not my problem, thankfully. Never had been, and never would be as long as I did my part and kept myself and everyone else out of prison for any term length of time. Even then, we had sheltered assets that were untouchable from our legitimate ventures, held in offshore accounts and invisible to nearly any but the most elite of forensic accountants.

"Corvus, for Luca Di Maritzi," I told the hostess at the podium greeting guests and looking up reservations. This was the kind of place that reservations were all but required, but if you were *very* lucky, or willing to wait; you could snag a seat in off the street. Typically, the wait was two hours or better, though.

I'd had yet to try the food here, but I was told by Torment it was a treat – and that was high fucking praise indeed coming from that epicurean snob.

I was led to the upstairs of the place, which held tables all around the outer edge looking down over the tables below. There was a secluded round book set back behind a fountain at the top of the stairs, the gently tinkling water loud enough to foul any parabolic microphones in employ anywhere in the restaurant.

The fountain was a heavy marble piece of work, and a small-scale replica of one of the famed fountains in Italy – no doubt the same region where the food was from. Torment would certainly know; but I didn't really particularly care. I was here on more pressing business; the food was just a bonus.

I slid into the booth beside Synister, who was already waiting with Di Maritzi.

"I told you he wouldn't be late," Synister intoned, and I glanced at my watch. It was two minutes to the appointed hour we were to meet. Of course I wouldn't be late. I abhorred being late as much as Synister did.

"Would have been ten minutes early, but parking was a bitch," I said.

"Corvus, this is Luca Di Maritzi," Synister made the introduction. "Mr. Di Maritzi, this is Corvus, the man in charge of our real estate dealings."

"Please, please, we're all friends here – call me Luca." Luca snapped his fingers. He was younger than I had expected. Late twenties, maybe – when I had expected late thirties to early forties. I glanced at Synister as someone nearby came and dropped a drink at our table.

We didn't tend to fuck with the Italians, so this was pretty much highly unorthodox. What's more, these Italians happened to be new to the area. The Mancini's were the usual game in town, and we'd had a rather unfortunate run in with them about eight months or so back when one of their presumed stiffs had ended up on Grim & Reaper's table. Except she wasn't dead. It'd been a major headache and had taken some real doing to untangle the Gordian Knot of chaos that'd become our problem.

Hangman wasn't complaining, though – that's how he'd gotten with his Lorelai, and she was a sweet girl. Tended to keep Hangman's head above his depression and PTSD flare-ups. They were a match made in heaven and it worked.

Of course, thinking of them, my thoughts trailed back to my bright-eyed kitten.

I slammed the door on those thoughts as quickly as they attempted to manifest in order to keep my head in the game.

"I understand you have some real estate you'd like to talk about leasing," I said.

"That I do, friend. A toast," he raised his glass and I raised my eyebrow. "To a profitable future."

Synister snarked a laugh and said, "Let's not get ahead of ourselves. A deal has to be made, first."

"I guarantee you'ns guys 're gonna want what I have to offer," he said.

"We're listening," I said cautiously. If it sounded too good to be true, it probably was.

"You use our places for your fights, no money up front, ten percent, and you uh, maybe owe us a favor or two here and there."

Synister and I looked at one another, and a silent accounting passed between us. We sat in silence for several moments and I tapped Syn's foot with my own under the table to signal he should *definitely* take this one; I certainly didn't have anything nice to say.

"The last family came around here treating us like their errand boys were the Mancini's. You, no doubt, heard how that worked out for them..." he said, and it was as deadpan as I had ever heard him. He was even less impressed with their bullshit than I was.

"Ten-thousand down, as a gesture of good will, a single event, you can have five percent, and this is a onetime deal," I said. "To see how things work out – a trial if you will, and nobody owes anything to anyone. That's just clean business."

"Alright, alright," Luca looked like he was mulling it over. He sipped his drink and stared plaintively at me.

"Twenty-five down if you're only offering five percent, ten down if you're offering fifteen percent," he said.

"We'll do fifteen and ten," Synister said quickly. "That's if you really do want to be friends..." I smirked and hid it as best I could behind my glass.

We turned a few hundred thousand, sometimes as far upward as a mil on a good fight. The percentage would far outweigh the cost of renting a venue. Our fights were popular and we had good talent.

Luca looked thoughtful and said, "Open to renegotiation after this inaugural investment?" he asked.

"Sure," Synister said.

He raised his glass, and we clicked ours to his, sipping before setting them down.

"A deal's a deal," he said. "Sorry if you'ns thought I was gettin' cute."

He snapped his fingers twice, and plates were brought out. The rest of the negotiations, locations, legal and forward-facing contracts etc., were worked out – which was all me and my job.

On paper, we were renting the warehouse for a month to store shipments going out to parts to be decided. It was, of course, all a shill just to get things done on the back side. Of course, this did make for a handy opportunity to change things up with the Colombians. Easier access and all of that, which why not kill two birds with one stone?

The chess pieces were constantly moving across the board, and it wasn't really paranoia if they were out to get you. The "they" in question? Law enforcement, of course. While we'd done a fair bit of investment into Savannah PD there were any number of a veritable alphabet soup of government agencies who were likely out there lurking. FBI, ATF, hell when it came to the South Americans, I was hazarding CIA, not to mention with the Marines involved there could possibly be NCIS and JAG in the bowl too.

See... alphabet fucking soup.

Dinner was fabulous, of course; and Synister was rejoined by this evening's wrecking crew as we headed out the door.

"Shade," I gave a polite nod. "Death." I spared him the nod – but that was just how things were with me and Death. He'd been the one that Courtney had set her eyes on back in the day, which who could blame her? He definitely had the looks to go along with his money. We were good, don't get me wrong. We'd squashed that shit years ago; but with Savannah so new and now firmly in the mix thanks to Synister? Well, old ghosts... you know?

"You good?" Synister asked me, because of course he didn't miss a thing.

"I'm good, just personal shit," I said. "I'll get to that with you in a moment." I scowled at him, and the fucker grinned.

"Let's walk," he said. "Where'd you park?"

"Lot down the street," I said.

"Good," we fell into step, Death and Shade bringing up the rear.

"You know I'm just ripping the Band-Aid off. She had to meet the majority of them sooner rather than later."

"Thought that was what tomorrow night was for," I said and he chuckled.

"I was just saving you a few grand on moving expenses."

"Fuck you, a few grand is nothing."

He laughed.

"There's a reason I'm here tonight, man." Death chimed in quietly from behind me.

"I kind of figured, and I appreciate you leaving the introductions to me," I said with a sigh.

"No problem," he said.

"Bros before hoes," Shade pitched in.

"Always," I said and Synister slowed.

"First time I've heard you even come close to hesitate with that one." My best friend stopped and turned to me.

"I have no idea what I'm doing here," I confessed. "The pull is strong with her and it came out of nowhere," I told them.

"One day at a time," Shade put his hand to my shoulder and gave me a nudge. "Keep moving, boys – before the Italians think this is some shit it isn't."

I laughed at that, and nodded, "Fair point, my brother in blood. Fair fucking point," I said. We kept moving.

We talked about it a little more as we moved down the sidewalk and ultimately, I was surprised the rest of the guys were being so easy on me with this.

"Why is it, none of you have been giving me a ration of shit?" I asked as we reached my Porche.

"Maybe we just think you deserve a shot at happiness, too," Death said with a shrug and Synister gave me a look like 'duh.'

"Thanks," I murmured, and they said their farewells until tomorrow night as they wandered on down the street back toward Luciano's and whatever vehicle they'd ridden in to get there.

I drove home and wondered to myself how Savannah's day had been, hoping like Hell that Tor and Fear hadn't given her a run for her money.

Chapter Twenty-Five

Savannah…

The apartment above the garage at Corvus' was a *tiny* one-bedroom, if it could even be called that.

I led the way up the stairs from the tiny side door in the garage and keyed my way into the little studio and then some.

It let right into the small living room, which was open concept with the kitchen and a small area enough for a four-person table if you were pushing it.

There was a fireplace, set back under the overhang of the bedroom loft which overlooked down here, and one of the features I appreciated the most? Was the fireplace down here shared a chimney with a fireplace up *there*. So, it was sort of a two-fer. Of course, I didn't think either of them were functional, as many fireplaces and chimneys around the south; especially in Savannah, weren't. Usually due to old age, disrepair, and modern HVAC systems.

Still, I would happily do the same as I'd done in my old place and put a small heater set back in them to give me the aesthetic.

"Oh!" I turned at the sound coming from the kitchen. A man

looked up from where he'd had his head in the fridge and he shut the door.

"Hi," he said with a grin that could only be described as wicked.

"Um, who're you?" I asked.

"Yo, Reap." He gave a nod to Reaper behind me. "I'm Torment. I'm here to satisfy your every kitchen need..." He looked me up and down and his grin became lascivious. "And any other need you might like to have entertained."

I rolled my eyes and said, "I'm good, I promise. It's nice to meet you."

He laughed and said, "Where do those go?"

I turned and Reaper stood, just holding the boxes still.

"Um, upstairs in the loft. I need to check out the closet up there."

"Original to the place, so tiny," Torment called after us.

Shit.

The rest of my afternoon was spent trying to spirit away what was my wardrobe – which was *not* inconsiderable, away into what was the closet space up here and working out what I would do with the rest of it.

It was furnished, the apartment, but Torment had assured me this was all going to come out and my furniture would be moving in – which was at least slightly comforting. I had enough dresser and armoire space to work with up here, and the bed was indeed a queen – as mine had been.

There was a bathroom up here, with a shower; and downstairs, just off the kitchen, there was a water closet with just a toilet and a sink.

I was trying to adjust to my new surroundings and get things unpacked and put away as quickly as possible in at least the bedroom so that I could function throughout the rest of the week and get to work on time and dressed to the nines.

For the most part, the men stayed out of my way just bringing things up and down as needed and leaving me with boxes to sort through of my personal belongings. I just heard an occasional "Dude what the fuck?" from my kitchen and Torment as he judged just about everything that came out of my kitchen boxes as he sorted the kitchen out for me.

I wasn't going to complain. I was just grateful for the space; they could be as judgy as they wanted over my cheap Faber ware cookware.

It was late, my furniture was in, boxes still piled on the kitchen counter, dining table, and couch. I was exhausted, but blessedly alone, and went in to take a shower.

I stood under the hot spray for a while and got into my comfiest pair of pajamas I owned.

I hated the mattress here; and missed my own, but it would be something I would have to get used to as my old one was definitely done for.

I texted Fabian and let him know all about the afternoon adventures, but after five minutes or more with no response, I figured he had retired early. Which was a little bit of a bummer, because I honestly wanted his perspective on all of it.

I mean, if Corvus didn't care more than just a little, he wouldn't have gone to all of this trouble, would he?

I thought it would take me a long time to fall asleep, it being a new place and a new to me bed, and all, but I must have been more tired than I thought.

I slept, hard, dark and what I thought was dreamless; only for the night to be shattered by a hand over my mouth and lips next to my ear growling out, "Don't scream, Bright Eyes, I'm not in the mood to listen to it."

I froze, heart hammering in my chest, and I couldn't see the mere inches in front of my face. There wasn't enough light for that, just a hulking dark figure in the dark, darker than the deep shadows of the room behind him.

"Good girl," he murmured. I swallowed hard and waited for him to take his hand away from my mouth, but he didn't.

Instead, he let out a low and appreciative sound somewhere

between a purr and a growl and moved the blankets off my body to get a better look at me.

"Now I'm going to make you come, and you're going to be a good girl and take it, aren't you, Kitten?" he asked.

I made a muffled sound from behind his hand and he chuckled, a decadent sound and said, "I'll take that as a 'yes, sir.'" His free hand slid into the waistband of my satin shorts, and his fingertips found my pussy, delving at the apex of my thighs to stroke at the heat and gathering wetness there.

"Oh, I like that very much," he murmured, and he started stroking me slowly, working me up, drawing the wetness from my opening up and around my clit.

I made sounds behind his hand, and felt almost as though I couldn't get enough breath through just my nose, but he seemed to like it that way, his fingers pressing against my tender flesh, making a circular motion that he knew would drive me absolutely *wild.*

I wrapped my hands around his wrist, but he wouldn't take his hand away. I made pleading begging moans behind it, and he just smiled harder, his teeth white in the dark, a Cheshire cat's smile.

"Mm-mm," he said. "I have you right where I want you."

I panted, and writhed against the sheets, and he was relentless with his sweet tortures, working my clit expertly, my body his instrument, a symphony he played just to himself and the captive audience of one that I was at his hands.

He eventually took his hand away from my mouth, and I cried out his name; "Corvus!"

He traded having his hand over my mouth to holding me down by my throat. Not choking, not cutting off my air or the blood flow to my brain, just pressing, just enough to let me know that he could if he wanted to; that I was thoroughly at his mercy and whatever dark and twisted desire lay at the heart of him.

"That's it, baby, sing for me, sing my name," he urged, and I cried out as I shattered completely in his hands. I writhed, my body convulsing on wave after wave of pleasure as he laughed in triumph, that rich raucous sound like a murder of crows – at which point I really *did* wake up, to my own hand at my pussy and my own hand at my throat, and the real Corvus leaning against the wall at the top of the stairs down to the living room.

I shrieked and jumped up onto my knees on the bed, half-assedly covering myself with the blankets and clutching them to my chest as he laughed and applauded me.

"That was wholly unexpected and quite the fucking show, Kitten!" he cried as I tried valiantly to swallow my heart back down into my throat.

"What are you *doing*?" I demanded.

"I didn't intend to wake you or to interrupt. I just... hm," he hung his head, hands buried deep in his pockets and I glanced at the glowing numbers on the bedside clock. It was a little after midnight, pushing half past the hour but not quite there.

I swallowed hard and looked at him.

He was still dressed in his slacks from that morning, and I recalled the expensive Armani suit he'd worn. His jacket was gone, as was his tie, but the sleeves of his tailored to fit dress shirt were rolled back over his forearms and he looked... *tired.*

"What's wrong?" I asked, and I held out a hand to him, beseeching him to come sit by patting the bed beside me.

He pushed off the wall and meandered over, taking a seat beside me, putting an arm over my waist, and leaning in for a kiss, which I gave him.

"I missed you today," he whispered against my lips.

"Missed me?" I asked softly, and searched his eyes in a room that was much brighter than the one from my dream, the shadowed blue light of the moon pouring in through the windows along the exposed brick wall on either side of the room.

"That doesn't sound like *no strings attached,* friends with benefits, or whatever you would call us," I said when the silence had pooled between us for too long.

"I think it may be time to upgrade you to the girlfriend package," he murmured, tracing a finger along my hairline, tucking a long length of it behind my ear.

"And what comes with that package?" I asked with a faint smile, because honestly, that sounded really good.

"Well, we still maintain our own spaces, for now. I'm not exactly sure that I make for the best boyfriend material. It's been a long time."

"Yeah?" I asked softly. "How long?"

"Twenty years give or take," he said.

"What? Why so long?" I asked.

He was silent, and dropped his eyes to my hand, pressed against the bed by my hip, tracing a fingertip over my left ring finger.

"She cheated, with one of my brothers, and I never got over it."

"I'm... I'm sorry," I stammered, in part because that sounded a little excessive. I mean... I've heard of heart break but *holy shit.*

"She wasn't who I thought she was, and I'd given my heart over to her completely. It was the kind of pain that... Well, it wasn't very easy to get over it. The broken trust something even more so. I swore never again..."

"Then..." I formed it as a lingering question, because I wasn't sure what I had done to break the curse so-to-speak.

"Then this obnoxious blonde with a fake-as-hell souped-up southern accent showed up and made my work life *actual work*," he said with a chuckle and I had to laugh.

"Oh, the horror," I said rolling my eyes.

"You have no idea, I *hated* that she was better than me at the real estate game, and then, one night, I got a text from her that was meant for somebody else and I found out in the intervening weeks that she was *nothing* like I thought she was. She was something entirely different. Entirely *wonderful*... and I almost missed out."

"Well, I'm sorry to say," I said lightly and dryly, "You were *everything* I thought *you* were."

"Oh, yeah?" his smile was almost shy and he tweaked my nose. I jerked back with a laugh and he said, "This, I've got to hear. Please, do tell..."

"Overbearing, arrogant, insufferable, incorrigible, oh, and gorgeous..." I ticked off each point on one of my fingers and his eyebrows went up in amusement. "But what I hadn't counted on, was just how *useful* those things could be and how they also equated to, *protective, confident, tenacious, unstoppable,* and that you were as gorgeous on the inside as the out when you wanted to be."

His expression was inscrutable as he searched my face.

"You know, I found myself thinking the other day that I would gladly let you put me through no end of trouble and hell just for those moments where you were so gentle with me. The way you hold me, the way you wash my hair, and the way you sometimes forget when we're in the thick of being intimate and it almost feels like loving rather than fucking."

He snickered then and said, "Busted..."

"I asked you this morning if it would be so terrible if you loved me and could only be with me... I've been second guessing your answer all day."

He hooked a hand behind my head and pulled my mouth to his, kissing me thoroughly until I was all but totally breathless.

He pulled away and murmured against my lips, "No need to guess, bright-eyes. I love you, and you're mine. You've been mine from the second I first licked that delicate pussy of yours on that dining room table."

"You say the sweetest things," I murmured, and then we were kissing again, hands roaming, and before I even knew what I was doing, my fingers were at the buttons on his shirt, undoing them one at a time.

"No condom," he whispered against my lips.

"Shit," I swore softly.

"You're on birth control?" he asked.

"Yes, I have the five-year implant."

"We doing this whole commitment thing?" he asked and I pulled back and looked him in the eyes.

"Absolutely."

"Then it's just you and me, baby. I haven't so much as looked at another woman since you came into my life that night." He swallowed hard at the confession and I felt a soft smile paint my lips.

"I don't think any man could honestly measure up to you even if he tried," I murmured. "Only way any other man is getting into my pants is by force."

"They'd die for it," he said flatly and that *did* make me smile – some of his darkness rubbing off on me, I suppose... either that, or maybe being with him had woken some darkness of my own.

"I believe you," I whispered against his mouth, as we both slid down to lay with each other, "and I hope you'd make them suffer."

"That's even if they got to you in the first place," he growled and we were kissing again. Something primal, something feral, something that was a touching of souls that'd been laid bare.

We'd been quietly baring them for however many minutes in the freest exchange of words I think we'd had to date.

It felt good.

It felt even better when the clothes were off, and he was inside of me. He was gentler, more sedate this time than in past encounters, and I loved it, but I missed the Corvus of my dream at the moment. The man of surety and confidence who wouldn't hesitate to drive me into the bed so hard I thought we might break it.

I bit his bottom lip until he made a noise and let it go, begging him *"Harder."* And he obliged. Driving into me harder, deeper, but not faster and it was *perfect.*

"Yes, oh, yes!" I held him close, burying my hands in his hair, writhing in counterpoint to his movements and *oh, oh, oh!* There, right there.

I was breathless with anticipation, the pleasure mounting, my body his to play with how he saw fit, and *God, lord,* did he know how to play me.

He played me so finely, I never wanted him to stop, and the sounds of his moaning just served to push me that much closer to the edge.

We came together, both shuddering, both trembling finely in each other's arms, our bodies touching and essence mingling, and it was fucking *perfect.*

Chapter Twenty-Six

Corvus...

"Corvus..." her voice held just a hint of warning to it, and her eyes sparkled with mirth.

"I'm sorry, did you just call him *Corvus?*" my client asked and I chuckled.

"No, she called me Corbett, you misheard. Interestingly, both mean the same thing," I said.

It was contentious across the table, but at the same time this deal was done – and while both sides were getting what they wanted, neither were exactly happy about it. The sign of a perfectly performed negotiation. When both sides could live with it, but neither side were exactly over the moon.

Savannah and I were playing our parts, just trying to get the documents signed so we could get out of here. It was Thursday, and dinner was going to be served at the Manse. I found myself more excited than daunted about announcing her officially as my woman.

It was a big deal, and every one of the Wraiths had their own way of doing things. For Synister, it had been fucking Madisyn at the table. He did love an audience. Fear, it had been eating his woman out on the pool table at the club one night when all the brothers were there.

Hangman's situation with Lorelai was more sedate than that, as she'd had a very recent assault in her past that required a bit more of a delicate approach. So, he had settled for snapping at any one of us that dared to come too near her at a gathering at the Manse shortly after they'd settled into their life together at the caretaker's house at old Bonaventure. It hadn't helped that her mother had been there the first time all of us had gotten together. He made up for it later with a particularly artful display of Shabari, suspending her in the clubhouse garage with just us boys present to watch the show in silence. She'd been blindfolded to make it easier, and it had been a beautiful display.

I had something of my own planned tonight. A game for my little kitten to play; one of *cat and mouse* that would serve three purposes. One, to show her off as *mine*, two, to get me off, and three, to prove to the men of the Wraiths that the past was in the past and that I trusted them.

We wrapped things up and when both clients had left the parking lot, and we were satisfied we were alone, I opened the passenger door to the Porche.

"After you," I murmured, and she slid into the passenger seat, setting her laptop laden Italian leather briefcase at her feet. She had confessed her ability to thrift shop, and had confessed that it wasn't a thrift store find but rather had been a gift from her little brother upon her college graduation. Her purse, on the other hand, had been a particularly good thrift store find that had only required a little bit of saddle soap and some TLC to restore.

I had to compliment her on her fine work; I never would have been able to tell that it'd been thrifted. She'd laughed and had told me that one had been professionally handled, and had cost her more than the purse itself – but she was responsible for refinishing all of her furniture.

I drove us back home so that we could change into something more casual and shed the workday.

We parted ways at the garage, her to go to her apartment, and me to my kitchen door. I went upstairs, and lingered at my closet for a moment, smiling softly to myself as I pulled down my favorite, well-worn Henley, and a butter soft pair of jeans. I dressed quickly, changing out my dress socks for something thicker, that would withstand my heavy motorcycle boots and went downstairs to the coat closet for the rest.

I donned my chaps, jacket, and cut, and sighed, shrugging into the road worn leather like a knight would his armor. I felt more like myself in my gear, and as I stepped out the back door to head back to the garage, I paused to take Savannah in.

I realized, I'd never actually seen her in anything this casual. She wore jeans, rolled up at the cuff over dark blue Keds and low white socks that barely peeked over the line of the shoe. The jeans were a medium denim in color, and whole – no holes, which I was surprised she found anything without in this day and age. Over them, she wore a light blue men's dress shirt, rolled back at the wrist and I swear it suspiciously looked like one of mine...

"Is that my shirt?" I asked her.

She smiled a little shyly and said, "Maybe. A tee shirt just didn't feel right." She hitched her purse a little higher on her shoulder and I couldn't help but grin.

"It's perfect," I said and she eyed me just a little suspiciously on her own.

"What, ah... what's this?" she asked, waving vaguely in my direction.

"This is what I wear when I ride," I told her.

"Shall I follow you, then?" she asked and I grinned wider and shook my head.

"Oh, no. You're riding with me."

"I don't know..." she said and looked skeptical.

"Never been on the back of a bike?" I asked, curiously.

"Does a four-wheeler count?" she asked.

"No," I shook my head.

"Then, no," she said with a laugh.

"Well, if you're going to be with a biker, there's no time like the present to learn," I held out my hand and she looked dubious, but took it. I took her over to the bike and said, "Wait here."

She trailed fingertips along the leather seat, as I went into the garage to the set of shelves built over on the side with my Porsche. I picked up my helmet, and the spare I kept for the odd occasion I needed anonymity. It was solid black, the facemask a deep dark tint. It was hers, now if it fit like it was supposed to. My everyday wear was my usual brain bucket.

I put mine on, holding hers between my knees and then went back out to her, lifting the facemask so I could see what I was doing and helping her put it on.

"It feels tight," she complained, and I nodded.

"Like it's smashing your cheeks in?" I asked.

"Yeah, forcing me to have fish lips," she crossed her eyes. I laughed. I couldn't see her mouth, but I imagined she was pulling her cheeks in and making the face.

"That means it's a good fit," I told her. "You'll get used to it."

She laughed and it was more than a little nervous.

"Don't we need to pull out the cars?" she asked.

"Nah," I pointed to the double side gate.

"It's a minor inconvenience because I've got to hand-lock them up after us, but the curb is so low it's nothing to use them to get out when cars are parked in the garage. I'm just going to have to bite the bullet and get them automated."

I went over to them and unlocked them, swinging them inward. It used to be the original entrance to the place, horse and carriage would ride in, make a loop around the round brick drive, back the carriage under the carriage house on one side, horse stalls on the other. Neat and tidy.

Back at the bike, I instructed her to lean with me, not against me, to hold on tight, and to watch her feet – I didn't want her shoes melted to the pipes. Above all, I told her, to *watch those pipes.* They get hot, and I didn't want her to burn herself on them mounting or dismounting.

She listened with rapt attention, her blue eyes wide through the open visor of her helmet, and when we were ready to go, I closed it for her, told her how to breathe to keep it from fogging up on her, and went over to the bike, starting it up. She got on and settled behind me, which was a bit of a process for her first time as she carefully minded both the pipes and where she placed her feet.

The ride to the Manse was a woefully short one, and only required we take surface streets, so no freeway. It had been a good long while since we'd taken a group ride anywhere or had gone to do anything that wasn't just a short ride through Savannah, and I realized just how much I'd been dying to go for a real ride.

It was certainly something to bring up at dinner.

We arrived on the back side of the Manse and I noticed that Savannah's attention was on the pool. I smiled and made a mental note that a swim should be in our future. It was one of the surprising things we had in common, after all.

There were a lot of things I wanted to do, just her and I, and I realized how long it had been since I'd really gotten to do any couples' things and also, that I had missed it more than I realized.

I pulled into line with the bikes already present and it didn't take much more than a quick count to see everyone was already here.

We left our helmets with the bikes, and I threaded my fingers through Savannah's, walking with her up to the kitchen doors.

Several of the guys were in the kitchen with Tor who was whipping up his magic in a metal bowl. I saw Requiem, Death, Revenant, and Specter – so all that Savannah had already met.

I didn't know how much exposure she'd really had with each, but I know she'd met them.

"Hey, hey!" Torment called as we entered through the doors.

"Hey, boys. How's it hangin'?" I asked.

"Short, shriveled, and a little to the side," Revenant said and he shook one leg where he was standing at the end of the counter.

Savannah snorted indelicately and covered her mouth.

The guys tittered with laughter at her expense and I shook my head.

"I had to ask," I said, ruefully.

"Dinner'll be up in ten," Torment declared. "Y'all get the fuck out of my kitchen; we're officially over capacity."

"Yeah, yeah; you're such a fuckin' girl," Specter said and he was the first to relinquish his seat at the counter to stand and head for the dining room.

The rest of us naturally fell in, and Torment asked Savannah, "What'll you have to drink? We got wine, beer, that shitty hard seltzer – anything you could want, really."

"Oh, uh... what's for dinner?" she asked.

"Beef Bourguignon," he said.

"Ah, then a red if you've got it."

He narrowed his eyes and asked, "French or Italian?"

"We're having French, so French, of course."

"Okay, that was easy." He looked thoughtful.

"Got a good Malbec?" she asked.

"Oooo, a girl after my own heart. You may pass and I'll bring it right out; have to go to the cellar for that one."

"Me too, if you please," I said and Tor threw me some chin.

"Absolutely," he said at our retreating backs.

We found the club in the dining room, as well as Madisyn, Lainey, and Lorelai. So too was Madisyn's bestie, Valory.

The table was enough to seat twenty-five, and it seemed to be filling more and more.

There was Synister, and at his right hand was me, and at my right hand was now a place setting for Savannah. To Synister's left was Madisyn's place, but right now, she was in his lap.

We were all at our usual places according to club position, however, shifted down a spot to make room for Lainey, and Lorelai beside Fear and Hangman. Valory was seated at the far end of the table near the prospect in one of the extra seats at the grand table.

"This is beautiful," Savannah murmured as we made our way down the table's length and I pulled her chair out for her.

Indeed, the Manse as a whole *was* a beautiful specimen in early turn of the century architecture. It was a Greek revival mansion built in the early 1900s and painted a cheery yellow on the outside, but inside? It was all classic hand carved wood paneling and crown molding. The original ceiling medallions above the hanging chandeliers.

"I've always wanted to see inside this place," Madisyn said quietly. "I just never bothered to look up who owned it."

"That would be me, and Synister, in partnership," I murmured back.

"You?" she asked, surprised.

"Only half," Synister said with a smile, "And it was bought with my money."

Savannah looked to me and I nodded.

"It's really very beautiful," she said. "I would love to see more."

"Certainly," Synister obliged. "Give you a tour after dinner."

"Actually," I piped up, "It's been a while since we've taken a group ride, and I'd like to head on over to the club after dinner with everyone if it's cool with you... there's something I'd like to get out of the way."

Synister cocked his head ever so slightly and I put my arm around Savannah pulling her into my side with a slight nod.

"Club ride to the club house after dinner!" Synister boomed, and the rest of the table fell silent and looked to our president.

"Hua!" the men chorused, which stood for 'heard, acknowledged, and understood.' Something several had brought back with them from their military service and had handed to the rest of us.

He'd been so loud, I was sure Torment had heard all the way in the kitchen.

Savannah looked at me curiously, and I smiled down at her, realizing that sitting I was several inches taller, which just meant my girl was all leg – which I definitely appreciated. Especially when they were wrapped around me.

Dinner was a lovely affair; Torment really outdoing himself, as always. Most of it was spent talking and getting to know Savannah, who I had told to just be her real self. It turned out, that my little bright-eyed kitten had a lot in common with Madisyn's best friend, Valory.

They got onto the topic of fashion and that took up a good portion of the evening with even Madisyn, Lainey, and Lorelai at a loss for words when it came to the designer names and years being tossed back and forth between them.

"I just thought you had a love for semi-vintage fashion," Valory said at one point.

"Ah, sort of," Savannah laughed nervously. "Just turns out I was poor, and trying to fit in... yay me..." she sounded meek and embarrassed and it was Synister who laughed.

"You certainly fit right in like you were born to it, if Corvus' bitching about you is any indication."

"That was *before*," I argued jovially, and Syn winked at her.

"Never let up on him in the real estate arena, it's fun to watch him squirm," he told her.

She laughed and said, "We have a deal, we argue about work at work and at home – but we never argue about home anywhere *but* home."

"It's a good rule," Haint toasted her with his glass and took a good-sized draught of the wine in it.

As soon as dinner was concluded, and the table was cleared, most of the dishes handled to the point a load was going in the dishwasher, and another waited at least rinsed in the sinks, we departed.

It was full dark now, and I needed that – ready for the games to begin and to work off some of that rich meal.

We arrived at the club and lined out the front with our bikes, heading inside. I'd quietly asked that the women be excluded for this set of games, and Hangman gently led Lorelai off to their house at the end of the street, just inside Bonaventure's gates.

I'd taken the time to quietly inform the guys of my plans while the girls and Synister had gone to take Savannah on a short and private tour of the Manse, where I guess she had filled their ears with her enthusiastic knowledge of history and early turn of the century architecture.

We'd left Mini-Syn, Valory, and Lainey at the Manse while Hangman had brought Lorelai to tuck her in at home, and I'd brought Savannah to be the evening's entertainment and to initiate her into life as my woman.

I took the opportunity to take her aside now, and fill her in on my expectations.

"What is it?" she asked, curiously as I closed the door behind us, sealing us into the downstairs room she'd given me that *incredible* blowjob in just a few weeks back.

"I want to play a game with you and the guys tonight, but only if you're willing to be my dirty girl for me."

Her cheeks rosy with wine and the ride over in the chilling evening air as summer finally gave way into fall, she stood stock still and murmured, "Go on." I took it as a good sign she was willing to hear me out.

I explained what I wanted, and she listened, rapt, and said... "For real?"

"Too much?" I asked, and she grinned, shaking her head. "That honestly sounds like *so much fun!* You're sure that none of the others will uh, take liberties?" she asked.

"It's as much to prove I trust them as I trust you," I said, "If any of them push it, or go further than you're comfortable with – we discuss after, and I handle it; how does that sound?"

"We're talking just a kiss, maybe grab my ass or pinch what passes for my tits, right?" she asked; and it took me a minute to recover from laughing at the 'what passes for her tits' comment. She definitely made no illusion about her lack of anything bigger than an A or B cup.

She grinned at me, and I said, "Yeah, that sounds about right, of course, these kinds of games, they might opt to scare the shit out of you to up the ante, but it's more of a haunted house thrill than anything. They're getting their own set of rules."

"Okay," she drawled, a little uncertain about that one. "I'm in – but *where* are we going to do this?" she asked.

"Bonaventure," I said plainly. "We have access."

She gasped, "In a *cemetery?*"

I laughed, and said, "You're agreeing to let us hunt and strip you in the dark, and it's doing it in the *cemetery* that's got you hitting the 'pause' button?" I asked.

"I mean..." she scoffed and rolled her eyes and asked, "Doesn't that increase the likelihood of us getting caught?"

I shook my head, "Hangman is the live-in caretaker, and any calls or complaints would come to him. It's handled. If anything, it monumentally *decreases* the likelihood anyone outside of us will see you or catch you out."

"Okay," she said thoughtfully, and then nodded.

"Okay?" I asked.

She smiled and nodded once, happily, "Okay." She agreed, and I pulled her in and kissed her thoroughly.

I'd been fantasizing about doing something like this for a long fucking time.

Chapter Twenty-Seven

Savannah...

It was dark, and the slight breeze held the kiss of fall along with the damp and green smell of the nearby river.

The branches of the trees swayed in the slight wind, rattling like bones, the Spanish Moss swaying like the tattered remains of a wedding dress.

I wasn't sure if Bonaventure had a ghost bride legend, or a woman in white. I know that it held the grave of little Gracie Watson, but she didn't haunt her grave that I knew of, but rather a bank downtown... or at least that is what Lainey had said at dinner. She was some kind of a ghost tour guide and enthusiast, I guess.

It was cool, but not cold, but I was sure that as soon as my clothes started coming off, it would definitely get cold...

Was I really doing this? I asked myself, and the surge of excitement in my breast said, *absolutely.*

I stepped over the threshold of the gate that Hangman held open, and shivered but not with the chill on the air, but rather anticipation.

The rules were simple; I got a head start, a full minute, to run and to hide. After a minute, the men fanned out. The goal was to avoid them, but *especially* avoid Corvus for as long as possible.

If I was caught, I lost an article of clothing, and I was subjected to light foreplay – the men's choice. No penetration, though. No fingers, no cocks, nothing inside me except maybe a tongue from a deep kiss.

I didn't quite know how to feel about that, but Corvus had asked me to do it for him... I'd reluctantly agreed on that front, but voiced my unease, which had seemed to please him in some way.

"Off you get," Hangman said when I lingered inside the gate for a hair too long. I looked at him and he smiled warmly, through his longish beard and said, "Clock's ticking."

"Run rabbit ruuuuuunn!" someone called out behind me, and I bolted, into the dark, sprinting for everything I was worth up the center drive, before darting off to the right along one of the walking paths. I carefully stealthed between mausoleums and tall grave markers, and surreptitiously tucked myself behind one of the gnarled oaks, trying to catch my breath.

I heard echoing laughter from up front, and heard the boys fan out, slight whistling calls flitting between graves and trees, as I stayed still and listened to them advance.

I swallowed, and worked on controlling my breathing, to quiet it, and bring it down so I could listen but my heart still thundered in my chest, the blood rushing in my ears.

A branch snapped, entirely too close, and I froze, listening, ears straining, and when I heard a rustle, I ducked low and took off, running up the path in the opposite direction, dodging onto the gravel and sand drive as a shadow loomed off to my left. I *sprinted*, rushing through the night past the arch with Jesus and the beautifully carved marble woman sitting near him.

I slowed down, looking back, and ran right into a wall of muscle and leather in front of me. I'd been so focused on who may be coming up behind me, I'd forgotten to remain situationally aware of what was in front of me and around me.

Uh-oh.

Hands went to my elbows to steady me, and I looked up into a wicked smile, very white teeth set in a scruffy jaw, shadowed with deep dark hair. Equally dark eyes penetrated into my very soul as Synister thrust his leg between mine, making me rise to my toes. I swallowed hard and he said, "Got you little rabbit."

"So, you do," I whispered.

"I'll take this," he said lowering me to my feet, his hands leaving my waist to pluck at the buttons of the shirt I'd stolen from Corvus.

"Okay," I stammered carefully.

He jerked his head in a direction and said, "He's that way, I don't want him to catch you too soon… let the boys have some fun and make it good for him." He pushed the shirt back off my shoulders and took it from me and I shivered as the cool breeze caressed my heated skin.

He put his lips near my ear and captured my earlobe gently between his teeth briefly before breathing into it, *"Run little rabbit, run!"*

I went past him, and ghosted through a walkway to the left, heading back toward the front of the cemetery.

He stood watching after me, stuffing my shirt into his back pocket as he put his hands to his mouth and made a soft mourning dove call with his hands.

"This is *not* fair!" I hissed under my breath, but of course they would be communicating with each other somehow.

I smiled, and slid down to hands and knees, crawling very carefully between stones as I heard footfalls on the path. I huddled in place and heard two of them come together.

"You see her?"

"Synister caught her."

"Fuck, of course he would be the first."

A slight laugh. "Just means fewer clothes when we find her."

"*If* we find her – she's good at this game."

"I know right?"

"You go that way, I'll take this way."

"Copy!"

They parted ways, and I couldn't be sure which one of them had been which – I hadn't been around them long enough to be able to identify their voices.

I waited until their footfalls faded, breathed out the breath I'd been holding, and shifted slightly, peeking out into the walkway. I could probably hide for quite a while, but that would get cold, quick, so I knew I needed to keep moving – still, I definitely had an advantage of being able to hold still for a time.

The coast was clear, so I crawled out from my hiding spot, and moved further down back toward the river, opposite of where one had gone, the other having struck out toward the fence line shared with the cemetery next door.

I swallowed, and stepped carefully, and wandered for who knew how long before I hit the main drag and the line of oaks that towered over the long drive.

I thought I might actually have this thing, when a flicker of light went up near one of the trees, and I felt my shoulders drop.

He snapped the cap of his zippo closed and the coal on the end of his cigarette glowed red.

"Well, well, well, what have we here?" his voice was oily and left a film on my senses that I didn't like.

I drew breath and made to bolt but Specter lunged at me, and caught me around the waist. We both went down and I put out my hands to stop my fall on the gravel. I tried to get away, struggling to wiggle out of his grip. I kicked out, and tried to be careful about it, connecting with his shoulder. He grunted, and I got my legs mostly free. I kept moving, kept crawling, and kicking and finally kicked free!

He got my left shoe and crowed in triumph as I bolted in another direction blindly, trying to get away from him. Of all the people I *didn't* want to meet out here, his crude ass was definitely it.

Like with Synister, I was too focused on making sure he wasn't coming after me, I crashed into another set of arms, a pair that gripped me, turned me, and fetched my back up against a tree, the bark digging into my skin.

Like with Synister, a knee went between my legs, and pinned me to the spot. My pussy let out a throbbing ache, and I swallowed hard. *God, why was that so hot?* I thought to myself.

Fingers twined gently between mine, and my arms were raised and pinned above my head.

I looked into a pair of hazel-green eyes leeched nearly colorless by the slight moonlight out here. A swipe of medium light hair swept across his forehead, and his smile was a slow and easy parting of lips to bare straight white teeth as he pressed himself against me, letting me know just how hard this was making him.

I swallowed hard and Torment breathed, "Relax, baby. You're safe with me."

He transferred my wrists to one of his hands, and easily managed to hold both with the one, his fingers long. The other fingertips he trailed along my skin in such a way to leave fire in their wake.

I shivered and he smiled and whispered in my ear, "You're much too hot to be cold..." he chuckled darkly, the sound dangerous and sharp, like a very real blade pressing against my skin, about to cut, but not quite – a threat of pain, a pain so sweet you could become addicted.

"You like the way I touch you like this?" He trailed fingers along my ribs and I gasped.

"Yes," I confessed, and he smiled even bigger.

"I'll let Corvus know," he said and kissed the tip of my nose before whispering, "Gimme the other shoe."

I kicked off my other shoe and he said, "Watch where you step, baby. This is supposed to end in fun, not blood; more's the pity."

He let me go, swooped down, and picked up the shoe, backing off me.

"Run rabbit, run rabbit, *run, run, run*," he sang out softly, the old 1940s British tune, and I did, I ran, partly because it was the game, but also because there had been a glint in Torment's eyes, a savage darkness of a type that said if I didn't he might not want to stop, and he might not want to be gentle – everything about his countenance a silent threat.

I hid and caught my breath.

The game would end at dawn, and if I won, I was guaranteed a shopping spree on Corvus' card. If I lost, I was going to get some wild sex in a cemetery... so honestly, either way I was winning. But now I was fully invested in not losing any more clothes if I could, and I was particularly interested in not getting too scratched or bruised after Specter's spectacular tackle.

The way he had taken me down, I was guaranteed to at least have some scrapes if not a plethora of bruises; more than likely on my knees where I'd taken the brunt of the fall. I was glad I had my jeans on, landing like that on my bare knees would have left me bloody.

Unfortunately, it wasn't looking good for me making it to dawn; not that I really wanted to, because again, that mourning dove call, and again, bootsteps and the rustle of leather closed in on me.

I slid around the monument I'd hidden myself against, and stood carefully, edging until it was between me and the sounds of the hunt.

I walked carefully, I didn't run, as walking created less noise. I had reached the view of the caretaker's house, and was nearly to the locked front gate, when a large shadow detached from the rest to my left, and stepped into the aisle. I groaned at having been caught again, when arms closed around me from behind, and a hand went over my mouth.

I squeaked from behind that hand and practically went limp against the hard chest at my back.

"Gotcha, baby," the voice in front of me said, and with a chuckle and a few steps forward, it resolved into Grim.

I leaned my head back against the shoulder behind it and craned my neck, trying to see who was behind me, but I'd been told that where Grim was, Reaper wasn't far behind him. Sure enough, Reaper held me fast, his chest rising and falling at my back a little rapidly for my tastes, as though he was wrestling with his self-control.

"Oh, will you look at that... there's two socks on two perfect feet. Lemme have her." Grim held out his arms and I was pushed, unceremoniously into them, he spun me around and held me fast the way Reaper had held me the moment before, my back to his front. I bit my lips together to keep from making a sound to draw anyone else to us as Reaper got really close, looming in front of me. He took my face between his hands, lowering his lips beside my ear and murmured, "How'd this happen, huh?"

He took my hands and turned them palms up, stroking his thumbs over the heels of my hands. I hissed from the sting and brought them up to my face. They were skinned pretty bad, but I hadn't noticed. Partially from the adrenaline swirling through my veins, and partially from the chill in the air, numbing them.

"Must have been when Specter tackled me," I whispered.

He lowered his face over my hands, his tongue flicking out. He tasted the dirt and the blood and I gasped at the sting in the wake of his warm, wet, tongue against the small wound, the sting intensifying.

"That is *so* unsanitary," I murmured, slightly horrified, and Grim chuckled.

Reaper went to his knees in front of me and looked up as though in worship, which made me still, and my heart quiver in my breast.

"One for Grim, and one for me," he murmured up at me, and took first one sock, then the other, stuffing them in his pocket.

I shuddered and gasped, as Grim's teeth lightly set in the side of my neck and he flicked his tongue over that sweet spot that sent goosebumps down my arms.

"You smell like peaches and sunshine on this starless night," he whispered in my ear, as he breathed me in. I closed my eyes at the poetic words, Reaper's fingertips skimming up the outsides of my denim clad thighs as he stood. My eyes flickered open in alarm, and I shrank back into Grim who dropped his hands from my waist and took just a slight step back.

Reaper whispered, "Close your eyes, and count to ten."

I swallowed hard, doing as I was told, counting silently in my head slowly from one to ten, and when I opened my eyes? Both were gone.

I gasped, and turned, this way and that, but neither were anywhere that I could see.

I moved carefully, picking my way over the gravel in my bare feet, hugging myself and heard from under the front porch's overhang, "Guess it's my turn... let's make it a little more fun."

I froze and Hangman jumped down, over the few steps, and crunched over the gravel to me. He undid my belt, whipping it through the loops on my pants and quicker than I could follow, he had it twisted and pulled through on itself and he said in an authoritative voice, "Hands."

I brought them up, palms up as I had for Reaper, and he looked at them in the diffuse light coming from one of the upstairs windows, pausing and saying, "Come sit, I'll run in the house and we can clean that up." He made a noise, out into the dark, and he led me to the porch and had me sit down on the steps.

"The game's not done," I said. "I could get more scrapes."

"True, but we take care of our women, even when we do play these fucked up reindeer games. Hang tight."

He keyed his way into the house and went to a first aid kit just inside on the wall. He came back with antiseptic spray and some gauze.

"Gonna sting," he warned, and he spritzed my palms, focusing on the heel of my hands. I hissed between my teeth, and he chuckled, wiping at them with the gauze to get the worst of the grit off.

"How'd this happen?" he asked. "You trip?"

"Tackled," I laughed lightly.

"Who?" he asked.

"Specter," I said quietly. "I think he has it in for me or something, our first meeting was... uh... *less than polite*. He was rather crude, and I, uh, told him to go fuck himself."

Hangman laughed and said, "He's a dick to everyone. Good on yah for not taking his shit. Still, it'll be handled. This is a bridge too far, Corvus is going to want a word. This is supposed to be a haunted house thrill ride, not actually damaging."

"I mean, it's been more fun than it hasn't," I said with a dry chuckle.

"Good, come on out here – resume the position if you will."

I went out to roughly where we'd been standing and put out my hands, palms up, like I had before he'd hit the pause button on our little game of cats and mouse.

He put my belt around my wrists and pulled the free end and the cuffs he had fashioned out of them cinched down tight. Like *really* tight, holding me fast. It would be impressive if it wasn't so… *how did he know how to do that? Better yet, why would he know how to do this?* I thought.

He stepped back, made the mourning dove call, and said, "You better git, the pause on the game is over."

I moved carefully in the direction of the Jewish portion of the cemetery, past the caretaker's house, and was relieved when I found less gravel, and more sand and grass.

I twisted and pulled at my wrists, but whatever he'd done with my belt wouldn't budge. I crouched behind a grave and fucked with it, trying to see what he'd done, but there wasn't enough light. If it hadn't been so dark, I wondered if I would be able to figure it out and if I'd have been able to free myself.

Shit, I was disadvantaged as hell, but still – I was holding my own against how many of them versus me? At least, I'd like to think I was. They were honestly probably just playing with me.

I checked my watch, which was always present on my wrist and was riding higher, over where my belt acted like cuffs. It was too dark and too hard to read to get an accurate time but it felt like I'd been in the same spot for too long and that I'd have a better chance if I moved, so I moved.

I didn't know how long we had all been out here, but the more I slunk and hid, the more the chill in the air was starting to affect me.

My nose starting to run a bit. I meandered carefully through things, hiding and dodging anymore encounters for what felt like a while.

I was outside little Gracie's grave plot's enclosure, looking through the bars at the lighter white of her marble carving when a body pressed me into the enclosure.

"Bella," a voice I didn't recognize murmured in my ear, and it lit off in a string of Italian which was beautiful to listen to, but I had no idea the meaning behind any of the words except the first... Bella meant beauty or beautiful.

He turned me and pulled my restrained wrists up and over my head, hooking the belt that held them fast on the spiked iron bar above me. I swallowed hard as Death made me rise on my tippy toes and I was held helpless by the gate.

He trailed warm hands over my shoulders, and in a caress down my ribs, and stopped at the waistband of my jeans.

"Time to lose these," he whispered, and he pulled the button through the loop loosening them, and lowered the zipper sensually slow.

"Shit!" I gasped as he pulled the denim off my legs, slow, so painfully slow, my desire increasing with the eroticism of his gentle strip tease.

"You've been out here driving us all crazy for a while now," he said, placing a kiss on my panties, over my mound at the apex of my thighs. He drew a deep breath, scenting me, and made an appreciative noise.

"Well done, you," he pulled my jeans off my feet completely, and took his time kissing his way back up my body in light butterfly kisses that started at my knee and stopped at my chest, just above my bras' band between my breasts, his eyes rolled up to meet mine.

I was down to bra and panties, but the look in his eyes? I might as well have been nude and I was scared he was going to take things further than the game allowed for. I didn't want that. I wanted Corvus between my thighs, inside me, but in the moment, I was very afraid that if he *did* go further, I would be caught up in the moment and welcome his cock as long as he promised to make me come.

The cognitive dissonance was real as my pussy ached to be filled.

Death stepped back and looked at me appreciatively, a thumb at his bottom lip as he looked me up and down, hanging there, helpless.

He had my jeans dangling from his other hand and he slung them up and over his shoulder as he said, "Ciao, Bella."

"Oh, you!" I cried pulling at my wrists. "You're not even going to get me down?"

He walked away, whistling softly, and I thought to myself, *oh, shit...*

"That's cheating!" I hissed. "Unfair advantage!" I pulled at my wrists and tried to gain enough height by standing on my very tippy toes to push my hands up and over to let myself down, but it wasn't happening.

The sense of fun evaporated in an instant, and I was suddenly terrified.

I tried everything I could think of to get myself off the fence, but it wasn't working. I couldn't get on my toes high enough or get enough of a little jump to disengage myself from where I was caught by the leather of my belt.

I struggled for several moments, until I was out of breath from my attempts, but try as I might, I couldn't do it. I was just about to call out for help when Revenant stepped out of the shadows looking like if James Bond were the villain in his own movie.

"You'll have to excuse Death, I think he wants you to steer clear of him." He came to me, and put hands to my waist and said, "Help me out." He lifted and parted my thighs. He was fully clothed and so I wrapped my legs around him, trying not to gasp at the very clear erection pressed against me as he lifted me off the fence.

I made a noise, my shoulders screaming as I rotated them back forward and put my arms around his neck. He lowered me to the ground and ducked out from under my hands.

"Hangman's work," he said, and it didn't sound like a question.

He undid my wrists and said, "C'mere," and pulled me into a hug. I hugged him back, trembling, but not with cold.

"That scared me," I said, and he pulled back, brushing my hair back from my face. "Death and Corvus have an ancient history," he told me. "I think he wanted to ensure that old adage, 'bros before...'"

"Hoes," I finished for him unimpressed.

"Yes, well, you aren't that." He rubbed feeling back into my hands and made sure my wrists were fine and said, "Bra's mine," I obediently turned around, and he unclasped it, taking it from me.

I hugged over my chest and he said, "If you need to stop..."

I shook my head, "No, thanks for coming along as quickly as you did."

He chuckled and said, "Death told me right where to find you. Now run along little rabbit – there's still four of us out there."

"How long have we been out here?" I asked and he chuckled.

"Better go, you're cold to the touch."

"I don't feel cold," I said.

"Better go," he reiterated, and shifted in his stance to indicate his discomfort.

I nodded and moved away, and he walked back toward the caretaker's house.

I looped back around and returned to the spot we'd been in, watching his dark figure, darker against the dark return to the main gate, where Hangman slipped out from under the porch and unlocked it, so that Revenant could leave.

I walked back up the aisle, back toward Gracie's plot and stared at the angel nearby with the broken top part of her wing. I thought to myself that I could relate, that I was feeling like I'd fallen pretty far, pretty hard, and pretty fast into the debauchery of this game. I couldn't say I was sad about that. Not with the way my nipples tightened in the chill and I ached to have any one of them take them into their mouth.

I was just about to really start moving again when Fear found me.

"Boo!" he murmured and I yipped, to a masculine laugh out there further in the dark. Shit, they *had* to be moving this way.

"I get the panties," he said. "Nice."

I said, "You *better* give this back!" I unclasped the necklace Corvus had gifted me, handing it over to be ornery.

He pouted and said, "Aw, clever girl." He smacked me on the ass as he went by, heading for the cemetery gates. I yipped again at the stinging handprint he left and he said, "Fuck, Lainey's gonna get it when I get home." He shook his leg to re-seat himself in his pants and I gave a slow blink.

All of a sudden, I was *really* in it to win it, whether it be by holding out until dawn or finding Corvus because damn I felt that. I wanted it, and I wanted it badly.

I pressed on, and it wasn't long until I was captured again. "Shit! You all are *sneaky*!" I cursed as leather-clad arms went around me and I was pulled back into a jacket that was wrapped around me.

"Oh!" It was warm, the spice of his cologne pleasant as he said, "If we were half as sneaky as you, this would be over by now," he said. "You're giving us a fairly decent run for our money, beautiful."

I craned my neck back and said to Haint, "Well, it's definitely almost over now."

He chuckled and said, "Panties or watch?"

"Watch isn't going *anywhere,*" I murmured.

"You got earrings on?"

"Yes," I said with a slight titter of laughter.

"I'll take those. Those panties come off, I can't guarantee I won't want a taste. Because *damn*, mm-mm-mm, you look like you taste divine."

I took my earrings out and he palmed them, but before I could step away, he said, "Just a minute more," and kissed my temple. "Let's get you warmed up."

"Whoa, can I get in on this cuddle sesh?"

"Sheesh!" I rolled my eyes as Shade appeared out of the dark.

"Absolutely, bro. I'm sure she'd love to be the ham in this man sammich."

Shade chuckled and opened up his jacket and I found myself pressed between them.

"Watch or panties?" Revenant asked me again, and I laughed.

"Looks like Shade's the lucky winner of my last piece of lingerie," I said with all sarcasm intended.

He chuckled and dipped down to his knees, ghosting my panties down my legs, almost too careful not to touch me with his fingertips.

"Fuck, that's nice," he praised, standing after I'd stepped out of them. He dipped his head and kissed me, and I felt an electric jolt from it. Not necessarily one of *pleasure,* but more one of something akin to guilt. It felt *naughty,* wrong somehow, and I wondered if Corvus was somewhere out there watching.

He pulled back, and said, "Corvus is a lucky one."

"Thank you," I whispered, uncertainly.

They let me go, and I wandered carefully, grateful for the time to warm up, but also *very* determined to see this through. The shadow of being hooked to the fence had passed, and the lighthearted fun was back and I was grateful for that, too.

The only men I hadn't seen yet were Requiem and Corvus himself, which I found more than a little convenient. I mean, it was all a little too contrived that I had encountered everyone *but* them and I felt like they were talking me up and, well, gaslighting me into believing that I was doing well at hiding from them.

I also found it strange that I didn't run into anyone twice, had they left like Revenant, after catching me? Honestly, though, I was glad for that in the case of Specter and Death. I didn't feel so bad about Death thanks to Revenant's explanation about his history with Corvus, but Specter I definitely didn't want to run into twice out here.

I breathed out, and struck out in another direction, listening, ears straining, and I made it to one of the main drags through the cemetery again. I closed my eyes and listened, the sand gritty beneath my feet, and I heard movement somewhere up the way toward the gate. I went the opposite way, back toward the river.

I saw him standing out in the parking lot, looking out over the water. The sliver of moon had reappeared from behind the clouds and cast its white-blue hue across the rippling river and it was a picturesque scene.

It wasn't Corvus, so it had to be Requiem.

I stilled and watched and he called out softly, "I got a bum knee, don't make me chase you."

I stilled and he turned to look at me.

I gave him an impertinent smile and called back softly, "That's the game."

He growled and took off like a shot and I bolted, running up the way, back past Jesus and following the curve of the man drag.

My feet were tender, and he had on boots, so it wasn't long before he overtook me, catching me up and intentionally spiraling with me in his arms. We went down, but he took the brunt of the fall, landing on his back, me on top of him, protecting me from the ground.

"Oh, shit! I'm sorry!" I cried and he laughed.

"That's the game," he said and he kissed my shoulder. "Now do me a solid and get off me."

I scrambled to my feet and he got to one knee, he pulled me into his arms and placed a chaste kiss against my pubic thatch, darting his tongue out against my clit. I gasped, staring into his eyes and he drew back, a look of awe on his face.

"God, you're gorgeous," Requiem said. "You better run, because I guarantee Corvus heard that, and he's on your scent."

I tried to cover myself as best I could and he smiled and shook his head, "Sooner rather than later, Savannah. I'm not made of self-control."

I booked it, continuing to follow the curve, up and around the main drag going back toward the front gate, my hair whipping behind me. There was something oddly freeing about running nude in the moonlight; and I had the thought that *thank God* it was the changing of the seasons, and it was too cold for mosquitoes and no-see-ums.

I stopped, back to a tree, hiding behind it and heard the thunder of booted feet on the track just the other side of it.

I waited, listening, and held my breath, lungs burning and begging for oxygen as whoever it was breathed freely.

"Where are you, Bright Eyes?" I smiled and put a hand over my mouth to keep from giggling.

He moved up farther and I kept the tree between us and peeked. I could see his back, and my heart ached at how his shoulders were outlined against his well-worn and well-fitted long-sleeved shirt.

He wasn't wearing his jacket and vest. I bet he was overheating in them, which was funny because out here everything swinging in the breeze, it really was starting to get cold! I doubted I could make it to dawn if I wanted to. Not like this.

I slipped between graves, and hid behind statues, but he was close. Turning back and following me. Scenting the wind at some points and listening for the barest rustle of plant.

I found myself back over by some statuary and mausoleums and waited for him to pass.

I don't know how long we played cat and mouse, but I did a fairly good job of evading him.

Finally, we ended up in a full tilt run and I banked left, and he followed, catching me, and taking me up around the waist. He kissed my shoulder and turned me in his arms and we were kissing, his shirt soft against my skin, my skin, no doubt, cool to his touch. He pulled me in close and took a seat on the bench nearby, pulling me into his lap, one arm around my waist, the other hand going between us, working at the front of his pants.

He freed himself from his jeans and worked his cock against my pussy, and then he was inside me.

"Fuck, yes, baby. Ride me," he ordered, and he slapped my ass.

I rode him, my knees and shins planted against the cold marble, and he helped me. I kissed him, and he kissed me, and our passion quickly warmed me to my soul.

God, he felt so good inside me, all the little nicks and scrapes, the stinging little cuts were quickly forgotten with the feel of him inside my pussy, filling me, pressing out against my walls and his hands on my skin? Divine with the warmth of them.

We changed positions after a time, and when we'd reached the pinnacle of what this one would do for us and it just wasn't getting us there. He bent me over the bench, and reentered me, and *oh, yes.* Please, God, yes! He thrust into me, taking up my arms and pulling back on them and *oh, Jesus Christ!*

It was intense, the sweetest pain as he bottomed out against my cervix, his body deeply entrenched in mine, and he wasn't gentle – at all. I didn't want gentle though. I wanted it all. I wanted him so deep he owned me; I wanted his touch to outshine every lingering little touch I'd been given. I wanted to touch myself; I wanted to put fingers to my clit while he worked himself in and out of my body, but I couldn't form any sounds beyond the feral, begging, wordless cries that poured from my mouth, spilling into the inky black night.

Of course, there would be time enough for that later – for the rest of our lives in fact, if he could tolerate me that long. I didn't think it would be a problem to be honest... I could live like this forever. He was so incredible, so thrilling, and I couldn't get enough.

Chapter Twenty-Eight

Corvus...

She was tight, wet, but her skin was so cold beneath my hands. I'd been tracking her and watching her encounters with my brothers – as many as I could anyway, and yet I'd missed the one with Specter and the one with Death.

Specter would pay for that. Hangman had gotten with me and told me he'd cleaned her up, but I wanted desperately to get her home and into a hot bath once our fun was through.

It was wild to me, how proud I was of her for following through, and for trusting me and the rest of the Iron Wraiths... and yet, now that I'd captured my prize, all I could think about was getting her home, getting her warm, and loving her right.

I fucked her over the bench at Johnny Mercer's grave, and she panted, doing her best to keep quiet, even as both of our orgasms built and crested.

When she came, it was a beautiful thing, her willpower and desire an earth-shattering thing, the pieces of her falling like stardust from her lips as her feral little groan left her body. I was shaken to my foundation by the beauty of her, as I felt her clench around me rhythmically and I smiled to myself, pleased. She'd lost the game, but she'd won. I pulled from her, and she sat down, making a small sound of protest as her pretty little ass hit the cold marble.

I got myself handled, tucked back into my pants, the perfume of her essence on my body reaching my nose as I shoved myself back in my fly.

I stooped and picked her up, arm beneath her knees, the other around her back, her arms twining around my neck as she held herself close to me.

I'd carried heavier by way of packs, backpacking across Europe; but a man couldn't do this forever. I made our way to the front, where Hangman waited with a blanket. I set her carefully on her feet, and we wrapped her up. I lifted her once more as he unlocked and opened the gate for us to slip through. Spooky waited in the Land Rover, just steps outside.

"Syn said to drive you back to your place," he called through the open and waiting back door.

"Good looking out," I called, and Hangman held the rear door as I helped Savannah down to her feet and urged her to crawl into the back. She did and settled in the rear driver's side seat, holding out a hand to me to join her, which I did swiftly, pulling her into my arms.

"She alright?" Spook asked as I settled into the back seat with her.

"I'm good," she mumbled, spent.

"Good deal," he said turning back front, Hangman shutting the door on us, closing us into the vehicle the warmth enveloping us as Spook had the heat blasting.

Spooky drove us home, pulling up to the side gate and hopping out to unlock it for me as well as the French doors leading into my kitchen.

"Upstairs, get a warm bath running for me, Prospect." I told him when he came back and opened up the back door of the Range. He nodded and jogged back into my place, went upstairs, and did what I asked before coming back down. It was nearly two a.m. and the streets were empty, so we didn't sweat the Rover being out there for a few.

"Anything else?" he asked.

"No, see yah," he gave a nod and went out, closing things up behind him.

I had settled in my chair with Savannah wrapped in the soft blanket across my lap.

"How you feel, Kitten?" I asked her softly.

"Exhausted," she said. "But happy."

"Yeah?" I asked her.

"Yeah – that was fun. I want to do it again some time."

I laughed, softly and asked, "Can you make it upstairs?"

"Mm, hm." She slid from my lap and stood, holding the blanket around her. "I'm cold," she complained.

I said, "I got a bath going, come on upstairs and let's warm you up, get some of these scratches and scrapes taken care of."

"Oh, shit. I hope nothing is too bad. I have work tomorrow."

I laughed, and said, "We'll figure that out. Even if I have to do both your job and mine tomorrow... or later today as it were."

I followed her upstairs and she laughed softly and said, "Anyone asks me, I'll tell them I fell off one of the rental bicycles. They aren't very well maintained, you know."

"Never used one," I said.

"I fell off one once when I first moved here."

I helped her into the bath and she hissed, and I couldn't tell if it was because it was too warm or if it was her bare feet.

"Sit, let me get you cleaned up so I can have a look at you – I heard Specter got a little rough."

"I didn't expect a full body tackle to the ground," she said, "but I'm fine."

"You're tough," I praised and she smiled, leaning back in the bath. I plucked a twig and some bits of Spanish Moss from her hair and she wrinkled her nose at me.

I got my comb off the side of the sink and sat down on the stool behind her and carefully started picking the tangles and debris out of her hair while the tub finished filling and she hugged her knees.

"You okay?" I asked slowly.

"Death really scared me," she murmured.

"Oh?" I asked.

"Yeah," she whispered. "Don't be mad at him, though, Revenant explained—"

"Did he now?" I asked mildly.

She told me what was done and what was said, and I nodded slowly. "Not mad at him, baby. I promise. I'm sorry he scared you."

"It's okay, he sent Revenant relatively quickly. I was safe, I just didn't know it. Like at a haunted house, just like you said..."

I chuckled softly and felt more relaxed than I had in a very long time. She was in that vulnerable state, her voice soft and lilting, almost childlike in her fragility. After some rough and tough play like that it was only natural, and aftercare was an important part of the process. So, I made sure she was warm, and I gently combed her hair, and took my time doing it.

She was quiet, and I realized she was very nearly falling asleep. I had intended to wash her hair, but it could wait until morning. What I did do, was gently wash out her scrapes, took stock of the rest of her, a bruise on her hip, some chafing around her delicate wrists, and then took the time to wash her feet really well so I could doctor them up as needed.

She rose from the bath with lightly perfumed skin, as soft and supple as I'd ever felt, thoroughly warmed, and cuddled into my chest as I rubbed her gently through the towel that I'd wrapped around her.

"I don't know why I'm so *tired*," she murmured and I chuckled.

"You had quite the workout, and the adrenaline crash is always a bitch." I kissed her forehead and led her to bed and told her not to cover up just yet. I switched on the bedside lamp and looked at her feet. They were in surprisingly good shape, just a small cut on one of her little toes. I put a little antibiotic ointment on it and wrapped it in a Band-Aid while she giggled and tried to pull her foot from my hands, complaining that it tickled.

I tucked her in on my side of the bed, closest to the bathroom and whispered that I would be back soon.

"Where are you going?" she asked.

"I need to get your things from the club, you left your purse, remember?"

"Can't it wait until tomorrow?" she pleaded and I smiled and asked, "You don't want me to leave?"

"No," she reached out a hand. "I want you to cuddle me."

"Okay, can I at least grab a shower first?"

She sighed, and said, "Okay, but hurry up."

I laughed, kissed her, and took myself into the bathroom to shower. I texted the guys while the water warmed and Requiem offered to run the things by and leave them on my kitchen counter. He was headed to the riverfront anyway. I thanked him, and got in, letting the hot water sluice down by back and over my head.

I washed up, warmed up, and went to bed. Savannah drowsing already by the time I crawled in behind her, and pulled her back into the curve of my body.

She was so beautiful, brave, and tolerant. She'd given me exactly what I'd asked for and had been a good sport. Excellent sport in fact. I held her tightly and she turned in my arms, holding onto me.

I loved her. There was no going back on that. I guess when I told myself never again, I really should have never said never...

I snickered at the thought and she held me tighter and I kissed her forehead.

I didn't know exactly how any of this was supposed to work, but I figured that honestly, one day at a time was the best way forward.

She was tired the next morning, fairly exhausted, but she insisted on toughing it out and going to work.

I asked her if she wanted a quiet night in at my place or hers, and she cocked her head and said hers if I didn't mind. That she wanted to get used to the new place, finish unpacking. I smiled and suggested ordering in. She liked that idea. I just liked the idea of spending a quiet evening alone with her.

I took the Porche and drove down to the riverfront, got through my day of writing up contracts and reviewing listings, spoke to the odd brother that called to crow about how much fun last night had been, and had a heart to heart after reaching out to Death.

He apologized for scaring Savannah, but he hoped I understood why I did it. I did, and I thanked him, even though it had been wholly unnecessary.

Truth be told, everything felt *different* with Savannah. Easy in a way I couldn't define. I just felt comfortable with her, it was like this extra sensory *knowing* that we were on the same page, and that there wasn't really anything to fear. She wasn't going anywhere... which was honestly something that I didn't deserve.

I knew that, and I felt very fortunate indeed that she was a part of my life.

I think she felt it; this draw or this pull... While I know she was perfectly capable, strong, intelligent enough, and certainly had been doing the damn thing for a year or two now; I also knew she was a sweet and submissive soul who craved guidance and to be told what to do.

That was a huge responsibility. A sacred thing. One deserving of deep respect and love for the trust placed in me as the dominant figure.

With great power over someone, came great responsibility, and discipline. You couldn't let your frustration win or overpower you in the moment. You had to be firm, but gentle. It was such a vulnerable state to put yourself in to hand someone such an absolute power over your psyche and wellbeing.

I recognized I had been careless in the beginning. A reckless child; little more than an immature boy ripping the wings off a fly. I hadn't recognized what a true gift she had been. That she was handing me so much trust and wasn't playing pedantic games like so many of the disposable little darlings that had come before her.

I would spend a very, very, long time making things up to her, if they could ever be made up at all.

We texted throughout the day, and she was happy. She'd cleverly worn long sleeves with a long and tight cuff that morning to hide her chafed wrists, and I felt genuinely bad about that.

I checked on her several times and she was always quick to get back to me, which I appreciated.

At closing time, I gathered my things and headed downstairs.

Specter was outside our gambling den, smoking a cigarette. He nodded at me and I gave him a stiff smile and a polite nod back.

I put my briefcase in the Porche, and stopped, went back to him, and sucker punched him right in the gut. I leaned over him as he retched into the gutter and said, "You ever disrespect my woman like you did last night again, I'll fucking end you. You have any complaints about this, take it to the table. See what fucking happens."

"Hua," he gritted out, and I walked away, got into my Porche, and headed to the spot Savannah and I had agreed upon to pick up our dinner.

Once back at home, I climbed the steps to the apartment above the carriage house, letting myself in.

I found Savannah in her stocking feet, standing by the built-in bookcase surrounding the fireplace. She had a stack of books out of a box and was carefully shelving them.

"I *love* this bookcase," she said.

"I do too, it was one of the features of this place that I liked the most, I just keep my books in my little library in the main house."

"Well, I hope you don't mind if I fill this one, then."

"It's your apartment, love. Your space. You do what you want with it."

A serene little smile played on her lips and she asked me softly, "Do you mean that?"

"Mean what?" I asked, sliding the takeout bag onto the kitchen counter. I opened cupboards and found plates.

"What you just called me," she said.

"What?" I asked, distractedly.

"Love," she said and I stopped what I was doing.

"Did I?" I asked, and I really had to think back on it, and realized she may be right.

"You did," she said, her smile growing.

I smiled back at her and said, "Well, if that wasn't just some kind of Freudian slip," I said and she laughed.

"It's not the first time I've said, 'I love you,'" I said and she nodded.

"No, I know... it *is* the first time you've said it so casually."

"That's fair," I said.

I moved about her kitchen taking down plates and gathering silverware and she said, "In case I've not said it," she murmured and I turned to look at her. "I love you, too," she said softly. "So much."

I smiled and nodded, a warm glow suffusing my whole being, as I plated our food and brought it over to the little table that had come from her old place. It only seated two, and it was nice and cozy for this place. She'd redone it and most of her furniture in a French Provincial style and while it was semi-out of place with the stark, undecorated walls of the place, I knew she would make this place feel like a home soon enough.

She'd done wonders with polishing the turd she'd come from – though I still hated that she'd lived in that condemned monstrosity for so long.

"This looks great," she said with a serene smile as she settled in her seat.

"Do you have anything to drink?" I asked.

"Oh!" she got up and went to the fridge pulling out a bottle of wine she'd left in it to chill.

"It's cheap, but it's my favorite," she said twisting off the cap. I must have looked horrified because she laughed.

"Just try it!" she cried, and she poured a couple of stemless wine glasses.

"First of all, those glasses are a monstrosity. Wine glasses have a stem for a reason."

"Oh, really?" she demanded. "And why is that?"

"To keep the warmth from your hand from affecting the wine in the glass. Some wines are meant to be savored chilled, and stemless wine glasses defeat the purpose."

"Oh, you know, that actually makes sense," she said, bringing the glasses over.

I took the one she offered me and sniffed the contents, which honestly smelled like fruity rubbing alcohol. She laughed at the face I made and sipped hers.

I sipped mine and while it wasn't *terrible* it wasn't great, either.

"Ah! Yeah, no, that's no where even close to 'pretty good,'" I said. "It's barely drinkable."

She laughed and shook her head, taking her seat.

"We can add Wine Snob to the list of quirks I love about you," she said.

"Oh? Endearing, is it?"

"Mm," she nodded, chewing the bite of food she'd taken thoughtfully. "Adorable," she said.

I laughed and shook my head. *She* was adorable.

"You know, I've been thinking about last night all day," she said after a short but comfortable silence.

"Oh, yeah?" I sipped the wine which did *not* get better with more consumption – if anything, it got worse.

Savannah laughed at the face I made and I stood up, "Yeah, no, I can't do it," I said and tipped the contents of my glass into hers. I went to the fridge to find something palatable, even if it was just water.

"I would like to go home for a weekend," she said as I pulled a bottle of Perrier out of the fridge.

"To South Carolina?" I asked.

"Yeah," she said and I returned to the table with my glass of sparkling water.

"I don't see anything wrong with that, at all – has the tax attorney reached out to your family?"

"Oh, yeah! Yes, my dad called me about that today, actually."

"Good, good!"

"I just really miss the farm and I would like to go see my family."

"Well, certainly," I said.

"Which is why I've been thinking... I feel as though I've already met yours; and while mine is certainly more sedate and far less sexually charged... I would love for you to come with me," she looked hesitant, like she was almost afraid to ask.

I looked across the small table at my darling, my girl, and I smiled.

"Make you a deal," I said.

"I'm listening," she sat back, attentive.

"First available weekend, we go, but I'm long overdue for a long ride – we take the bike."

She looked thoughtful.

"It's two and a half hours," she mused. "I can agree to that."

I pulled up my calendar on my phone on the spot, "If it makes you happy, then let's figure it out now. There's no time like the present," I said.

We went back and forth for a time and settled on a weekend that was three weeks from now. Both club and real estate life preventing us from doing anything sooner.

"Thank you," she said with a smile as she typed it into her phone.

"Of course," I said, and I would be lying if I said that for some reason, I was exceedingly nervous; but honestly, it would be a good dry run because I was almost certain that introducing her to *my* family would be a minor disaster. Notwithstanding, she worked for our main competition. My father could quite possibly go apoplectic on that fact alone.

I didn't care.

We finished our supper, washed the dishes together, and curled up on the couch which was very strange to me. Comfortable, for sure, but with no rigidity or structure.

She covered us with a chenille throw and we cozied up in front of the television, where we discovered we had similar tastes in what we liked to watch. We settled on a true crime documentary on the Murdaugh scandal out of South Carolina, and I'm not sure when it happened, but we both woke, late into the night, warm and cozy together; the television asking if we were still watching.

"Come on baby, guess I'm staying at your place tonight," I murmured, and kissed the top of her head. She groaned and shifted against my side and sighed.

"I don't wanna move, but we have to," she said.

I chuckled and murmured back, "Me either, and no, we don't." I set the documentary to keep playing the next episode and we cuddled on her too-comfortable couch and slept.

Chapter Twenty-Nine

Savannah...

The next few weeks crawled by at points, and sped past at others.

It was a bit tumultuous in places, the club demanding Corvus' time on several evenings, but I quickly realized that living as neighbors and having my own space really did have its advantages. I didn't feel... lonely and as totally in a strange place as I would have if I was in Corvus' apartment. Somehow, being in my own space, even if it was new and only steps from his door, as I was surrounded by my belongings as I was? It was less weird for me somehow.

I was grateful for that as we adjusted to this new normal of being so together, and so quickly.

Still, I don't think I'd spent but a single night alone in my bed, or his... every night, he would come to my room and crawl into bed with me, or I would be at his place, in his. The one night, he came in, just as I was leaving, looking worn as he went to change to get ready for work.

I'd asked what'd happened, and where he had been, and he'd held me close, kissed my forehead gently, and had simply said it'd been club business; and club business meant it was none of the ladies' business if they could help it.

I'd took his meaning perfectly and had touched his face and told him that if it was a heavy burden, that I would listen to what he could impart; that I didn't want him to carry everything alone. Even if I didn't understand it. Even if I couldn't necessarily contribute in any meaningful way, I was *always* here to listen.

He'd held me tight, kissed me gently, and said I was getting the ride of my life that night for that answer, which had made me laugh – and boy did he deliver; even given how exhausted he was.

Now today was the day, and I nervously packed a backpack he'd given me with outfits to last me the weekend that wouldn't take up too much room, as he had to pack his clothes in it, too. Thankfully, he had packed first, so I just had to fit my things into the bag that was left, which there was still a considerable amount of room since I didn't have to pack certain things like toiletries. I still had plenty of that sort of thing at the farm.

I was dressed to ride in almost all new leather gear. The jeans and the shirt was my own, but the leather jacket and chaps were a gift from Corvus, as were the boots and the gloves. I met him downstairs.

In the intervening weeks, his bike had returned to the courtyard and he waited at it for me, looking as nervous as I'd ever seen him.

The skies were overcast, but the forecast hadn't called for any rain. At least not today, and it was supposed to be sunny and clear at the farm.

My family didn't know we were coming, it was going to be a surprise, and I could almost already hear my mother's outrage when we pulled up on the motorcycle.

My room was my own at the farm, and always would be. It was a family rule that we always had a room, a place, at the farm.

"You emptied those of everything but the bare necessities, right? Mom is going to send us back here with all that we can carry and then some," I warned him and Corvus laughed lightly.

"Heard, acknowledged, and understood, my love; and yes.

Nothing but the roadside emergency kit which barely takes up half of one of them," he said of the hard sided cases on his bike. I didn't know what you called them.

"Think I'm ready for a ride this long?" I asked skeptically. Truth be told, I needed the pep talk. Freeway speeds on that thing scared the shit out of me. Worse than a rollercoaster, because there was nothing between me and the rushing pavement. No safety measures to speak of.

"Baby, you're ready, and I promise, I'll keep you safe and it's going to be fine."

He held out his hand to me, the side gates already open and waiting for us to depart.

"Okay then," I shouldered the backpack and slipped both arms through the straps and took his hand. He helped me put on the helmet and I shooed him with a motion of my hands. He got on and started the bike, pulling out the courtyard, and I closed and latched the gates behind us, running the chain and closing up the padlock tight, pulling on things to make sure there wasn't enough give for anyone to slip through.

He watched me, eyes unreadable behind his sunglasses as I pulled on my gloves and went up to him, just half chilling on the sidewalk, and climbed aboard behind him.

I lied. Freeway all the way to my family's farm was fucking *harrowing*. I much preferred the lower more sedate speeds riding through Savannah traffic as compared to dodging rampaging drivers and even semi-trucks on the interstate. Actually, the worse part was dodging shredded tire pieces from the semis.

Thankfully, Corvus took pity on me, and we stopped every half an hour to forty-five minutes for a drink or to use the restroom. Which while I could appreciate the breaks, it was almost worse than just getting there! The anxiety of climbing back on the bike nearly worsening every time I had to re-mount or re-board it or whatever.

Just my luck I would wind up a biker's girlfriend and would low-key hate riding his motorcycle.

The best part about it, really, was being close to him, and holding on tight.

Pulling under the arch that said *Kittridge Farms* had me breathing a sigh of relief, even as going up the dirt and gravel track to the house was a harrowing ride.

The drive split in two at one point, an old-fashioned handcrafted picket sign pointing to the left saying *Farm Stand* and to the right, *Private Property*. Then another to the left saying *Orchard*.

My grandfather had made it, and someone had freshened it up with new paint, and very recently. We took the right track to the house, pulling up into the drive around the giant weeping willow tree in front of the wrap-around porch. My mom and dad were sitting on the porch swing with their peach sweet tea, as they did in the evenings, and my mom jumped up – presumably to holler at us that we had taken the wrong drive and that the farm stand was closed.

I was so excited, as Corvus cut the engine and leaned the bike onto its stand as my mother gave her spiel in her polite southern drawl.

I took off my gloves and shoved them in my pocket and undid the clasp under my chin, pulling off the helmet to shake out my hair.

"Savvy!?" my mother cried.

"Well, I'll be!" my dad crowed, as I rushed up the steps to hug them.

It'd been almost a year. I'd been keeping very busy to keep things going.

We hugged and squealed and Mom started to cry she was so happy, and I pulled back.

"Mom, Dad, I'd like you to meet my boyfriend Corvus. We hope you don't mind, but we thought we'd come up and surprise you for the weekend."

My mom and dad looked past me to Corvus coming up the steps. He stuck out his hand to my dad, and said, "Corbett Prescott, everyone calls me Corvus." He shook hands with my father, and you never would have known how nervous he was except for a slight tightness around his eyes.

"Corvus? It's a pleasure to meet you." My dad said his name like a question, just trying to get it right, and Corvus nodded when he did, giving my dad's hand a hearty shake.

"Are you hungry?" my mother asked, ever the proper southern hostess. "We just finished up supper, and there's still plenty."

"I could eat," Corvus said with an almost shy smile. "Savannah's done nothing but brag nonstop about your cooking, Mrs. Kittridge."

"Oh, please, call me Sally," she said beaming. "And you." She turned to me. "What have you been eating down there? You're nothing but skin and bones!" She put her arm around my shoulders and led me into the house.

"Chance!" my mother called out for my younger brother. "Chance! You'll never believe who's here!" she called as we passed the stairs.

My little brother came thundering down the stairs and hopped the banister.

"Savvy!" he cried and wrapped me in the biggest hug.

"Woah!" I cried and looked up at him. "When did *that* happen?" I demanded. He was nineteen and working the farm – learning from dad and taking some classes at the community college now. Still, apparently, he was still growing, because last time I had seen him, I didn't have to look quite so far *up*.

"Dude, I know, right?" he said and looked past me and Mom curiously at Corvus.

"Chance, this is my boyfriend Corvus," I said and he looked at him skeptically.

"Boyfriend?" he asked. "So you mean you're not a lesbian, or a nun?" he asked me, and Mom smacked him.

"Ow! Child abuse!" Chance declared, and I laughed, shaking my head.

"Most definitely not," Corvus said, and I blushed, deeply.

"Gross," Chance said, but eyed Corvus with some respect for the quick comeback.

We piled into the dining room, past the kitchen and Mom had us sit while she fixed us some plates and Chance poured us some glasses of the farm's signature sweet tea.

"Oh, my God, I've missed this," I said, taking a deep draught from my glass.

"We'll have to send you home with some bags," Mom said, and I winked at Corvus.

"It has begun," he murmured with a slight chuckle.

"So, what's Corvus mean, if you don't mind me asking," my dad asked.

"So my real name, Corbett means 'crow' and I guess some of my buddies from back in the day at boarding school think my laugh sounds sort of like a crow, so they tried nicknaming me 'crow' but our English teacher – who we all highly respected, said that was too easy and suggested 'corvus' which is the genus or species of bird that crows, rooks, and ravens belong to and it's stuck ever since," he explained.

I blinked, and said, "You never gave *me* the full story on that!" I stuck out my tongue at him and he laughed, and I *loved* that sound.

My dad nodded and said, "I can see what your pals were talking about!"

"I love your laugh," I said, and not for the first time. Corvus winked at me and settled back in his seat.

He hadn't worn his cut up here – we figured my family didn't need to know about that part of our lives. The less, the better on that front.

Mom fed us, and my family and I caught up, with the odd question thrown Corvus' way to keep him included. The mundane things like how did we meet, and how long have we been dating.

We told the truth on that front, that we were competitors in the real estate business down in Savannah, and that we hadn't always liked each other.

"What changed?" my mom asked.

We decided less was more and stuck to the truth, with a few embellishments.

"A showing went bad, and I accidentally texted Corvus instead of my assistant and he got there faster than the cops and threw the man out."

"I was closer," he said with a shrug.

"I worried about that," my mother said, leaning back in her seat. "I told you; real estate is *so dangerous* for women."

I nodded.

"It's also lucrative and what's keeping us going right now," my dad said quickly, so I didn't have to.

My mom looked apprehensive and I said, "Corvus is who put us in touch with the tax attorney who is working on our case," I said.

Dad leaned back in his seat, "I'm grateful for that," he said. "Truly. So, thank you."

We finished our late suppers and talked about the farm. Mom insisted we leave our plates and I show Corvus around the farmhouse and see Nana.

We took our leave and followed Chance up the stairs. He went to his room to carry on with his video games or whatever, and I slipped past Nana's room. She was asleep, so I put a finger to my lips and crept past, leading Corvus to my room where we'd be staying.

I slipped inside first, switching on the light, the ceiling fan beginning a slow and lazy spin, but quickly picking up speed.

He stopped just inside and I turned to look at him, waiting to see what he would say...

Chapter Thirty

Corvus...

Her room was a time capsule of her life, and honestly, just what I expected. The wallpaper was outdated, light pink and white stripes, with big pink cabbage roses. A little girl's room, and likely had been the wallpaper since she was a small child.

Layered over it was well crafted white furniture, a couple of dressers and a queen-sized canopy bed with a quilt in a pattern similar enough to match the wallpaper and tie the room together.

Pictures were tacked to a cork board mounted to the wall above one of the dressers in here. A mirror above the other, and there was a small vanity table, likewise with a mirror scattered with old makeup and perfumes that had accumulated a light layer of dust.

There was a bookshelf, the top decorated with trophies and accolades, several medals for her swim accomplishments dangling from one or more of the trophies to one side.

"Is it strange that this is *exactly* what I expected a childhood room of yours to look like?" I asked and she laughed.

"Oh, is it now?" she asked.

"Right down to the pink everything and white furniture," I said.

She hugged me around my waist and let me pull her in.

"How about it?" I growled in her ear. "Going to let me fuck you on your old bed?"

"Absolutely," she breathed. "Only if we're quiet though, it can and does squeak."

I snorted and laughed and she giggled with me, and we kissed.

"Come on, I want to show you the rest of the farm before it gets dark," she said, and she took my hand and after depositing our pack by the bed, took me back downstairs.

We went back through the kitchen, and she pulled down a set of keys off the hook by the back door, and led me out to the pool deck back here.

I gave a low whistle. "Nice," I said.

"I've got a suit here," she said, and I grinned.

"Really?" I asked. "I think I can come up with a pair of shorts that'll work."

"Pfft! Chance has a million – I'll make him lend you a pair of proper trunks."

"Deal," I said, and she led me past the pool and out the surrounding enclosure, down the way until we spilled out of the trail through the thicket by the house and I had to stop.

"Wow," I said impressed. We were at the top of a rise, overlooking the rows upon rows of carefully cultivated fruit trees down below.

"Impressive, right?" she asked.

"Hell yeah," I said.

She led me down among the trees and toward the big red barn that no doubt held the equipment required to maintain the orchards.

"You can't see it from here, it's on the other side of the barn, but we're headed for the farm stand," she said.

"Yeah?" I queried.

"I want to put together a box of things to take back with us; perks of being the owner's daughter," she laughed and said, "Besides. I've missed this place. I need to stock my kitchen for nostalgia purposes."

I laughed at that, and said, "Torment would probably have a field day."

"Oh, trust. I'll get him *all* the things come season."

"I think he'd like that," I said. "He's always said that South Carolina peaches are superior to Georgia peaches."

"Okay," I said. "My respect for him has gone up a notch."

I laughed at that again, and asked, "How many varieties do you grow?"

She smiled and said, "Good question," and told me all about which trees were which and grew what fruits, and how the perfect ones went to market, and the imperfect ones that were deemed un-pretty enough for grocery stores, they kept here and made into jams, jellies, and other sundry peach things for the farm stand.

We reached the barn and rounded the corner and I had to say – the farm stand and giftshop was *impressive.*

She keyed our way in, and turned on the lights, locking the door behind us.

"Here," she handed me an old-fashioned peach flat crate with a leather handle attached.

"Nice re-purpose!" I said, and she giggled.

"Thanks. My pop-pop, Chance, and I spent a whole summer making them for the farm stand and you wouldn't believe how many people try to take them home or buy them from us."

"They're well made," I said.

"Over a decade and still going. We have to replace the handles every once in a while, but they're sturdy. Yeah. They don't make them like they used to. Everything is plastic nowadays."

We wandered the aisles, shopping together, and she told me all about how recipes were made, and how far back they went in the family line. There were jellies, jams, and even chutneys on the shelves, and I picked up the latter and said, "Now *this* is Torment's speed. I bet he could come up with something amazing using this," I said.

"Put it in the basket," she said, and I raised an eyebrow.

"You know he would need like *six* to feed the whole club," I said.

"We can order online for that," she said. "Or come and pick it up. I'm sure he'll want to try a recipe on a smaller scale first."

"Hua," I said and put the single jar in with the others in our little shopping crate.

We loaded the thing, and I kept tabs on what we'd picked up, adding it up in my brain.

We finished our little spree and she set it on the counter up front and said, "We'll come down and get it tomorrow, I want to make sure we don't throw off the stock numbers."

"Good call," I said, and we went out and she turned out the lights and locked up.

It was getting past dusk and deepening into night, so we stopped to take in the light breeze and insect song.

She tilted her head back and breathed in deeply, sighing out in utter contentment, and God, she was beautiful.

"Homefield advantage," she said with a smile on her lips.

"What?" I asked. Her smile spread into a grin and she cracked the eye closest to me.

"Catch me if you can," she said and she took off running.

"Oh! Oh, ho, ho, ho!" I laughed, and gave her a head start.

Challenge accepted.

Also by A.J. Downey

The Sacred Hearts MC

1. Shattered & Scarred
2. Broken & Burned
3. Cracked & Crushed
4. Masked & Miserable (a novella)
5. Tattered & Torn
6. Fractured & Formidable
7. Damaged & Dangerous
8. Brother to Brother
9. Her Brother's Keeper
10. Brother In Arms
11. Between Brothers
12. A Brother's Secret
13. A Brother At My Back
14. A Brother's Salvation

The Virtues

1. Cutter's Hope
2. Marlin's Faith
3. Charity for Nothing
4. Stoker's Serenity
5. Justice for Radar
6. Lightning's Honor

Sacred Hearts MC Novella

Christmas with the Brotherhood

Indigo Knights

1. Her Thin Blue Lifeline
2. His Cold Blue Command
3. A Low Blue Flame
4. His Wild Blue Rose
5. Her Pained Blue Silence
6. A Cold Blue Call
7. Her Reluctant Blue Cavalier
8. Forged Under Fire
9. Under A Blue Moon
10. Sound of Blue Thunder

Sacred Hearts MC Pacific Northwest

1. Over the High Side
2. Wind Therapy
3. Apex of the Curve
4. Low Sided
5. Eating Asphalt
6. Hammer Down
7. Only Fool Riding

The Voodoo Bastards MC

1. Bourbon & Blood
2. Whiskey Shivers
3. Moonshine Lullabies
4. Cognac Secrets
5. Tequila Damnation

6. Absinthe Dreams

Iron Wraiths MC

1. Original Syn

2. Love & Fear

3. The Hangman's Rope

Royal Bastard MC: St. Augustine Chapter

1. Iron Hearts

Paranormal Romance (with Ryan Kells)

1. I Am The Alpha

2. Omega's Run

3. Hunter's End

Indigo City Darker (with Jared KingPacal Lain)

1. Triple Threat

2. Double Shot

Standalones

Synchronicity

About A.J. Downey

A.J. Downey is a Pacific Northwest girl living in an East Tennessee world who finds inspiration from her surroundings, through the people she meets, and likely as a byproduct of way too much caffeine. She specializes in real and relatable romance stories featuring that real-life kind of love that everyone craves.

Stalker Information:

Website
www.ajdowney.com

www.ingramcontent.com/pod-product-compliance
Lightning Source LLC
LaVergne TN
LVHW010054110826
845155LV00028B/333

* 9 7 8 1 9 5 0 2 2 2 5 9 9 *